THE MAYOR, THE TOWN AND THE MONEYTREE

BY RANDY WHITTLE

ISBN: 1449918034
ISBN-13: 9781449918033

ABOUT THE AUTHOR

Randy Whittle is a native of Roanoke, Virginia. In college he chose to pursue a career as a city manager. After military service in the navy, he became city manager of Bluefield, West Virginia, a community somewhat like Plain Oak in the novel. (The fictitious Plain Oak, however, operated under a modified strong-mayor form of municipal government and therefore had no city manager.)

Whittle's career has also taken him into regional planning and state government. He has authored a two-volume local history, "Johnstown, Pennsylvania—A History." Part One:1895-1936, was released in 2005. Part Two: 1937-1980, came out in 2007. The publisher was The History Press of Charleston, South Carolina.

DEDICATION

"The Mayor, the Town and the Moneytree" is dedicated to Mary Lee Umberger White (1923-1968), the executive secretary in the City Manager's Office in Bluefield, West Virginia, from 1941 until her untimely death in January 1968. My many memories of Mary Lee White served as a basis for one of the book's characters, Allie Eller, the mayor's secretary in the novel. Mary Lee White was a uniquely fine person.

RANDY WHITTLE

TABLE OF CONTENTS

CHAPTER 1
A SUMMER DELUGE

In the dense daytime darkness seen from his office window, everything faded and returned then faded away again as shifting veils of rainfall deluged the town. Rapid flashes of lightening prompted cracks and booms of thunder. Downtown streets were becoming swift, muddy streams.

If the phones kept working, his more irate citizens, the "I'm a taxpayers" Mayor John Fern called them, soon would be hot after him. "Just come out here and look!" they would be insisting once again. Meanwhile as he suffered through another countdown to disaster already ticking away, all he could make himself do was to watch an occasional car creeping along with its headlight glare muted in the gray downpour. Unless the rain soon stopped, whole sections of the South End were fated for waist-deep water. The cleanup to follow was certain to strain an already meager city budget. Delegations of angry citizens would be retracing earlier visits to city hall demanding solutions he was powerless to deliver. Once again, being mayor of Plain Oak, West Virginia, would be irksome, stressful and unmanageable.

Tense and helpless, he quizzed Allie Eller, his secretary. "How did we rate this, Allie? Haven't we been good lately?"

"You musta done something, Mister Mayor," she jested. "Probably had to do with liquor."

"That's hitting a bit too hard, Allie. If I got to give up liquor to make it stop, it might rain forty days and forty nights."

"Maybe if you'd cut down a wee little, Yer Honor, the Lord would ease up a bit and we'd all be better off."

Fern lit a cigar and rolled up his sleeves. He began wondering whether the city might have to execute an evacuation plan. Next the street-crew foreman, Doug Rodmeir, came in sopping wet. "Its awful out there," he reported. "The South End's good and flooded and cars are stalled on Tulip Drive. We can't even keep the catch basins open."

"Make sure no kids are playing around in them ditches," Allie instructed. "They fool around in rain like this for kicks or something. Remember the Raymond boy what got killed a few years back?"

"Okay Allie," Rodmeir agreed. "Boys, it's gonna be some night if this don't let up and quick about it," he added before leaving.

As Allie and the mayor watched water sweeping over the streets, the telephone rang and Fern's stomach sank. "Mayor's Office, Allie Eller," she answered. With her hand covering the mouthpiece, she announced to John Fern, "Guess who."

Mrs. Lilley was nearly always the first person to call in about anything whether it needed to be reported or not. Knowing who it was, Fern's reply to Allie Eller was intentionally loud enough to be picked up by the telephone, "Our good friend, Mrs. Lilley, I bet." He next took the telephone and spoke, "Hello, Mrs. Lilley, how are you?"

Fern listened a few moments then put the receiver on his desk. Occasionally he picked it up and agreed wholeheartedly with her about something, "Yes Ma'am," and "You're right." Finally after a pause in her chatter, he decided he needed to say something more substantive so he announced, "Mrs. Lilley, the first thing we've got to do is to get them to stop this rain. I'm working on it."

Allie's eyes twinkled as she witnessed her boss taking on the champion telephone griper in Plain Oak—a person who complained about everything from teenage rowdyism to automobile speeding, the need for a snowplow whenever it started to snow, pornography and even once about UFOs. Allie chuckled when she heard Fern insisting, "Now Mrs. Lilley, the flooding hasn't gotten worse just because I got elected mayor." Soon his voice took on a rapidity and harshness. "All right, Mrs. Lilley, I'll look at it, but my looking may make it get worse. If you're willing to run the risk, I'll come on out there and just see all that water."

In her twenty-seven years with the city, Allie Eller had worked under five mayors. She rated each of them as terrible, fair or good. She considered John Fern to be a very good man trying to face up to an impossible job. Like many Plain Oakers, Allie could recall his throwing the winning touchdown pass on the last play of the 1940 football season when Plain Oak High School came from behind to win a championship game. She also remembered the war veteran and ex-naval lieutenant commander who began managing the Fern-McCoy Seed and Feed Store on Market Avenue which his uncle, Herb McCoy, had tried to operate between heart attacks throughout the war. Allie Eller knew John Fern craved being liked. The years had also taught her that whenever a mayor sought popularity, he inevitably soured in some way. She had seen them come in with glory, hope and applause. A few months later something always happened and the public would turn against them. The ones who liked to be liked usually quit trying to run the city, and someone else would be mentioned as an ideal choice to serve as the next mayor of Plain Oak, West Virginia.

When the telephone rang once again, Fern seized his raincoat and partially broken umbrella. "You take 'em, Allie," he ordered. "They'll—everyone of them—will be wanting me to go out and look so I'm heading to the South End to look. They probably think I can stare hard enough to make a hole open up in the ground big enough to drain the place dry."

"That's the stuff, Mayor," Allie agreed clapping her hands as if she were approving an important point in a political speech. "Go on out there and look. Be sure and look down and not up. You got it going hard enough already."

When Fern was almost into the hallway, she answered the phone once again, "Mayor's office... Yes siree! He's on his way down there now to drain all that water away."

Hearing Allie's remarks, Fern poked his head back inside the office and asked, "Who's that?"

With her hand over the mouthpiece, she answered, "Old man Varn."

"Tell him to quit chewing his tobacco. Him spitting is causing…"

"You best get going, Mister Mayor," Allie offered. "At the rate you're moving, we'll see high tide before you bucket off a drop."

Despite his efforts to maintain a cheerful calm, Fern was shaken. This was evident in the way he handled the car. When he finally got it moving, he nudged into a signpost. Once the automobile had reached the more flooded streets, poor visibility forced him to creep along at a snail's pace. The drum-roll sound of the torrents striking the car and a continuing need to wipe the inside windshield added to his tension.

Heading south on Elliott Boulevard, Fern saw water gushing out of catch basins and manholes. After turning up onto Victory Street, he headed for a spot where one could view much of the South End. Even in the higher places, the flat streets held more than an inch of water.

How did I get into this mess? Fern pondered as he began reflecting upon the perplexing reasons for his mayoral ambitions. He had truly wanted to do great things for Plain Oak. The campaign promise to solve the South End's flood problem had been sincere. Before announcing any proposal, he had gotten Elton Bristow, a general construction contractor and an old friend, to work up a crude culvert design and cost estimate. The price tag was just over one million dollars and while some omissions were acknowledged, Bristow was confident a good job could be had for two million or less.

Soon after he had taken the oath of office, Fern persuaded city council to retain Barton, Callahan and Riley, the best consulting engineering firm in the area, to develop a general plan and feasibility assessment for the South End project. The new and hopeful mayor almost cried when the firm had priced the job at four and one-half million dollars plus right-of-way easements and engineering fees. Bristow's earlier design had assumed culverts and channels that were too small. He had skipped over the need to undertake extensive rock excavation in a residential area and had omitted relocating several hundred feet of water main plus a short but difficult section of the sanitary sewer.

Four and one-half million dollars plus! John Fern calculated, went over the location with a tape measure, refigured and persuaded every builder and engineer he knew to review the estimate. No one was able to develop a credible figure that was much lower.

In a follow-up meeting with the firm's professionals, Jerry Callahan told John Fern the project was infeasible. "You could probably buy up all the property down there and move the people out for what it would take to do this one job," he advised. "Given your tax-rate and debt limits, there's no way the city could float a loan to raise five million dollars assuming the voters would vote favorably in a bond election. Even if you could, you've got other needs in Plain Oak just as important as taking care of flooding in this one part of town."

Next Fern had sought help from the state, the federal government and even private foundations. Harry Bowles, the congressman who represented a big part of West Virginia including the Plain Oak area, got the U. S. Army Corps of Engineers to look into the situation. The district engineer's office roughed out some complicated numbers and concluded that the benefit-to-cost ratio was too low to justify a corps project. Bowles wrote Fern a cautious letter explaining that the federal government could do nothing under present programs and funding.

Governor Cutler Burns advised the mayor that the problem was local in character and if any trace of encouragement were given about possible state aid, Plain Oak might defer solving its own problem. His letter had ended with frankness:

Certainly for now and in the foreseeable future, your city should not count on any state aid for your South End Flood Reduction Project.

Fern continued thinking about his present disenchantment with being mayor. The day he met with the senior staff of Barton, Callahan and Riley, opened their report and read the four and one-half million dollar figure, he seriously thought of resigning. Within three months of his having taken office, the new mayor suddenly lost most of his enthusiasm for the job.

The pounding rain finally softened into a misty drizzle. Mercury Drive had been covered with two to three feet of water in most places. At half past six, the lowest part of Oakdale Place was flooded by almost four feet.

Fern waited patiently as the waters slowly receded. Listening to the evening news on his car radio, he learned that just over three inches of rain had fallen in about three hours as recorded by the rain gauge at the airport. There had indeed been a deluge but Plain Oak had experienced worse storms in the past and would certainly suffer them again.

By seven-fifteen the August sun was shining with extra clarity. The waters were now confined to overloaded sewers, swollen creeks and swampy lowlands. Once again Plain Oak was becoming hot and sticky.

More relaxed but somewhat subdued, John Fern continued touring the city that had elected him. A few homes on Mercury Drive had horizontal water-stain lines about a foot and a half off the ground. Most streets were coated with a reddish-brown slime. Garbage cans had floated around before coming to rest on streets and lawns. Tree limbs littered yards and roadways. A few smaller trees had been completely uprooted. Some automobiles were ruined.

Fern knocked several times on Mrs. Lilley's front door. There was no answer. She had apparently experienced some water in her home. Mrs. Lilley was known for never being around when city officials made the visits she had requested of them. Fern placed a calling card above her doorknocker and made a hasty exit.

Returning to his car, he observed the Jiggs on the opposite side of the street putting furniture and rugs out to dry. Margaret Jiggs, a cheerleader in high school when Fern had played football, was weeping. Her recently retired husband, Frank, hailed the mayor.

Fern tried to think of an excuse not to spend time with this couple but there was no polite way to avoid it. Frank Jiggs was hard-of-hearing and usually seemed nervous. Loud, verbose and having a smattering of engineering knowledge, he would declaim ceaselessly that the city's public works projects were poorly designed, inadequately inspected and almost always generally unsatisfactory.

After shaking hands with Fern, Jiggs opened in his deep voice, "All this is getting worse, Johnny, lots worse. We had a hard rain but nothing out of the ordinary. It could have gone on another hour or two and we would have had four feet of water in our house. This is another sad day for Plain Oak.

"You know where all that water comes from?" he continued in a voice loud enough to be heard seventy-five yards away. "All those new developments outside town, that's where. The Fairway Mall and Tone's subdivision with his new streets and houses. Not long ago all that was woodlands. Now it's paved over and we get the runoff, Johnny. Why doesn't the city sue the bastards and make them take care of their own damned water?"

"We'll look into it, Frank," Fern replied.

"Look into it! Look into it—hell!" Jiggs shouted as if the mayor were a block away. "There's got to be some action. Any damned fool knows this problem gets worse every time somebody builds a house up there. The rains didn't do anywhere near this much damage twenty years ago. Those people up there—and Tone's stuff is right in the middle—are responsible. They won't come into the city because they don't want to pay your high taxes. Our homes were here long before any of that opened up, and now we're being forced to sell out if we can get a buyer, but who'll buy a home in a swamp? We've lived here over fifteen years and it's gotten steadily worse, Johnny—lots worse."

Frank Jiggs sniffed a few times and then screwed his face so as to reveal a sour frame of mind. "Do you smell it, Johnny?" he asked condescendingly. "Sewage. Vintage shit is bubbling up out of the sewers. This is one hell of a mess, Johnny. I calculated we'd need an eighteen-foot diameter pipe to handle a one-in-ten-year storm. Make the mall pay for it. That's where it comes from. The mall takes trade away from the taxpaying businesses of this city and puts its runoff down here. And I'd bring that new development into the suit, Johnny. They should carry their weight too."

The mayor could think of nothing more to say. Jiggs began lashing out at some other new construction. After a few neighbors recognized their mayor, they began wandering across the squishy lawns to learn what, if anything, was going on.

One of the more articulate of the gathering was Sam Steinman, a balding forty-year old labor lawyer. "How are you going to keep your pledge, John?" he probed. "Four and a half million bucks isn't chicken feed for a little place with fifteen thousand people and six millionaires."

Steinman frequently wrote letters to the city council and to people in leadership positions. His contributions to the Readers' Forum were so numerous Plain Oakers almost viewed them as a special column in the Dispatch. He did, however, know the community and kept up with its current events. Steinman believed the city could do nothing to solve the South End problem and derived a trace of satisfaction by asking questions that unveiled the mayor's helplessness.

A bit depressed, Fern was in no mood to say anything. He did manage to utter in a quivering voice that featured a restrained but angry dignity, "What would you do, Sam, if you were in my place and were the mayor? What would you do?"

No man to be put in a corner for want of words, Steinman hastily replied with an air of comic satire, "Why I'd build the damned drains, Mayor, just like I had promised since I would be you. All you need is about five million bucks. I wouldn't let it stop something like this. Look at all the mud and crap out there. Smell the sewage. Someday someone's going to get electrocuted or drown. Then you'll be sued for more than the five million."

Steinman had probably expected the several persons standing around to applaud or cheer. His pronouncements were so familiar, however, there was no reaction whatever.

Moreover he had been upstaged quietly by Eleanor Stacey, a young pretty mother of two who, barefoot and carrying what seemed to be a gin-and-tonic, stepped around several broken branches to join the others.

After a commanding entrance, she opened in a soft, southern accent, "John, let's all go for a swim in our basement. Come on over. The water's fine."

Fern tried to think of a fitting reply but all he could manage was, "No thanks, Lena. I've seen enough water today to last a lifetime, but if I were in a mood for a swim, I'd certainly pick your basement."

"Poor Mayor John," Eleanor Stacey soothed as she teased. "Don't let a little old tempest spoil your day. Do all you can for us. Go home and kiss Margaret. Have a drink and get a good night's sleep."

For some reason Fern's perspiring face flushed a light red. Eager to leave, he felt a duty to say something but lacked an idea to shape into words. Almost impulsively he exhorted, "Were going to build this project—no matter what. It will get done." His words seemed to him almost as if they had been forced through his lips. Even while he was uttering them, Fern felt cheap. Better than anyone, he knew of no way to honor the renewed commitment.

After his fanciful remarks, Fern gasped, "Good-by," and eased over to his car. Several persons were staring silently and as he perceived it, disapprovingly at him. Having forced a smile on an otherwise deadpan face, he waved a jerky farewell and drove away.

CHAPTER 2
A CONCERNED PUBLIC

The Plain Oak City Council met every Thursday evening in a large basement assembly room at city hall. Some sessions lasted almost until midnight while others would be over in a very few minutes. Because most people who came either wanted something for themselves or were there to complain about things the city was doing or ought to be doing, John Fern hated the meetings and considered them irksome, tense and often boring.

There were a few "regulars" who attended almost every session to complain in general and to heckle the council and the mayor in particular. Whenever anyone criticized the local government, the regulars would clap and shout, "You tell 'em," or "That's right." Council members usually tolerated these outbursts, but Arch Kidd, the forceful chairman, typically reacted by tapping the gavel and calling for order.

One of the leaders of the regulars, Emily Sailspur, had thin gaunt features and always wore black. Among his close friends, Fern referred to her as "the witch." The most recent Halloween just happened to have been on a Thursday and Mrs. Sailspur was not in attendance. When someone asked where she was, John Fern butted in, "It's Halloween. She's out testing her new broomstick."

Many of the regulars criticized him for the remark and demanded an apology. Fern held his ground. "It's Halloween," he answered back. "Lots of folks have things to do on Halloween."

As with any meeting that followed a severe thunderstorm, people from all over town had flocked to the council chamber. The regulars arrived early and were mostly seated together. Anticipating a barrage of protests over his failure to deliver on a campaign promise to install a drainage system in the South End, Fern dreaded the session.

Hot and stuffy already, the assembly room was warmed all the more when a television cameraman turned on high-intensity lights exposing wall displays of framed documents and memorabilia from Plain Oak's past. There were photographs of past mayors, championship teams, beauty queens, and such visiting dignitaries as former governors, two U. S. senators and John Kennedy campaigning in the 1960 primary.

The council hastened through its prepared agenda like clockwork: minutes, resolutions, introduction of a non-controversial ordinance, the financial report, and the like. Time was always reserved for citizens to speak. All anyone needed to do was to fill out a card, give it to the clerk and wait being called by the chairman.

The first speaker was Mrs. Mildred Frei, speaking for the Plain Oak Garden Council. A stylish and beautiful woman in her mid-seventies, she was wearing a blue dress with an ornate lace collar. Her late husband had been president and board chairman of the First National Bank of Elliott County but Mildred Frei was well-known in her own right.

Using no notes she began eloquently, "They tell me a five-year flood means there's supposed to be one chance in five that one as bad or worse will happen in any year. Isn't that right, Mayor John?"

"That's correct, Mrs. Frei," Kidd answered. Fern also nodded affirmatively.

"Ah so," she resumed. "We've had one five-year flood this year, one last year, a thirty-year drought two years ago, and both a five-year and a ten-year flood the year before that. We've had four five-year floods or worse in the last four years. The way I have it figured, somebody doesn't know what they're talking about!"

With this, the regulars broke into a strong applause and there was wild cheering from the audience. When the chamber became silent again, she continued, "Now we in Plain Oak have got to lick this flooding business. There are no two ways about it. I don't care what the thing costs. I'll go down there with my garden spade and do my bit. The thing is if everybody digs a little, we'll all get it done."

At this point there was laughter and cheering. Mildred Frei continued, "Mayor John, we're counting on you. We're all with you. So let's all get the job done!" Again the chamber broke into a brief pandemonium.

After the noises had subsided, her tone became more serious and she announced, "Now as important as all this is, it's not why I'm here tonight for the garden clubs—not the main reason. I'm here because of that ark business—Snidow's ark. They haven't got a building permit. The thing he and his brother and the boy are doing is ugly..."

"Excuse me, Mrs. Frei," the chairman interrupted, "but what's this ark you're talking about?"

"Herbie and Dexter Snidow and Herb's boy are building a flood ark like Noah in Genesis I suppose, only in their front yard. They've got wood all over the place and they're using a loud power saw late at night. For all we know, they'll be gathering male and female animals..."

The audience roared in laughter. The ark was a protest symbol directed at the city's inability to solve its flooding problems especially in the South End. A large reddish man about forty years old immediately stood and barged in, "Me and muh brother, Herb, we're fixing up a flood ark. If the city won't help us, we's a doin' as the Lord said unto Noah. When another five-year flood come along next month, we'll all..."

"You're out-of-order," Arch Kidd shouted as he tapped the gavel. "If you want to speak, sign up and wait your turn like everybody else."

"I thought you all wanted to know about our ark," Snidow quipped before being cut off by Kidd's gaveling.

John Fern displayed a sour look. Dexter Snidow, one of the candidates who had run for mayor, had been badly beaten in the primary. Despite a heavy vote against him, he continued spreading word all over town that he would be Plain Oak's next mayor.

Most sensible citizens considered Snidow to be too hotheaded and irresponsible to serve them. Fern's campaign strategy had been to ignore him. The television camera was now focused on the two brothers. Mildred Frei had aided their publicity stunt unwittingly.

"We'll check into this, Mrs. Frei," Kidd announced, "but a man probably has a right to build a boat in his yard so long as he isn't creating a nuisance."

"I never said a boat," Mildred Frei retorted. "I said 'ark, ark.'"

With this the whole council chamber exploded into laughter. A few people began shouting in unison, "Ark, ark, ark," and Kidd pounded his gavel again and again.

After some calm was restored, Mildred Frei continued, "Now seriously, the garden council wants to know if the ark needs a building permit and has to be zoned right and all. It's an ugly mess. It's more than a boat and not so much as a house—a proper house, that is."

"I don't know, Mrs. Frei," Kidd admitted. "Maybe our mayor knows. I haven't seen what the Snidows are doing. I entertain a motion that the mayor look into this and if the Snidows need to comport to the zoning and building codes and get a permit, that they be so advised. Do I hear a motion?"

"So moved, Mister Chairman," Edward Fiske, a black councilman, volunteered.

"Moved by Mr. Fiske. Do I hear a second?"

"Seconded by Mr. Hawkins. Any discussion? Any discussion? Hearing none, all in favor say ..."

"Aye," all sounded together.

"The motion carries, ladies and gentlemen. Mr. Fern will be making a report, Mrs. Frei," the chairman advised as she returned to her front-row seat.

"Mr. Elmer Feightner," Kidd called out. "You have the floor, sir."

Feightner, a short somewhat stocky man of fifty, was slightly nervous but managed a smile as he approached the podium. "Thank you, Mr. Kidd," he began. "Now I don't want to take anything away from the South End folks' problem. I saw the pictures in the paper and everyone knows about the flooding down there, but we in Cherry Corner have a bad situation too. I'm not saying it's as bad as in the South End but it won't take anywhere near the money to remedy." Feightner passed around some photographs taken during Monday's storm.

"Mister Mayor," Kidd asked, "didn't the city engineer do a plan and cost estimate for drainage in Cherry Corner? Do you remember the figure?"

"Yes, Mister Chairman," Fern replied as he stood up. "He figured it'll take about three hundred thousand dollars to put in a fifty-four inch pipe needed to correct the problem."

"Mr. Feightner," Kidd continued, everyone here wants to help you folks out there. You've made a good case. One picture is worth more than a thousand words. Our city simply doesn't have the money right now. We all hope we can work up a program to get this project built somehow."

Feightner nodded politely but there was an impression of hopelessness on his face as he returned to his seat.

Sam Steinman was spokesman for a large delegation from the South End. When called, Fern braced himself for a verbal attack on his promises and vain efforts. Steinman, however, was tactfully polite. Knowing the mayor and council all wanted to deal with the problem positively, he opened, "Mister Mayor, Mister Chairman, Councilmen, ladies and gentlemen. I am presenting a petition signed by one hundred and eighty-nine persons. It's a simple request for a realistic solution to the flooding we experience all too often in the South End. Another petition may soon be in circulation asking for legal action against a few developments located outside the city limits. Another lawyer is doing some legal research into this before we draw up the petition. Tonight we don't want to bore you with a lot of speeches all saying the same thing. You know the problem. Our mayor saw it firsthand late Monday. I'll simply ask the many people here on this matter to stand so you can see them."

About thirty persons stood and politely sat back down. Pausing for a few seconds, Kidd announced that the council appreciated the petition, Steinman's statement and the show of concern from the South End.

At this juncture about two-thirds of those in attendance left. The extra bright lights were turned off and things seemed more relaxed. Fern recognized an elderly, thin but rugged man sitting alone near the back wearing khaki clothes, boots, and a cowboy hat. It was Harry Sneed, a distant cousin and his wife's uncle. Sneed lived all alone on an immense tract of land twelve miles outside of town. Having never seen him attend any sort of meeting in Plain Oak, Fern wondered why this man was there.

When the chairperson of the library board was giving her quarterly report, the mayor watched Sneed leave through the rear exit. Perplexed, Fern tried to concentrate on the meeting but began wondering when he had last seen his uncle-in-law. Finally he remembered it had been at the Bailey Family Reunion which must have been fifteen years in the past because the Fern's only daughter, Amy, had attended in a girl-scout uniform.

Refocusing on the session, Fern heard someone offer to answer questions. There were none. Glancing over the library report, the trust-account balance had grown to three hundred thousand dollars—all stipulated for use toward a new library on the old Williams property downtown. A truly adequate building would cost almost one million dollars.

At long last the session started winding down. Those still attending were getting edgy and city officials were tired of listening. Kidd finally asked, "Is there any other business to come before this council?"

The brief pause following the chairman's question was interrupted by Dexter Snidow who stood, grinned menacingly and then almost shouted, "You know what I think?" After a brief pause he continued, "I think Plain Oak's a zoo a bein' run by a bunch of monkeys!" The few remaining regulars whistled, clapped, laughed and cheered despite Kidd's loud gaveling and pleas for order.

Fern stood, stared first at the regulars and next at Dexter Snidow. He then waited for some calm to come over the audience. With a crimson face and a slight tremor in his voice, he announced loudly, "I'd rather be in a zoo run by a bunch of monkeys than in a barnyard run by a bunch of jackasses!"

Fearing a free-for-all, Kidd pounded his gavel vigorously and shouted, "I declare this meeting adjourned!"

Afterwards a small number of persons were standing about chattering. Fern's impulse was to get out of city hall right away. Pretending to be late for another meeting, he tucked a few papers into his briefcase and hastened for the exit. Two people wanted to talk with him but he allowed no opening. "Call me at the office tomorrow," they were told curtly.

Fern started his Pontiac and pulled onto Elliott Boulevard. The streets seemed dirty and the traffic light at Marshall Avenue changed colors in a strange way. Fully half the streets in town needed resurfacing. Driving down Elkins Place, he was reminded of the crumbling sidewalk along the park. Briarwood Plaza was still caked with dried mud, an aftermath of the storm. Every street, sidewalk, manhole, catch basin, street light, vacant lot overgrown with weeds, stray dog—all were steady reminders of his duties and responsibilities as mayor.

Once inside 327 Oak View Drive, Fern would seek to divorce himself from public officialdom and its potholes, the "I'm a taxpayer" people, endless complaints and old friends and campaign supporters begging him to cancel their parking tickets.

Following most of the council sessions, he needed to go through a ritual of unwinding or otherwise spend a sleepless night. He would pour a highball, light a cigar and talk for a while with Margaret. Even if it were late, she would keep company with him.

This evening Fern was quite agitated. The Snidow brothers despised him and the exchange at the end of the meeting raised a concern that there might have been a fight. Holding a glass of bourbon and water, Fern sat in his favorite rocking chair. A minute later, Margaret, wearing a light-green robe, took her place on the sofa.

"I could give you a thousand guesses," he began, "and you'd never come up with a special someone who showed up at the meeting tonight."

"Millie Frei," she answered. "Today's paper said she'd be there speaking for the garden clubs."

"That's not who I had in mind. Millie was there all right, but she comes around every now and then about something. The guy who showed up I'll bet had never been to a council meeting in his entire life. In fact he doesn't even live here in town."

"I can't imagine, John, pray tell who."

"None other than one Harry Sneed, your own uncle and I guess some kin to me, but I'd have to go through a stack of family Bibles to figure what kin he is."

"He's your third cousin," she answered quickly. "His great-grandfather and your great-grandfather were brothers."

"Now what in Sam Hill would possess old Harry to show up on a hot August night to hear a bunch of people bitch about too much water?" Fern expressed in wonderment. "Sitting there, I figured we hadn't seen him in fifteen years. What do you think he wanted, Margaret?"

"Maybe he's in trouble and wants you to help him out. Probably he just wanted to see Millie. He had read she was going to be at the meeting and I'll bet that's why he was there."

"Ain't no way," Fern countered. "If he wanted to see Millie, he'd go and see Millie. He wouldn't show up all alone at a meeting, say nothing and leave before it was over."

"How did he look?"

"Same as always," he replied. "I didn't look close and I never said a word to him, but he's the same. I didn't see anybody talk to him. I reckon few there, if any, even knew who he was."

"Well Millie Fox Frei sure knows him," she reminded her husband. "He was once dead in love with her and they're some kin though not close."

"That doesn't answer the riddle. She was first to talk and last to leave and they didn't swap one word."

Margaret smiled, picked up her knitting bag, and proceeded to knit away at something. "You men don't know anything. I'll just bet Uncle Harry wanted to look Millie over before starting to court her once again. Maybe we'll have a romance in the making. Now you know old Harry never wasted a word on anyone and Millie, she'll talk your head off. Being a widow, she wouldn't think of striking up a conversation with Harry."

"But they're kin, Margaret."

"Third cousins, same as you and Harry," she advised, "but you're no kin to Millie Frei."

Fern rocked gently in the chair, puffed leisurely on his cigar and began to reminisce, "You know, old Harry…he got a raw deal. Anybody who knew anything about him knew he wouldn't hurt a flea but when that revenue agent disappeared, lots of folks thought he was getting' onto Harry and Harry had killed him. I remember it when I was a boy."

"Harry was paying for the wages of sin," Margaret asserted.

"Then when this agent turns up in Chicago married to another woman, nobody paid any attention," he continued. "Everybody liked the mystery about a man suddenly disappearing from down at Harry's. That was the big talk. It was all over the papers but when the guy turned up alive, the big story was he had left his wife and had taken up with another woman. That made big news back then. Nothing got written to clear Harry about what people had been saying about him. They were almost sorry the poor bastard was still alive but were glad he had gotten himself another woman. This had given them something else to talk about. People are people, I guess."

"Are you going to call on Harry?"

"I ain't got time for Harry," Fern answered. "He sure never said a word to me. If he wants to see me about something, I can be reached. I certainly have no plans to go out there to that jungle of his."

As Fern sipped on his bourbon, his eyes sparkled and he chuckled to himself and continued, "You remember old man Taylor Toms, don't you—always going hunting? He met up with Harry somewhere—this was years ago—and asked him if he and his brother, Joe, and their two boys could go turkey hunting down there at Harry's place. 'Sure,' Harry had told him, 'come on out real early before sunup.' Now old Taylor, he had probably bought as much moonshine off of Harry as any, so he figured they could go down there and do some real hunting. Most folks were still scared to go near Harry's place on account of that revenue man dropping out of sight. Well anyway, they all got down there early one morning when it was still real misty. Out come old Harry carrying his gun. He was as nice as he could be. He had 'em all come in and gave them coffee and told them to stop back when they were done hunting and he'd give them some really good liquor. Then when they were on their way out, he said to them, 'Just two things—don't shoot any mountain lions and don't shoot my prize turkeys.'"

Fern was chuckling almost to a giggle. "Well they went out and old Taylor and them, they tried to figure how to tell the difference between wild turkeys and Harry's tame ones. Didn't any of them know how, and when they got to talking about big cats and they couldn't shoot 'em, they all decided to leave. There they were. They were all at what was supposed to be a great place to hunt and they went away before loading a gun, and old Harry—he wouldn't hurt a flea." Fern laughed and laughed while Margaret, having heard the story before, merely smiled.

"To change the subject," she interrupted, "Amy called tonight and told me she and Tommy are coming for the long Labor Day weekend. They'll be staying with us this time and should get here for supper Friday a week from tomorrow. They won't have to head back 'til Tuesday morning."

"Halleluiah!" Fern cheered. "Now that's the sort of news you and I both need." He rocked confidently and paused to take a deliberate sip from his drink and a few short puffs from a cigar. As this activity slowed, his face became more serious. "I don't suppose," he asked softly, "we've heard anything from Jack?"

Margaret stared calmly at the floor and replied gently, "No, John, not a word. We'll hear something before long. Might be he'll come in with Amy and Tommy."

"Might be," he agreed pensively.

For a few moments all conversation stopped. Margaret stood, ambled over to the rocker and kissed her husband gently. Yawning quietly, she excused herself saying, "I'm bone tired."

After she had gone upstairs, Fern made the rounds locking the windows and doors. He poured a shot of bourbon and sat back down in the rocking chair. His son's photograph on the mantle caused him to wonder about the young man's whereabouts. Jack had last called two months earlier from California to say he had hopes of getting a job. There had been no word since. The Ferns had been assuming their son had been unsuccessful and was too ashamed to let them know. Thinking of Jack made Fern sad so he shifted attention to Amy's coming. Rocking gently with his eyes closed, he *took the pass from center, faked to the tailback and dropped back to throw. Andy Weems was moving fast and motioned so Johnny Fern heaved a long pass. A loud roar came from the Plain Oak side. Everyone cheered the mayor.* He next experienced a renewed compulsion to double-check the doors and windows before mounting the stairs.

Fern hated getting ready for bed. Little chores like undressing, washing, brushing his teeth and putting on pajamas all seemed like major obstacles until he was actually doing them. He especially disliked taking off his shoes. Being barefoot gave him a sense of powerlessness.

Once in bed, he dozed away until he *was a salesman searching frantically for a committee of important buyers all waiting impatiently for his sales presentation. He raced up the stairs and entered an imposing office with tall ceilings and tasteful eighteenth-century furniture. After greeting everyone, he forgot his company's name and its products. A clumsy search through the briefcase turned up old faded newspapers. Embarrassed, he passed out his calling cards but all of them were blank on both sides.*

Troubled and sweating, he remembered Amy and Tommy would be home for Labor Day and everyone still liked him because of the touchdown pass. *He wandered to the forward part of the flight deck. As the carrier turned into the wind, a cool mist blew over his face. He then remembered the war was over and the ship was heading for San Francisco. There would be cheers and happiness…*

Suddenly he was jolted by the telephone ringing. *Jack's dead*, he thought to himself in a panic. "Maybe it's a crank call or a wrong number," he mumbled. Margaret opened her eyes and briefly sat up in confusion.

Fern reached for the phone, "Hello, …Who's this?…It's Harry Sneed," he informed Margaret so she could go back to sleep. "Harry, it's always good to talk to you but it's 4:20 in the morning… No, we plan to be in town… I'll go down there… Early this Saturday… No we won't say a word to anybody…That's right Margaret won't mention it to a soul… Okay. Good-by, Harry."

Fern put the phone back on the receiver. Margaret rustled in bed and inquired softly, "Pray tell, what does Uncle Harry want?"

"I really don't know," he answered, "but he's sure got my curiosity. When I said, 'Harry, it's 4:20,' do you know what he said? He said he wanted to make sure I'd be home when he called, and he figured I'd be here after four o'clock in the morning."

"There can be only one Uncle Harry. What happens Saturday?"

"We're going fishing way early in the morning. I'm to be alone. No one's to know about me going. It's a family secret. I'm to be down there at 5:30 for breakfast and it's very important. Remember, no one is to know."

"Try and get some sleep, John." Soon he heard a steady breathing from her side of the bed.

CHAPTER 3
A VISIT WITH HARRY SNEED

Driving through the early mist and darkness, Fern kept a sharp lookout for the strange fence that enclosed Sneed's wilderness isolating its owner from the rest of the world. The structure was eight feet tall and had been made from abandoned fencing plus old sheet metal and other materials hauled away over many years from demolished buildings and dumping sites far and wide. As Sneed collected these materials, he affixed them to trees and other support structures. Eventually the barrier encircled his immense holdings. Once a conversation piece, the fence quickly became covered with graffiti and political signs. As time passed, the barricade soon became so entangled with vines and other vegetation, it had become hard to see in broad daylight and was completely hidden in the early morning haze and shadows.

After turning onto the entrance road, Fern's headlights lit up a volley of signs: **Private Property, No Trespassing, No Hunting or Trapping,** and **Trespassers Will Be Prosecuted**. The same fencing lined both sides of the graveled road up to a tall gate some three hundred yards in from the highway. As he halted to determine how to enter, the structure was lifted somewhat automatically, and a loud bell clanged in the nearby woods. After Fern's car had passed beneath it, the gate slowly dropped back into a closed position.

While everything seemed dark, the beginnings of day were visible in the eastern sky. At a bend in the road, a young deer scampered into the undergrowth. Three minutes later, the lights could be seen from Sneed's cabin located on a small knoll above Elliott Creek, a tributary of the Kanawha River.

As Fern parked, a floodlight was turned on and Harry Sneed came out from the porch carrying a shotgun and a lantern which he beamed all around the automobile. "I been looking fer a big rattler, John," he advised seriously. "A few days back I seen him near where we're standin'. It was big around as muh leg. Time I'd got muh gun, he'd gone."

On the screened porch, there were snakeskins stretched over boards, large hornets' nests and other features of a menacing wilderness. Sneed looked at Fern and declared bluntly, "You're an hour early."

"I thought you said five-thirty," Fern objected. "It's almost exactly that time by my watch."

"It's just four-thirty. You go by that daylight-savings stuff."

"I'm sorry, Harry," Fern apologized in amusement, "but the best fishing comes at sunup and you said you were going to feed me breakfast."

"No mind," Sneed countered seriously. "I get up real early every day. My favorite times is sunrise and when it's a comin' down 'bout to set. Besides, there ain't no point in fishing today. They won't be bitin'."

"Now Harry, how can you tell the fish won't be biting today?" Fern expressed in mild protest before easing into a tall-backed hickory rocking chair.

"Has to do with how hot it's been and the color of the water. All that rain got things stirred up. No, John, they won't be bitin'—not today anyhow."

Fern knew there was little point in arguing with Harry Sneed about anything, certainly not about fishing on his own place. Fern's curiosity as to what Sneed really wanted was beginning to intensify but he knew his distant cousin would unveil everything in his own unique way.

Without saying where he was going, the host disappeared for about ten minutes then reemerged with a tray of scrambled eggs, fried ham, sliced bread, saltine crackers, paper plates, a crude pot of coffee and two mugs. "Hep yuhself, John," Sneed offered graciously but seriously.

"Thank you, Harry," Fern answered and then filled a paper plate with eggs and ham. Next he poured a mug of coffee and sat at a table near the edge of the porch. Sneed fixed a similar plate for himself then joined his guest.

John Fern tried to think of things to say. Sneed said almost nothing but the absence of conversation did not bother him at all. Finally Fern thought to ask, "Do you still have any of those mountain lions out here, Harry?"

Sneed pointed silently to his mouth full of food, chewed deliberately, sipped some coffee and replied, "Yep, but don't let nobody know cause somebody'll want to sneak in here and kill one. They'd never find 'em without dogs, but I don't want them kinda trashy folks on this place."

"Do you ever see them?"

"You don't never know fuh sure you seen 'em but I'm pretty sure I have a few times usually about dusk. It's rare though. They're curious about me and sneak up on me. I know they're there by the feel of things and I might a caught sight of one a few times. They'd never hurt a flea. Ain't hardly any left. That's one reason I keep this place."

"How big's your place, Harry?" Fern asked as he lit a cigar.

"Sixteen thousand nine hundred and ninety-two and six-tenths acres, more or less," he answered proudly, "all together and all mine."

Once again there was silence. This continued to bother Fern who felt some compulsion to keep talking, but as he thought about Harry Sneed living all alone and unaccustomed to idle chatter, he resolved to speak only if there were something worth saying.

As the daylight advanced, a distinct rhapsody of bird sounds emerged. Fern could make out Western Run Mountain and thought he saw a trout leap and splash in Elliott Creek.

Prompted by no cue, Sneed opened soberly, "I'm getting old, John. I don't feel old and I still come and go like I did when I was a kid but the plain fact is I'm gettin' on in years. I put together something like a Garden of Eden out here, and I want ta help you to build a New Jerusalem. The two go together, you know. You're the mayor. Plain Oak is my birthplace. Someday I may lie there in the family plot next to Momma and Daddy and my two brothers. Plain Oak can be a New Jerusalem. It can be fuh me and you and if'un we do it right, fuh Almighty God."

Fern's expression was a curious blend of confusion and interest together with a slight impression his distant relative may have gone crazy. He put aside his old cigar and unwrapped a fresh one. After leaning back in his rocking chair, he stated softly, "Harry, you're leaving me a bit confused. What in the world have you got in mind?"

"What do you need to make Plain Oak as great and fine a city as this here place is a garden paradise, John?"

Fern rocked gently in the chair, stared at Sneed and answered, "About fifty or sixty of the right funerals and lots and lots of money."

Sneed focused his eyes on John Fern and announced seriously, "Only the Lord will bring on the funerals but I, with his hep, can get ya the money."

Mayor John Fern was dumbfounded. "Harry, you were there the other night. That flooding they were talking about—I need five million dollars for that one thing alone—five million! We can't raise that kind of money in Plain Oak. A new library would cost over a million. We've got other flood problems besides the South End and I'd like to see us get a great park. Hell, we could go through ten to twenty million dollars like a hot knife through warm butter."

"I'll get it fuh ya, John," Sneed announced calmly, "all you need. We'll make a new Jerusalem—not a comin' down out of Heaven—but a fine place."

"Damnit, Harry, Plain Oak isn't an old Jerusalem. It's a nice place with a lot of good folks and a few sons-a-bitches."

"Its my home, John. Here's where I live but Plain Oak's home. Let's make it a great place, John."

John Fern could scarcely believe what he was hearing. Sneed was thought of as being eccentric but quite sane, too serious a person ever to try practical jokes and anything but stupid. As he rocked in the chair and puffed on his cigar, Fern gathered up the nerve to ask the essential question, "Now Harry, how are you going to come by that kind of money?"

"Now John, that's my business."

Fern stood, paced a short distance and continued, "Now Harry, it wouldn't have something to do with moonshine money paying to make Plain Oak into some kind of New Jerusalem, would it?"

"Now John," Sneed answered calmly, "I haven't distilled a drop in about almost fifty years."

"Then how in the hell do you keep this place?"

"The Lord provides."

"Don't hand me that stuff, Harry," Fern protested. "The Lord provides for me too, but I get mine through a seed and feed business; and for serving at what's supposed to be a part-time job as mayor—which isn't part-time at all—they give me ten thousand dollars a year. It's not much but it's legal and honest. You were a big-time moonshiner once. I couldn't testify to it and I don't want to either but we all know it was true. Now you're telling me you can give the City of Plain Oak fifteen or twenty million dollars. Harry, folks are going to be asking, 'Mr. Sneed, where did you get all that twenty million dollars?' As I remember, you had more than a little bit of trouble with the income-tax people—when was it?—something like forty years ago. Why thanks, Harry, but if you step up and say,

'Okay Plain Oak, take this twenty million and go and do good with it,' you'll be up before more investigating and tax folks than I could shake two sticks at using both of my hands going at once."

"That ain't the way it'll happen, John," Sneed answered quietly but firmly. "I'll get ya the money, fair and square."

Beginning to perspire and feeling edgy, Fern started to pace the floor while Sneed, sitting motionless, stared through the screen toward the stream. John Fern stopped, looked at Harry Sneed and resumed his questioning, "Are you into something crooked?"

"Anything I do, John, is gonna be right."

"Is it legal?"

"Might not be to the letter of the law but it's fair and honest."

"Look Harry, there's one thing I got no use for at all. Honest to God, I wouldn't hurt a flea but I could damned near kill the sons-a-bitches that're pushing drugs whether it's smuggling or growing or doing some chemistry-laboratory stuff..."

"John," Sneed interjected, "I ain't got nothin' ta do with no drugs and I'm long gone out of liquor."

"Are you into bootlegging cigarettes?"

"Nope."

"Gambling?"

"No way."

"Something to do with women?"

"Of course not."

"Smuggling?"

"No.

"Stealing?"

"Never."

"Bootlegging liquor?"

"I said I'm long through with liquor and that means I ain't into bootlegging."

"Fencing?"

"No."

When Fern paused in his interrogation, Sneed filled in, "It ain't none of yuh business. I can get ya the money and it won't be immoral but you won't know nothin'."

"Harry," Fern resumed in a more subdued tone, "was moonshining wrong in your thinking? Was it immoral?"

Sneed jumped at the question with tenacity, "There never was any poison what come from muh stills. I always had me a chemist. When anybody dranked muh stuff, it was okay and they didn't get no sorehead neither. When they dranked that rotgut in lots a places and in speakeasies, there was people what died from it. Nobody never died from mine and if'n they hadn't got what I turned out, they'd a got some other stuff. I didn't take nobody an' say to 'em, 'Here, boy, drink this stuff. It's better than not drinkin' nothing.' They was a drinkin' all along. All I done was get 'em some stuff what was safe and cheap and free from hoodlum crime. Immoral? —not what I done. No suh."

"You could say all of that about drugs today, Harry."

"Ain't no way. Dope's dirty. Them what's in it are low-down trash."

"You never committed a crime, Harry? Don't you think moonshining was wrong?"

"If'n I had a thought it, I wouldn't have distilled one drop. Prohibition come in and couldn't nobody get nothing. Some was a thinkin' and talkin' like it was God's wish so they make it into the law. Alls I can say is them people never knowed their Bible. What was they a gonna do when the Master turned water into wine? Send the revenuers in after him? And don't give me none of that grape-juice talk. Wine is wine."

"Oh, I never would have been for Prohibition, Harry," Fern stated. "I can't see violating the law as being right."

Sneed answered, "When the law's a good law, I says obey it. When the law's sinful, I says treat it as sin."

"Well my question is, Harry, what sinful law are you either disobeying or figuring on disobeying to get to where you can give Plain Oak a huge sum of money so we can make it into some kind of New Jerusalem?"

Before saying anything, Sneed reached for a pipe and filled it from a small pouch of tobacco. He lit it cautiously then stood and gestured with his arms, "Do you see that paradise out there?" he began. "It's beautiful. It's clean. Someday the whole place will go to the state of West Virginia and be protected—a nature preserve with no huntin' and all wilderness. It cleans the air and purifies the water and enriches the land. I put it all together, piece-by-piece, with moonshine money. I don't go to Nevada and throw money around like some folks do. I give to the church. I do next to nothing fuh muhself. It's mostly been fuh right here." Sneed pointed to a flock of birds that happened to be flying by almost on command.

"You're not answering my question, Harry."

"Now you got folks what gets wet every time the Lord calls for a big rain. Water gets in their houses and can cause disease. It's dangerous and could kill. You make a promise. You're a gonna solve it. Then you find you ain't got enough money and you ain't got no way ta get it. What're you gonna do to keep yuh word? I come along and I says, 'I'll get the money.' Then you start a thinkin' how it's crooked money. You're a thinkin' maybe you don't want it. Well, I ask ya, Cousin John, supposen I told you that back in Prohibition times I made a whole mess a money and put it in them Swiss banks, and it's been a gaining interest to where I got a whole lot ta give away. What would ya say to that, Cousin John?"

"Is that the way it is, Harry?" Fern asked in a serious tone.

Refusing to answer, Sneed pressed with the same question, "What would ya do if that was it?"

"I'd want to talk to a lawyer before I give an answer to something like that."

"Bullshit!" Sneed shouted. "This is family business—man-to-man blood talk, me and you. I don't even now want Margaret in on this. You're twenty-one or whatever it is now—eighteen. What would ya do?"

"How does the city get the money?" Fern asked pensively.

"What do you mean?"

"I mean our city gets its money through taxes and fees, fines and licenses. Checks come in from taxpayers paying their taxes. People don't bring in five million or twenty million dollars or whatever in a brown paper bag like you did back when you were buying up all this land and putting big fences around it. People pay taxes they owe unless they can find a way to wiggle out from paying them. They don't go around paying taxes they don't owe—at least that's the way I've always seen it to be.

"Now Harry, if you want to make a gift to Plain Oak, that's fine. You come in and say, 'I, Harry Sneed, do hereby give unto this fine city the sum of twenty million dollars.' You can do that. It would be legal. But everyone including your friends at the IRS would soon be wondering where Mr. Harry Sneed got all that money. You could probably go through a lawyer, Harry, and make some sort of anonymous..."

"I don't trust no lawyers."

"All the same, people would find out with that kind of money."

"Okay, we'll get some taxpayin' businesses started in Plain Oak that'll pay big taxes. There's lots a ways. I'll get ya the money, John. What you gotta do is make up a plan. Get engineering plans and cost numbers done. Leave the gettin' the money part ta me."

Fern returned to the chair and began rocking aggressively. He cleared his throat and resumed in a somber tone, "Harry, you're into something that's not right. I don't know what it is and I reckon I don't want to know. I've never known you to tell a lie about anything, but there's lots of questions you plain don't answer. I don't want Plain Oak taking money from something that's not right."

"There's lots a things what's not right," Sneed retorted vehemently. "All your flooding—that's not right. Hungry kids with nowhere to go and nothin' ta do—that's not right.

"When I was a boy there was a goodly number of whorehouses in Plain Oak. You know what the city done? They fined 'em. They sent old Captain Hawks around ta collect their fine oncest a week. Fine hell! It showed up as a fine on the books. What it was was a license they was a payin' to the city. Old man Mayor Riley, he paved downtown streets, and concrete sidewalks got built with that money. You're too young to remember them old wooden walks. I can remember them a little bit. Well, that's how a lotta streets and walks got built and they're still bein' used today. What are ya gonna do, go out an' tear up them streets and walks 'cause it was whorehouse money what built 'em? Well anyhow, in come muh Uncle Ted Sneed as mayor. You don't remember it. Uncle Ted, he thought it won't right so he stops all the fine collecting from the whorehouses. Does he run the whores out of town? Heck no. They go on whoring all the same, but Plain Oak warn't gettin' no money from it and the streets stopped getting built. I remember when I was fifteen, a bunch of us would go 'an look at them houses. We knew what they was and where they was. We was always too scared to go in but we wanted to."

"Harry, why now?" Fern asked thoughtfully. "You've been out here all these years almost by yourself. Some people are even scared of you. Now you want to do a good turn in this strange, special way. Why? What's going on?"

"Like I said, John, I'm gettin' old and I kinda feel the Lord's a tellin' me to do this thing." While staring into the distance, Sneed puffed a few times on his pipe before continuing, "It's not like I'm having visions or dreams about angels a comin' ta visit me or anything like that. I just sort of feel strong it's the thing ta do an' I can't hardly get it outta muh head. That's the way I think the Lord talks ta me and I know—I just know he's a talkin' ta me."

"At times, Harry, I've thought I'd steal to fix up the South End and do other good things. When all's said and done, I'd never do it for real."

"No, stealin' wouldn't be right. Thou shalt not steal," Sneed lectured. "You get yuh plans done and let me know the cost. I'll take it from there."

"How high can we go?" Fern asked.

"Do the plans with no limit," Sneed replied. "Do everything right. Forget how much money. It'll come."

"Harry, I got to know."

"You can't."

"I'll tell you something, Harry, that'll be hard for you to understand," Fern confided. "I even need money the city hasn't got to get the plans done. That's how bad things are with the city."

"No problem," Sneed answered, "how much?"

"A million dollars—maybe even more than that."

"I'll get it straight to you," Sneed assured John Fern as if there were no problem whatever.

Fern became silent and began gently rocking. Thoughts of massive public works, hiring investigators to fight drugs, solving flooding problems, a new library building, buying and developing a massive city park, paving dirt streets and alleys—these visions all flashed through his mind. He began thinking to himself that the worst thing that could possibly happen to him would be to get caught in some illegal scheme as a conspirator with Harry Sneed. He could be indicted, prosecuted, convicted and sentenced—all for the good of Plain Oak. The punishment would be worth it, he reasoned. Pondering the morality of it all, Fern could see goodness in his going along with whatever crime Sneed might be into and a sin of cowardly selfishness in remaining lawful.

After an indeterminate silence, Sneed reopened the discussion, "There are a few things: You're not a gonna know how I'm a doin' it so don't try and find out cause you won't. Second, don't you talk ta nobody—Margaret, yuh children, yuh lawyer, yuh best friend—nobody. I mean nobody. Third, and this is important cause I'm seventy-six—don't poke around. I can leave a little bit of money when I'm gone but not a whole lot. Besides, I want to see these things done before I pass on to my reward."

"Harry," Fern pleaded, "like I said, I've never known you to lie. I've got to know for sure you aren't getting this kind of money from drugs or bad crime."

"You have my word—no drugs, no stealin' or fencing, nothin' immoral and no bootlegging. There ain't no moonshining neither but if there was, there ain't nothin' bad in that."

"Harry," Fern resumed in a more reflective tone, "all the money the city spends has to be appropriated by the city council through the budget. If all of a sudden the city treasury starts getting lots and lots of money in it, some of the council members will start pushing for pet projects of their own; and the workers, the police and firemen and the others, they'll start agitating for raises and by rights they ought to be paid more. The problem is we'll have a surge of money that won't keep up, and if we raise people's pay and the dollars slow down, the city'll get in a heap of trouble."

Sneed's nodding was an indication he followed what Fern had been saying. "You'll have to work it out, John," he declared. "You're the mayor. Put it in a special fund or something."

"Let me put it to you in a different way, Harry," Fern continued. "You said something like you might create some taxpaying corporations in Plain Oak, and they would start paying lots of taxes. If this got done, all the money would go into our general fund and would have to be appropriated before it was spent on anything. I make up a recommended budget but the city council has to pass it. They can and they will change it. With money like this, they'd put in their pet projects and raise everybody's pay all over the place."

Fern could tell from the look on Sneed's face that his third cousin understood the problem perfectly. Still staring at the floor and puffing on a pipe, Sneed answered, "It'll have to be given specially for what we want done with the money."

"That'll do it," Fern agreed. "If somebody gives or wills money to the city for a special purpose and the city accepts the gift, it'll have to be spent for what it was given to do so long as the whole thing's legal of course."

"Lessun somebody challenges it in a court of law."

"Let me assure you of one thing, Harry," Fern declared. "If anybody gives money to the city of Plain Oak to put a drainage project in the South End or build a public library, there'll be an awful lot of lawyer doings to make it happen."

"I'll have to get it ta ya dedicated somehow. Leave that ta me."

"It would be easy if everybody knows you're the one giving it, Harry. If nobody knows where the money's coming from, the whole thing won't be so easy."

"I'll work it out."

"I don't know, Harry," Fern began slowly and thoughtfully, "I was trying to think about the New Jerusalem. Seems like it's in the Book of Revelation."

"Revelation, chapter 21," Sneed affirmed. " 'And I John saw the holy city, New Jerusalem, coming down from God out of heaven, prepared as a bride adorned for her husband.' We can't do what only God can do but we can do our best to make our own New Jerusalem. It won't be perfectly square and have twelve gates and all but we can do our best here on earth to make a truly good city."

As John Fern began to pace the floor again, Sneed could read what was going through his cousin's mind: The money could be used to do a lot of good for Plain Oak. On the other hand, there was probably something illegal involved but all Fern would know was that it had nothing to do with drugs, violence, theft, prostitution or gambling. While Sneed was known to be a strangely righteous man who read the Bible frequently, he was definitely the sort who could and would derive from scripture almost any message he wanted.

After an extended silence, Fern announced decisively, "Harry, you get me the money into the city treasury in a lawful way and we'll make Plain Oak into the greatest place on earth."

Sneed stared toward the stream. Several ducks were floating but would submerge occasionally to feed. "Okay," he agreed, "but from now on, don't you ever call me. It's long distance and there'll be a record of the calls. I'll call ya when I'm in town but I won't be talking business to ya. When I first call, you go right away to the payphone at the A&P near the boulevard. I'll ring it and that way we can talk an' won't nobody be a buggin' us."

Sneed's remarks sent a chill through John Fern. "Harry, this is what bothers me. Why would anyone want to tap your phone or care if I call you long distance? You're Margaret's uncle."

"They wouldn't," Sneed answered factually. "It's just a precaution. People'll do anything fuh money. When Plain Oak starts getting' lots and lots, they'll want to get at it and they'll stop at nothing."

"Anything else?"

"Nope, that's it," Sneed concluded, "lessun ya still want to go fishin'. Seems the stream's cleared up. If them ducks can see around when they poke their heads under the water, I figure a fish can see to take bait. I know where there's a bass or two, big fightin' ones."

CHAPTER 4
AN UNUSUAL PACKAGE

The council chamber was almost empty. No one had signed up to speak. The only important business on the agenda was a late-season bid opening for repaving a few city streets. John Fern began to hope the session would be over in ten to fifteen minutes.

Since the Elliott Asphalt Paving Company had the only blacktop plant within a twenty-mile radius of town, it was usually a foregone conclusion that this firm, owned by two brothers, would win every paving contract for work in or near Plain Oak. This evening, however, there were two other submissions. One was from Road Builders, Inc. of Traylorsville, the recent low bidder on 40,000 tons of sheet-asphalt work on a nearby state highway. The other proposal had been delivered in a heavy, tightly wrapped package left outside the city clerk's office during the noon hour. It bore no sender's name or return address. On all sides of the box, typed labels had been affixed. These read:

> To the Honorable Mayor and City Council—
> Plain Oak, West Virginia—To Be Opened
> With the Paving Bids

This proposal did attract interest. No one knew who had delivered it. In addition, a paving bid wrapped as a package was unprecedented. They were usually mailed or hand-delivered in nothing larger than a nine by twelve-inch envelope.

Arch Kidd tapped the gavel and asked the city engineer to help the clerk with the bid opening. Since the work was all bituminous asphalt of a set specification, the figure everyone would be watching was the cost per ton of material, rolled and in place. The bid from Elliott County Asphalt was $44.00 while that of Road Builders, Inc. was $45.50 per ton.

City Engineer John Ruffy and Howard Sanders, the black city hall janitor, together lifted the package onto the clerk's writing table. Ruffy used his pocketknife to cut through the heavy tape and wrapping paper to uncover a cardboard box that was also well reinforced with tape.

"Whoever sent this bid must have wanted to attract a lot of attention," Kidd remarked to the seven private citizens who made up the audience. "It's probably some kind of publicity stunt."

"This beats anything I've ever seen," Ruffy added as he cut through the top of the cardboard. "Maybe this bid's been chiseled into a marble slab."

John Fern watched eagerly while the city engineer used his knife to slice through a few more pieces of tape. "It might be something other than a paving bid," he stated casually.

When the cardboard lid was opened, John Ruffy suddenly shouted, "Good God! It's full of money—big money!"

For a few seconds everyone was stunned into silence. "Get a couple of policemen in here quick!" the mayor ordered to Howard Sanders. "And tell the sergeant on duty to get the police chief down here right away!"

"There seems to be an envelope," Ruffy advised.

At this point the meeting broke into pandemonium. Everyone left his or her seat to peer into the box. Marion Walk, a newswoman who covered almost all council sessions, broke out laughing and started writing rapidly in her notepad. Kidd was so shaken he forgot his duties as chairman until the mayor shouted, "For God's sake, Arch, get this meeting back to order! Make everyone sit down. We've got some serious business here."

With this Kidd pounded the gavel and shouted, "Order! Order! Everyone be seated. We'll know quicker what this is all about the sooner everybody sits down and we have order."

After rapping a few more times, everyone sat down. The citizen spectators had all moved to the front row. Once calm was restored, John Ruffy advised again, "There's an envelope stuck to the inside..."

"Will the city clerk please open this envelope and read whatever's in it," Kidd instructed in a loud excited voice.

Before Elton Naylor could begin reading, two young policemen entered the chamber. "Chief will be here in ten minutes," one of them announced.

"Officers," Fern explained, "the city engineer has just opened this box apparently full of money. While we're trying to understand this, we want you here for protection so stand by."

"Yes sir, Mayor."

"Go ahead, Mr. Naylor," Kidd continued.

Elton Naylor was a quiet, officiously conscientious man of fifty-five who usually spoke slowly and softly. All the excitement brought forth a nervousness in his voice which he strained to conceal. "This letter is addressed to the Mayor and City Council of Plain Oak, West Virginia. There's no name given—sender's name that is. It's all typewritten."

"Please read it, Mr. Naylor," Kidd repeated.

Naylor began nervously:

> **The Lord gives all things. This is a gift to the city of Plain Oak to be used to make it the great city it deserves to be. Use it to do the engineering plans for the South End. Use it to hire an architect for a new library. Use it for planning whatever the mayor wants to plan and if the engineering is good and the planning is good, there will be much more money for building these things. If this money is abused, there will be no more.**

Naylor concluded by saying, "The only name given is 'a friend of Plain Oak.'"

The chairman asked, "You say there's no indication of who sent this?"

"Not from what I see here," the clerk replied.

Kidd looked at the mayor and remarked, "John, this beats anything I've ever seen or even heard about. What do you think we ought to do?"

"First we should get it into a secure vault," Fern replied. "The banks are all closed and the time vault at First National can't be opened until tomorrow morning."

Bill Willy, the city attorney, volunteered, "Mayor and gentlemen, you can store this money with police protection in the city treasurer's vault and I'm sure it'll be quite safe. Two things should be done right away though. The money should be counted with good witnesses so no one here gets accused of making off with any of it. The second thing is we should get the FBI in here right away. This could be from a bank holdup or something."

Everyone paused for a few seconds. "I think you've hit on the right advice, Bill," Fern added approvingly. "What about the serial numbers on the bills?"

Bill Willy thought for a moment and added, "Right, Mayor, we should probably have our own inventory of the bills by serial number. It would give us better control over this."

Fern added, "We will have to keep the inventory secret or somebody might get our list and use it to make a false claim for the money."

"It could happen, Mayor," the city attorney agreed.

"What else?"

"I'll have to be doing some legal research. Unless a valid claim is made that it really belongs to someone else and was stolen or something, I'm satisfied it'll belong to the city. Of course, the donor may claim temporary insanity and want it all back but the real risk is that it was stolen."

"Great God!" Fern added seriously. "If there's a lot of money here, claims could start coming in from one end of the world to the other."

"All the more reason to get it counted, inventoried by serial number and put into a secure vault for safekeeping," Willy advised. "Frankly, Mayor, the counting ought to be done tonight."

John Fern turned to the city clerk and instructed, "Elton, call Al Triere. Get him down here right away with as much help from his treasurer's office as he can get to come in. You and he'll count this money and list the serial number to each bill. Get the coffeepot going. Unless there's a bunch of bricks in the bottom of that box, this could be an all-night job!"

* * *

At 8:50 the next morning, several boxes of currency and a giant plastic yard bag holding the cardboard box and wrapping materials were placed in the trunk of the police car that also carried the mayor, the city clerk and the treasurer. When everything was ready, Chief Sacker started his siren and flashing light, and two patrol cars moved rapidly through downtown streets to the rear entrance of the First National Bank. Here a security guard and the bank's president, Terry Switsworth, were waiting.

"Good morning, John," Switsworth opened with a broad smile. "The paper said there was about a million. Was that right?"

"Just over a million, Terry."

"Let's get it good and locked up for now. We'll use a sort of vault within a vault. You can have the full use of a big safe we have inside our vault and you can add all the chains and locks you want to it. Your stuff will be all right."

"That's fine," Fern agreed.

"You'll have to sign a paper, John," Switsworth advised as they left the loading area. "We'll get it to you in a minute."

After everything was secured, the four city officials—Naylor, Triere, Chief Sacker and John Fern—stopped by the president's office for a brief visit. After they were all seated, the banker looked at Fern and asked him, "John, what's the city going to do?"

"We'll be guided by our city attorney," the mayor replied, "because there's a lot of law in all this. Personally I'm hoping we can make plans for the South End drainage, a new library, maybe a park and lots of things like that. Our giver wrote like more money would be coming and we should make good plans for using it."

"I know," Switsworth commented. "Marion ran the whole letter in today's Dispatch."

"Terry, we've instructed everyone to give out no details about all this to make it hard for someone to concoct a false claim that it was really theirs."

"That sounds like a wise move, John," Terry Switsworth stated. He then continued, "I hate to say what I'm going to say, John, but when big money appears suddenly and there's no explanation, there's probably been a crime. Nowadays this usually means illegal drugs or maybe some kind of money laundering. Whatever's going on, somebody's hiding something. Something's not right."

"I was afraid you would be saying that kind of thing, Terry," Naylor added.

"If no one can tie it to a rightful owner and you report everything to the authorities," Switsworth continued, "it'll probably be seen as an abandonment of personal property. This means that technically it'll belong to the city because you found it on city property and exercised control over it."

"Will we have to wait a long time before we can spend it?" Fern inquired.

"I really don't know how long something like this usually takes," the bank president replied. "You see, if you do spend it, you'd be doing so at your peril. The FBI and the Secret Service and maybe the state banking people will all come in here. It might be a good idea to try and get them in together and cut down on the amount of your time they'll take up. They'll be doing fingerprints and checking for counterfeits. Sometimes they can tell a lot about money from the serial numbers. They'll figure out things you and I don't even know about."

"I don't suppose we could go ahead and deposit it with you, could we?" Fern queried.

"Heavens no," Switsworth answered bluntly. "Every now and then some character we don't know shows up here trying to make a big cash deposit. If it seems fishy—and it usually does—we refuse him and report it. Taking in hot cash is something this bank won't do as long as I'm here. Now there are other banks around that don't ask the kinds of questions this one does."

"But if this is illegal money, why would the criminals behind it want to donate it to a city?" Naylor inquired. "It's hard for me to imagine any criminal wanting to give money away especially to a municipal government."

"I don't know about that," the police chief replied. "Lots of funny things happen because of criminal types. Giving away big money and watching all the confusion it causes could be someone's idea of fun. Even sending it done up in a package to be opened during a public meeting is clearly the work of a thrill seeker—someone who likes doing jokes for crazy excitement. The crime wouldn't be for gain but for the thrill and fun of doing it. There's even a little Robin Hood in all this because our city's always broke for money that could do a lot of good."

"It could be somebody like that," the banker agreed, "maybe a criminal, maybe not. We'll eventually know. For the city's sake I hope it's all legitimate, John, but don't count on it.

"One other thing," he continued. "You won't have to worry about somebody making a phony claim. Anybody smart enough to dream up a good case for it will have the brains to know there'll be a lot of questions to answer about how they got the money in the first place. If they can't figure that one out, they'll be too dumb to come up with a good story."

CHAPTER 5
A TROUBLED MAYOR

When John Fern finally got back to his home, Margaret was seated at the dining-room table. "So you've been out working?" she began.

"I've been watching other folks work, Margaret," he answered in a yawn before giving her a gentle kiss on the cheek.

"I reckon you'll want breakfast and then go to bed?" she continued indifferently.

"Sounds good, Margaret, only no coffee this time, please."

"Marion wrote there was a million dollars. Was that true?" she quizzed as if last night's happenings took place day in and day out in Plain Oak.

"Give or take," he replied while seating himself at the table.

"I never knew Uncle Harry was that give-or-take rich," she remarked casually.

"Who said it was Harry?"

"Who but Harry? 'The Lord giveth all things.' That alone giveth Harry away—and him showing up at the meeting two weeks back and calling you. No one else can know you went fishing down there after all these years. The whole thing's exactly like him. The only thing is he's never done anything like this before but every time Uncle Harry ever does anything, it's always something that's never been done before. I'll give him his due."

"Whoever it was doesn't want it to be known who it was," Fern stated emphatically, "and one million dollars spent right can do this poor town some real good."

"'And if the planning is good, there will be more.' Marion wrote it in her article. It's fine for Harry to be helping something besides his bears and frogs," she continued, "but he'll get picked up. You can't run white-lightning stills anymore and not get caught. Don't you let him get you ensnarled with him."

"For what it may be worth, Margaret, your Uncle Harry Sneed told me eyeball-to-eyeball he hasn't distilled a drop since way before the war."

"Then the Good Lord has undoubtedly seen fit to bless him in some other way," Margaret observed. "I wonder what Uncle Harry's turned to since he's turned away from turning out his holy mash."

"I don't know anything wrong he's doing, Margaret. I haven't heard tell of him being into anything. I asked and asked and he assured me anything he was doing was right," Fern argued. "Now I don't know what he's doing. He said something like he had a lot of money in Swiss banks earning interest. I don't know whether this is true because he was always using, 'for instance,' when he talked like that. But I do know whoever gave all that money—and I want to emphasize I never said it was Harry—whoever it was doesn't want it known who it was."

"Don't worry, John. I won't tell one soul. But mark my word, he's going to get caught and I don't want you getting trapped with him. Uncle Harry's one of those people who can do no wrong no matter what he's up to or however he's going about doing it."

After Margaret had disappeared into the kitchen to prepare his breakfast, he picked up the Plain Oak Dispatch to read Marion Walk's article. Dominating the front page was the headline: CITY RECEIVES ANONYMOUS GIFT PACKAGE OF $1,000,000 IN CASH—FBI CONTACTED.

Marion Walk's stories were always crisp and accurate. Fern's eyes skimmed ahead to the very end of the column where he was quoted:

> …Mayor John Fern would make only a few general comments. "I hope it turns out to be lawful money that can be spent for the good of our city," he said. "This could get us started on the South End Flood Control Project and other badly needed things. We will cooperate fully with any investigation. If this is criminal money, we won't use it."

After breakfast he mounted the stairs, got dressed in pajamas and went to bed. A gentle softness pervaded everything and he felt unusually comfortable. An early doze was interrupted by Margaret's disconnecting the telephone. Her tiptoeing was slow, soft and rhythmical.

At 5:30 that afternoon she shook him to partial consciousness but he kept drifting back to sleep. Something reminded him that Amy was coming. Maybe she had heard from Jack. Fern shook his head, sat up and finally stood on the floor.

After a difficult shower and shave, he descended the stairs and mixed a gin and tonic. He then sat in his rocking chair and confided, "I really buzzed off, Margaret. I don't remember a thing after you unhooked that phone. I'm still half-asleep."

"You're getting famous now, John," Margaret informed her husband. "NBC News, CBS, ABC and several newspapers have been wanting to talk to you but I told them you weren't available. A man from the FBI called from Washington. I told him you were sound asleep and he said, 'Good.' He said he'll call you this evening at six sharp. That's why I got you up. He said it was best for you not to talk to anybody, and he was telephoning everyone who counted the money last night. I gathered he's already talked to the police chief, 'Sad Sack' Sacker."

"That's interesting."

"So don't drink that stuff too fast. It might make your liver shiver and find its way on up into your brain."

John Fern rocked a few times, paused and gently sipped his drink. "Come to think of it, a foundling bundle of about one million bucks in the doorway of the city clerk's office in plain old Plain Oak is the kind of thing to make news," he informed his wife. "Maybe I'll look good on TV and run for president."

At two minutes past six, the telephone rang. Fern's stomach sank and his heart began to pound steadily. After two more rings, he stated to Margaret, "It's got to be for me. I'll get it." He stood, went into the kitchen and picked up the phone. "Hello," he answered calmly. "Speaking…Yes sir…That's right…It's all in a big safe that's in the big vault at the First National Bank here in town … No sir, the letter is in the city clerk's vault. It's an official city record so that's where it belongs…That's good…I haven't said much of anything to anybody. We were up all night and I've been sleep just about all day…She covers city hall and writes almost all the news articles about the council meetings. She was there and saw it all…Of course we'll cooperate. We want to get to the bottom of this same as you do… Certainly…Okay, we'll be looking for you sometime Tuesday morning. …Thank you, sir, and good-by."

"Now pray, what's that all about? Is the FBI still alive and well with old J. Edgar gone?"

"They'll be getting here Tuesday in the mid-morning. That was a Mr. Alex Parker who must be the chief assistant deputy to the deputy assistant chief."

"He's the one I talked to."

"They'll be flying a charter in from Washington and they'll be bringing FBI and Treasury Department people to count the money all over again," he informed her. "They'll be putting the bill numbers into some computer thing."

"That's good," she remarked. "This old town will start livening up and I bet old Harry's beginning to squirm."

After Fern returned to the rocking chair, a sense of terror gripped him all at once. Might he be involved in a criminal conspiracy? Surely he would be asked if he had any idea who had sent the money. How would he answer? Might the FBI and other agencies have a file on Harry Sneed and go after him? Still how would he, the mayor, be implicated? The money was for a worthy cause—solving city problems. It was not destined for anyone's pocket, certainly not his own.

Fern sipped his cool drink and became more relaxed. *Even if the whole thing got to be known*, he reasoned to himself, *I'd simply tell the truth. If I told anyone it was Harry, I'd be chopping down the city's money tree. Folks would understand*, he continued musing to himself. Next he announced once again, "I never said it was Harry, Margaret, and I'd just as soon you not mention his name to anybody."

An hour and a half later, an automobile entered the driveway, and the slamming of car doors and the trunk signaled Amy and Tommy's arrival. The Ferns both jumped up and greeted the young couple with warmth and affection.

Until his daughter and son-in-law actually arrived, the idea of their coming was a sustained and cheerful thought radiating warmth in Fern's troubled mind. After fifteen or twenty minutes of catching up which he viewed as a lot of nothing gibberish, this happy anticipation inevitably faded and the conveniently forgotten alienation would resume once again.

Before their coming, John Fern had a strong urge to talk alone with Amy—about Jack, about herself and probably about himself as well. As soon as they had settled in for their visit, Tommy began to remain around Amy like a secret agent charged with preventing a defection from an autocratic regime. To make matters worse, Amy seemed to be getting the same way and would not let Tommy out of her sight either.

Fern had always been able to suppress a latent dislike of his son-in-law. Ever since the wedding twenty months earlier, he had been laboring to accept the fact that Tommy

Webber had become a member of the family. There was no explanation for this silent disdain. A proud father, John Fern had probably wanted someone more outstanding for Amy. Also Tommy, like the other members of the Webber family, had nothing distinctive about him. He was not funny. He lacked originality. There were no colorful features or quirks. Any cartoonist would have trouble doing a caricature of him. Nonetheless Tommy was a "safe" person for his daughter. He was not the sort to chase women, beat Amy, become an alcoholic, take drugs, get fired or cause embarrassment to anyone in the family. Were there someone with whom he might confide about it, John Fern would explain, "Tommy Webber's just a damned non-entity."

When the "catching-up" talk was about over, the telephone rang. It was one of Tommy's aunts, and Amy went and stood beside her husband near the phone in a display of deep concern and interest in every detail about her newly acquired relative.

Tommy had a big family. The call reminded John Fern of another thing conveniently forgotten after previous visits by Amy and her husband—someone in the Webber clan was always getting sick prompting a multitude of inquiries and chatter to start back and forth by phone about how "she" and occasionally "he" was doing. On this trip it turned out to be Aunt Pearl's turn. "Poor Aunt Pearl's angina is acting up," he heard Amy telling Margaret.

The whole pattern was revived in Fern's memory like a recurring nightmare. *My God, here we go again*, he pondered to himself as he gulped a large swig of gin and tonic and began rocking deliberately in his chair. His anger quickly reached a flashpoint where Fern either could not or did not want to control himself any longer. He then thundered in desperation to Tommy Webber, "Why don't you send poor old Pearl a fifth of good bourbon and a box of fine cigars."

"Oh Daddy," Amy replied while managing a feigned smile and enough serenity to mask her inner shock, "that wouldn't do."

"Aunt Pearl doesn't drink, Mr. Fern," Tommy replied in a relaxed tone which contained a trace of well-managed anger.

"Then it's not too late for her to start," Fern retorted with a bitterness directed more at himself than at his son-in-law. "If she won't take bourbon, send her a case of cold beer!"

With his latest gibe, Fern stormed out of the door into the dark, humid evening. After walking down the driveway and into the backyard, he heard a faint sound of their telephone ringing again. He held his breath hoping it was Jack, but not hearing Margaret call for him, Fern concluded another member of the Webber family was seeking or giving more news of Aunt Pearl and asking the usual trivia about Amy and Tommy.

Three more days of this shit, he reminded himself in a sober realization that any thought of Amy's coming home was a sugarcoated delusion that would always be shattered as soon as she and Tommy arrived at 327 Oak View Drive.

He sat on some deck furniture but found it damp. There was also the feeling of tiny bugs being everywhere. A meteor streaked across the late August sky. His thoughts turned to Uncle Jake who had died twenty years earlier. When anything was seriously bothering him, Fern would visit Jake, pour out his soul and come away with absolute confidence about what to do and how to do it. All Jake ever did was listen intently, ask questions, say comical things and tell old stories that paralleled Fern's situation. For some reason tears blurred his eyes and drained down his cheeks. *Thank God for Margaret.*

Suddenly John Fern had a brief but terrifying compulsion—an urge to grab a garden spade and drive to the old city cemetery, dig up Jake's grave and open his coffin for one last reunion.

Realizing his impulse was nurtured in a streak of madness, he returned to the house to find Margaret. After rushing from room to room, he found her alone in their bedroom seemingly weeping. "Margaret, I love you," he sobbed as he approached to embrace her. "I'll always love you."

CHAPTER 6
NO COMMENT

After saying good-by and watching the young couple drive off, John and Margaret Fern stared soberly at one another for a brief, almost timeless moment. Their simple exchange unveiled an admission of problems weighing heavily on their minds: Had they been poor parents? Would the rest of their lives be one long wait for a telephone call from Jack? Should they go out looking for him? What will be the fate of the Harry Sneed affair?

This silent understanding was intense and disquieting in ways neither could endure. John Fern broke it by looking at his watch and saying, "Goodness, Margaret, here it is after nine and we're hosting a convention of FBI and Secret Service and heaven only knows who else."

After they entered the side door, the telephone began ringing. Although several feet away from where her husband answered it, Margaret could recognize Allie Eller's voice.

"Then I'll be going straight to the bank, Allie," John Fern said. "That's where I'll be until you hear something different." After hanging up, he repeated what had been told him. "They'll be here in forty minutes. We'll be meeting at the bank."

A few minutes later, Margaret noticed several persons on the sidewalk in front of their home. Someone was setting up a television camera. Her face betrayed an inner turmoil. She did not like a throng of people swarming around 327 Oak View Drive but the activity meant a break from the usual monotony. After regaining her composure, she announced, "Smile, John, soon you'll be on Candid Camera."

When John Fern looked out the front window, his face turned reddish. Next he sat in his rocking chair and lit a cigar. "I'm going to say nothing. I'll smile, wave to them and answer 'no comment' to everything they ask me."

"You'll do that very well, John," she teased. "I have every confidence you'll rise up and meet such a lofty challenge." Returning to the window, she observed, "I see they've placed a TV camera so you can't back out of our driveway. You'll have to order it moved. They can't do this to you of all people, the mayor. It deprives you of…what do you folks down at city hall call it? …ingress and egress? I can't wait for the evening news."

"I'll start the sprinkler over in that part of the yard," he advised.

"That's a wonderful idea, John," she persisted. "Of course, you'll have to go out into the yard, hook up the hose, move the sprinkler over there and turn it on. While you're doing all that, you can tell them 'no comment' so many times they might nickname you 'No Comment Fern'."

Fern continued rocking deliberately. About once every minute, he paused to look at his watch. Finally he mustered some nerve and walked outside through the side door. Seeing that the driveway was in fact blocked, he went forward and announced nervously, "I really don't have anything to say."

"Was the money stolen, Mayor?" one reporter shouted.

"We don't know. We hope not but we'll find out."

"Did you talk with the FBI, Mayor?" another asked.

"Yes."

"What did you all talk about?"

"They're going to investigate and we're cooperating fully. That's all."

"What will the city do with the money if it's all legit and you can keep it, Mister Mayor?"

"I really have no comment to make at this time," Fern answered. "Now you've got my car blocked and I've got to get on with being mayor."

"Do you know who sent the money, Mayor?" another announcer asked in a loud voice.

"No comment. No comment. We're cooperating fully with the authorities. No more comments. Please let me out."

With this, Fern got into his Pontiac, started the engine and began easing backward toward the street. The cameras were taken out of the way. One newsman holding a microphone asked through the car window, "Where are you off to now, Mayor?"

John Fern answered, "Out," and continued backing into the street.

CHAPTER 7
A NEW JERUSALEM

Harry Sneed drove through scattered thundershowers. A magnificent rainbow outside Fayetteville prompted a smile of assurance. God's will was being done exactly. Goodness is people living together and loving one another and loving God and the world he created. Sneed would help bring about a perfect city, a New Jerusalem. Plain Oak would be first. Later there might be others. John Fern would be an architect but God was behind the whole idea.

Just before Gauley Bridge, Sneed jammed his brakes and skidded across a snake killing it instantly—another sign, evil in retreat. Remembering how Moses was punished by not being allowed to enter the Promised Land, Harry Sneed once again vowed to remain free from sin.

After a short drive over a back road lined with maple trees, he reached the Hillside Mission Church of Prayer, Prophesy and Revelation. No one else was around. Dusk was settling into the mountains and scattered clumps of woods. He parked in a small lot and went inside.

The empty church had a quiet, simple beauty. Sneed sat meditating and staring into the shadows.

A half an hour later, another car stopped. Footsteps were heard mounting the wooden stairs and entering the church. A tall brunette man of fifty walked up and down the aisles seemingly searching for someone hidden. He kneeled at the altar and prayed for about two minutes. Next he enunciated in a deep voice, "Are you alone, Harry?"

"No Tom," Sneed answered in a quivering voice. "God's in here."

"Any one else, Harry, here or around?"

"No one else, Tom."

"Okay Harry, what can I do for you?" Tom asked in a stern but peaceful tone.

"I'm doin' the will of God, Tom," Sneed began. "I know it in my bones and soul, so when you ask what can you do fuh me, you're a really askin' what can you do fuh Almighty God!"

Tom rephrased the question perfunctorily, "What can I do for you and Almighty God, Harry?"

"Thomas, I hear yuh daddy is about to take his place in God's Eternal Kingdom," Sneed stated inquisitively.

"Yes, Harry, his time seems to be near."

"The faith still got big insurance on him?"

"Yes, Harry, quite a lot."

"Mightn't it be ten million dollars worth?"

"Yes, ten million, Harry."

Sneed gave a knifelike stare and remarked seriously, "Now here's what I'm a askin' ya ta do, Tom. I'm askin' you to get him to give eight of the ten to the city of Plain Oak, West Virginia. This means changin' the policy so when he's gone that city'll get the money. He'll need to have witnesses swear he's sane when he makes the change. It's for the glory of God and the salvation of men. Of course, the faith'll come into much more than the eight million it'd be a getting' from the policy, but this'll have to be scattered out over time same as pro'bly you'd be a gettin' anyhow. I don't reckon no insurance company gonna give up all ten million at oncest—in one big check, that is."

Tom Clair maintained a stoic expression. "So it was your doings giving that box of cash to that town."

"Not from me, Tom, no more than the money for a lot of yuh missions come from me or any of the faithful. It come from God and God's got a plan for its use—a New Jerusalem— same as God has seen to it yuh missions would grow and multiply, and they have and still are to this very day and will 'til the Second Comin'!"

Tom Clair appeared to be in deep reflection. "I'm troubled, Harry, by all this. Saint Paul wrote to Timothy that money is the root of all evil. Here you go giving money to some city. Did you ever think... did it ever occur to you," Clair began exclaiming loudly, "that you might be corrupting that city by giving money to it?"

"Tom," Sneed answered quickly, "Saint Paul ain't never said money was the root of all evil. You've got to read your Bible with greater care. He said the love of money was the root of all evil and he was right! There's a difference. I never give no money to no city and I ain't a gonna neither. God Almighty give it an' will give it, the same as yuh daddy givin' it ain't him a givin' it or Prudential Life or whatever one it is. It's God a doin' it fuh his plan fuh a New Jerusalem an' to work against sin and to clear a path fuh the Coming!"

Tom Clair began arguing earnestly, "Now listen, Harry, we been counting on that money someday to help us get on with Daddy gone so we can keep up doing good things and serving the Lord. This is the will of Almighty God."

"The faith'll get all those good things and lots more," Sneed answered tenaciously. "I'm a tellin' ya in the presence of God Almighty." He paused for a lengthy moment and his voice turned calmer as he continued almost in a whisper, "You see how it's misty-like all over in here—almost like it's smoky inside this church?" Sneed was looking at Clair as if he were expecting the reply he did not get. "That's Almighty God a bein' with us, Tom."

"What'll you do, Harry, if my daddy doesn't change the beneficiary to the policies? There's several policies. What'll you do? Are you going to stop your gifts to the faith?"

"God's gifts, Tom." Sneed corrected politely.

"God's gifts. Are you going to stop God's gifts, Harry?"

"Tom," Sneed replied in a reverent tone that still reflected a trace of condescension, "I ain't worried about that. God'll ask ya ta ask yuh daddy to change them policies. You get on yuh knees an' pray. Pray hard! Ask his guidance. You'll get it. Has God ever failed yuh missions an' the work? Has he? Course not."

Clair paced up and down the floor deep in thought. Darkness was beginning to settle into the small, slightly musty church. As he passed a candle stand, he struck a wooden match and lit a few of the candles. "I seen about that thing in the papers, Harry," he began cautiously. "Said FBI and all kinds of the law will be checking about that box of money. Now if daddy's insurance is changed to Plain Oak City, they'll think our missions give all that money. The law will be checking all over our faith. What will our faithful think? What will they think? They'll think why should we give to the Lord's work if they're just gonna take their gifts, take them and give them to some city somewheres. That's what taxes are for. 'Render unto Caesar the things that are Caesar's.' Taxes are for the city. The insurance money is for God. I can see how the law will start thinking all that money come from our missions. Harry, it isn't a good plan. You've got to think it through. Why would daddy be leaving eight million dollars to some little old place he's hardly ever been to? Why would he?"

"There'll be more and more after he's in Paradise and the Lord uses the eight million dollars to make his New Jerusalem," Sneed explained. "Yes, Tom, 'Render unto Caesar,' of course. But you've gotta see how givin' it to Plain Oak is givin' it from God back to God to be used where he wants. Pray, Tom. God'll guide ya and you'll see it all."

"Are you going to cut us off if we don't change the policies like you say?" Clair asked again.

"Whatever's the will of God," Sneed replied. "I just want to know and to do his will, Tom. That's all. His anger can be kindled when his will ain't done. You know that." Sneed next smiled serenely and added, "But I ain't worried about that, Tom. I ain't worried. Talk with yuh daddy. Tell him what I said or let me talk to him. Tell him I been seein' signs and I know this is the right thing. You'll get a lot more than the eight million to do the good work."

"I can talk to him, Harry," Clair answered, "but I'm thinking he won't be changing nothing."

"Yuh daddy an' me go back a long way, Tom," Sneed reminisced sentimentally. "He baptized me—not the first time but the first time with fire."

"He'll see you, Harry."

"Let me know the time and the place. I'll be there, Tom. I kinda want to see him anyhow," Sneed explained wistfully.

Still deep in thought, Tom Clair commenced a new line of inquiry. "Did you ever think, Harry, that in this New Jerusalem idea you might be a false prophet and somehow, without you knowing it, of course, you're being led by Satan?"

"God be my witness, Tom," Sneed replied confidently, "I think about it all the time. I pray to Almighty God to lead me straight and away from the ways of the devil. I tell you, Tom, I been seeing signs."

"Satan may be leaving signs, Harry."

"Satan ain't a leadin' me around, Tom," Sneed replied indignantly. "Some things you just know fuh sure. Can Satan make a rainbow?" he asked pausing for a reply that never came. "You pray. Ask yuh daddy ta pray. Don't worry about the money. You'll get all you need. You always have, haven't you?"

Tom Clair stared soberly at Sneed, looked at the flickering candle for a few seconds and glanced at the floor. Again he looked back at Sneed and declared, "Harry, we can't move no eight million dollars in cash no matter how perfect the stuff is. The insurance money was our way to get it into checks and all. We've been paying big premiums…"

"You don't never try to move no eight million or whatever gift you shall receive all at onest, Tom," Sneed argued as if he were instructing a small child. "Trade it around a little at the time. It improves with age."

"I don't like it, Harry," Clair stated shaking his head in the negative. " I don't like it at all."

"Where's Thomas?"

"Morgantown."

"University Hospital?"

"He's staying at the Mountaineer and goes in for a treatment every few days. He'll be there another month at least."

"I'm on my way, Tom. Are you comin' too?"

"I can't go there now, Harry."

Sneed walked out of the church and into the dark. He paused to look for another sign, but the stars and the moon were hidden in an overcast sky.

At ten minutes after eleven, Harry Sneed checked into the Mountaineer. "Is the Reverend Thomas Clair, Senior, staying here?" Sneed inquired as he paid for a night's lodging.

"Yes sir," the desk clerk replied.

"Can I send him a note?"

* * *

When 10 a.m. finally arrived, a personal secretary greeted Harry Sneed at the entrance to the hotel suite. "Reverend Clair will see you now, Mr. Sneed," he advised. "Take the first door on the right."

Sneed was both shocked and saddened at the appearance of his old friend who seemed emaciated, artificially tan and much older. "May the Lord bless you, Harry," Thomas Clair opened. "May the Lord bless you."

Sneed was gripped with silence and his eyes became moist. Fearing his own voice would break, he paused soberly and merely shook Clair's hand and then seated himself on a small chair to the side of the patient's chair.

"You've come to see me before I'm gone, Harry," Clair began. "I'm glad you come. I been thinking and praying about you, Harry. God made the missions, of course, but you was doin' God's will and of us all, you was the important one with all the money you give to get us going specially in the beginning."

"Thomas, I been…"

"Harry, I'm about to pass on and I'm troubled about the faith," Clair confided. "It'll go on without me but it's changing in ways I wonder about. The old faith is changing."

"I been seein' signs, Thomas. God's got a plan. I know about it and God wants my help like when the missions…"

"James wrote in his letter," Clair continued, " 'Now an answer for the rich. Start crying. Weep for the miseries that are coming to you. Your wealth is all rotting, your clothes are all eaten away by moths. All your gold and your silver are corroding away, and the same corrosion will be your own sentence and eat into your body.'" While quoting, Clair had managed to project his voice resonantly despite his illness. He fixed his eyes on Sneed and continued, "Harry, I wonder if our church will be corroded by wealth."

"God's got a plan…"

"Now we got business managers and advertising folks, Harry. James was speaking to us when he wrote almost two thousand years ago."

"James was speaking…"

"Harry, I'm sick of heart. Our one mission, its success may be its ruination. I'm asking you to pray for the faith, Harry, every day now and on after I'm gone."

"God's got a plan and I know what it is, Thomas! I've been seeing signs. All that insurance on your life, it's…"

"The insurance money, when I'm gone, Harry, is going to the missions. It may ruin them, Harry. It may rot them," Clair lamented. "They're waiting around—waiting for me to die. I don't mind dying, Harry. I'm ready to go anytime, but those businessmen we got, they're waiting and almost begging me to get gone."

"It'll curse the missions," Sneed added.

"James said rot and corrode," Thomas continued nodding his head gently in agreement. "It amounts to the same thing."

"God has a plan for that money, a New Jerusalem…"

'They've learned to love money and to worship money, Harry, but they know not what they do."

"Fear not, Thomas!" Sneed managed to exclaim, finally capturing Clair's full attention. "God has a plan and I feel strong he's been a talkin' to me an' givin' me signs and things. It's sort of like I felt at the start when you first showed me the way—the same feeling."

"You've seen signs?"

"Signs, Thomas," Sneed repeated in triumph. "God don't want the insurance money to go ta the faith. That's why he's a botherin' ya, Thomas. It's all part of his plan for a New Jerusalem. You stewin' and worryin' and readin' from James is him a talkin' to ya. God wants the insurance money to go to the city of Plain Oak. It'll be used to make a New Jerusalem out of that place and then maybe it'll be his plan fuh there ta be others—other cities…"

"Cities of refuge?" Clair asked in a full voice.

"Could be sanctuary cities, Thomas," Sneed resumed. "Now I hadn't thought about no cities of refuge but they could be parta God's plan. Maybe that's what we need nowadays is cities of refuge."

"Why Plain Oak City, Harry? Why not some other place?"

"I don't question the wisdom of Almighty God, Thomas," Sneed replied in a tone of elation. "My only question is whether this is what he wants. When I talked with Tom Junior yesterday, he didn't like it. He say maybe I'm bein' led around by Satan. Now, Thomas, I don't get led around by no Satan. I feel God's presence when this idea's in muh mind and soul and I've seen signs—rainbows—and I caught a fish what had a coin in the belly. In warn't in the mouth like Saint Peter done but it had to be in its mouth 'fore it got to the belly and that was after God sent me this idea."

"Harry, it was a big part of God's gifts through you that's been paying for this insurance," Thomas stated.

"Oh, I know all that," Sneed replied. "That ain't got nothin' ta do with it. I want God's will to get done, that's all."

"So you want me to change the beneficiary on the policies to the city of Plain Oak. Is that it, Harry?"

"Thomas, you are a true man of God. I want you to pray about it. I'm not a prophet and I don't claim to be neither but you're a prophet. If you feel the breath of Almighty God telling you to change them to Plain Oak, do it fuh him, not fuh Harry Sneed. I think it's God's plan and wish. He'll have to tell ya. He's a troublin' you by putting all them thoughts in yuh mind about whether all the wealth and riches is good fuh the faith. Ask him, Thomas. Ask him. If in yuh mind and soul it ain't the thing to do, don't do it."

"I seen in the paper and on TV where Plain Oak City come into a heap of money, Harry. Was that part of the plan?"

"It's fuh engineering' and plans, Thomas," Sneed replied. "Course, it's gotta stay secret same as a lotta the gifts to the faith had to stay secret. Don't nobody know and I'm sure you ain't a gonna tell nobody."

"And the insurance is for getting' the plans done, is that it?" Clair continued inquiring.

"Partly carry out. It'll take a heap more money than what'll come from the insurance," Sneed answered, "but it'll come."

"What do you do to Plain Oak to make it a New Jerusalem?"

"I don't know what all yet, Thomas," Sneed answered. "Fix it up. Get rid of floods. Get a library full of good books. Get rid of criminals. Make parks. Build churches. I'm sure God'll make his other wishes known, Thomas."

"But Harry, the New Jerusalem is to be perfectly square with twelve gates and walls a hundred and forty-four cubits high made of jewels…"

"That's when it's all done, and God Almighty will have to do some parts of it." Sneed paused for a minute and stated seriously, "You see, Thomas, Plain Oak's got twelve roads going in and out. Get a good map and look. There's twelve. It ain't perfectly square but it's square-like on a map. It ain't got no walls with gates cause cities ain't like that no more but, come a time, it'll probably get walls and gates. It's near the Garden of Eden…" At this Sneed paused and smiled as if the humor were directed at himself. "My place," he resumed, "that's in a lotta ways like the Garden of Eden, Thomas, and I love it and I protect it like God wants me ta do."

"You were born in Plain Oak, Harry?"

"Yep, born and raised there."

"And that money found over at Plain Oak, was it yourn or was it gov'ment?"

"It was all gov'ment money, Thomas, every scrap of it."

A sudden pain caused Clair to stiffen, grit his teeth and blow out some breath. Sneed grimaced as if the infliction were bothering him also. He managed to ask bluntly, "Are you gonna get well, Thomas?"

"I'm sure, Harry, I won't," was Clair's frank answer. "I've had dreams about death. These doctors up here are keeping me going but I'm weak. Some days are better than others but overall I'm fading."

"How long have you got, Thomas?" Sneed inquired with a trace of serenity in his voice. "Do you know?"

"They don't know for real sure, Harry," Clair confided. "Six months, a year at the most. Course they might get all this medicine agreeing with each others' company and I might stick around awhile but it seems to me the more I take, the worse off I am. When God wants me, he'll take me on out."

Sneed felt tearful and had a weakness in his throat. What he had to say was difficult but he managed, "Thomas, there's one important thing. If you got them business manager people hanging around like a bunch of buzzards a waitin' fuh you to get gone, they'll challenge you changin' the beneficiary to a city. They'll claim you was insane. If the Lord guides you to do what I think he will, you'll need to make a case fuh yuh clear sanity."

Clair focused his eyes on Harry Sneed and asked, "How do you do that, Harry? We all seem a little insane to somebody."

"Get doctors and psychiatrists an' all them folks to file papers sayin' you are clearly sane. You're in the right place for all that up here," Sneed asserted. "But if God wants you to do this thing, please get it all done quicklike."

As Thomas Clair continued to stare at Sneed, his expression changed into one of softness and melancholy. He then stated softly, "I don't know much about insurance, Harry, but I'm doubting we can change the policies like you're talkin'. They're on my life all right but we had an awful time a gettin' it written. Them companies took a long time and asked lots a questions. It seems we had to show I was worth the coverage to the faith and the faith would have a big loss with me gone. Them companies wouldn't make out policies on me for the money to go to some city oncest I'm gone. You see, it may be we can't change the beneficiary to Plain Oak City even if we figure it's the right thing to do."

"But you're in sole charge," Sneed argued.

"Of the faith on earth, that's true, Harry, but when I'm gone, there'll be another shepherd. It'll be Tom, of course, but he's like a businessman. He's all accounting firms, TV, computers and lawyers. I love my son, but I don't know about the faith getting so commercial."

Sneed gently ambled across the room and stared out the window. Continuing his logic, he spoke with a warm but maudlin smile, "Thomas, I ain't worried. I think this is the will of Almighty God. Of course, it may be he'll want the faith to get and use all the money. All I ask is fuh you to find out God's will. If he wants to use the insurance on makin' Plain Oak into a New Jerusalem, I ain't a gonna worry about no insurance man sayin' it can't be done. It will be done, plain and simple. If he wants it to pay for Tom Junior's businesslike ways—and he might want it like that cause it was the plan early on—then that's how it'll be and he'll show us other ways fuh the money to get to Plain Oak. It's as simple as that."

Sneed fixed his eyes onto Clair and announced confidently, "Yes, I can see it sort of in muh mind's eye—the New Jerusalem comin' down from God out of Heaven, beautiful as a bride…"

"Amen," Thomas Clair whispered, "amen."

CHAPTER 8
POLICE STRATEGY

As he prepared for the meeting soon to be held in his Washington, D. C. office, Alex Parker remained disappointed with the information assembled thus far. None of the serial numbers matched those in the National Crime Information Center database of stolen money. Out of some fifteen thousand items of currency, the newest bill of the lot was almost four years old, and most of the fifties and one hundreds had been in circulation for six years or longer. The crime-lab analysis of the box, wrapping paper and packing tape had revealed nothing noteworthy. All the fingerprints were from the city employees who had handled the package and counted the money. Whoever had done the wrapping was said to have been inexperienced. The types and makes of paper and tape were identified. Both were in widespread use. The box had once been used to carton powdered soap and could have been discarded by almost any grocery store in North America. The anonymous letter had been typed on a Royal portable typewriter model that sold new between 1964 and 1970. There were definite key characteristics. Its writer was a "hunt- and-peck" typist.

While any of this information might someday prove useful, there were no strong leads or cross connections with other investigations. Differing so completely from the auto thefts, background checks and special inquiries that took up most of Parker's time, the case was fun and challenging.

Parker's pet theory was that someone had begun stealing cash in increments about seven years ago. This had continued for the next four years or so when it halted. Too terrified to spend or deposit any of this money, the perpetrator then gave it to a worthy cause clearing a troubled conscience. The two pennies found in the box had been put there for good luck.

The secretary opened the door at eleven o'clock and three men entered—Ted Flynn, the FBI's resident agent in Plain Oak; Robert Kovach, an assistant to Parker; and William Jones, a senior currency investigator from the U. S. Treasury Department. They had all spent most of the week after Labor Day in Plain Oak.

When the men were seated, Parker began by asking, "I assume you've all read the files?" Everyone nodded in the affirmative. "What we need to decide today is the level of effort we'll maintain in this thing when, at least for now, there's no proof of a federal crime. Apart from Treasury's three memos—and nobody could possibly understand the one with all the currency-diffusion modeling—I'd like to ask how the folks over in your department see this thing, Will."

"That's a sweeping question, Alex," Jones replied cautiously. "If you don't mind, I'd first like to hear from your man on the scene—not the memo stuff—but his own candid, off-the-record assessment."

"Go ahead, Ted," Parker offered. "Don't hold anything back."

"I wish I had something to say, Mr. Jones," Flynn confessed, "but I don't have any leads at all."

"What about the mayor, Ted?" Parker coaxed. "Couldn't he be part of this thing?"

"We all heard him say over and over he didn't know anything," Flynn replied cautiously. "As far as I can tell, he's a very straight guy. He's honest, reputable, certainly hasn't got any money of his own, no bad habits and no debts that I can find out about. The Ferns are an old family in Elliott County. He's never once tried to hold the police back from anything. He's in the seed and feed business and goes to church regularly. He had a good record as a naval aviator in World War Two. I don't think there are any skeletons."

"Could he have agreed to look the other way about something?" Robert Kovach began. "He's mentioned in the letter almost like he can do anything he wants with the money. Whoever wrote it has to be in some sort of cahoots with him or at the least thinks a lot of him. Don't forget his political-campaign promises to put in a big drainage project in a part of town that floods a lot. The city never had the money to do it. Could he be offering a base for a drug operation or something else in exchange for big-time money?"

"What would be the offer?" Flynn queried. "What would be the front? Who would he be tied in with? How would it work? What would he as mayor be expected to do?

"He's got a boy," Flynn continued, "almost twenty-three years old. The kid was once into drugs pretty heavy. Last year he sort of wandered off. Fern and his wife were hearing from him fairly regularly—Jack's his name—every month or so. Here lately it's been a long time since anyone's heard from the boy. The whole thing has really torn Fern and his wife to pieces. He's put out the word to the police down there to bust every drug deal going. He came over and talked to me about it twice. He's been to see the narcs and the state police.

"There is a little drug trafficking in and around Elliott County but it's small-time, local-distribution stuff. There's a small county airport down there. The narcs keep a good eye on it for unusual work on planes and they know every flight in or out of that place. Right now there's not supposed to be any activity out there.

"No," Flynn concluded, "there isn't anyone in the Plain Oak city government, especially John, who's in a position to work with any kind of criminal element."

William Jones began reasoning aloud. "Let's look at what our currency data is telling us. We have a bundle of bills all at least four years old. This tells me they had been stashed away no less than three years ago and some of them even longer than that. None were counterfeit. Now how would anyone come to store a quantity like that for three years or longer? We should be looking for a fairly steady, bit-by-bit, cash embezzlement beginning six or seven years ago and ending maybe three years back. The ages of the bills form a dispersion pattern that indicates this very thing. Our suspect is probably a loner. All that religious stuff in the letter may be for real or it could be a phony ploy to throw us off his or maybe even her trail. Our person might be someone ripping off an outfit he or she thinks is wicked. The motive doesn't necessarily have to be for gain. It could be for revenge. It might even be someone inside city hall who handles cash and is in a position to siphon off some of the tax money as it comes in. He or maybe she would be keeping it away from the politicians and saving it for a pet project like John Fern's drainage job."

"Very, very plausible," Parker agreed. "Is there anybody or any situation like that down there, Ted? Could a bank or a savings and loan or even the city itself keep such poor records or have such a weak system of internal controls that a major defalcation could go undetected? Certainly we ought to look into the bank examinations going back at least seven years and talk with the examiners and firms that do their audits. From past experience I'd be looking for a situation where one person had done everything—cash intake, bookkeeping, reconciling checks and all that. We ought to review the cash intake system at city hall and see if there have been any cash-flow abnormalities through the years with special emphasis on the period Will's talking about. What do you think, Ted?"

"I certainly agree Mr. Jones has the most plausible theory anyone's suggested so far," Flynn acknowledged. "I've been resident agent down there for almost five years. I've never gotten wind of any big embezzlement. As for loners, Plain Oak's got them all right. I just don't see them in my work. We'll check into these sorts of things. Of course, the money could have been embezzled in Seattle and shipped to Plain Oak for all we know."

"Are there any big moonshine operations down near there, Ted?" Kovach asked.

"None that we know about. There's no market for it."

"That's what our alcohol and tax people tell us, Alex," Jones concurred. "We've been through twenty-five years of moonshining history throughout a big seven-county area down in there. There's nothing. There hasn't been anything since long before the Second World War."

"What it all boils down to," Parker concluded, "is we don't yet have evidence of a federal crime. Everything was reported in keeping with 103.22. We'll continue with our investigation and we'll be on the lookout for anything symptomatic of an embezzlement—maybe some business or firm that had gone belly up because of it. Something will break."

"Speaking for the Treasury Department—and this comes from the secretary who thinks this case is interesting—we want Plain Oak to go ahead and start spending the money as soon as you all at FBI give the green light. We're taking quite seriously the language in the letter about more money being sent. When those engineering plans get done, our patron saint of Plain Oak might happen to drop off another package and we'll nail him for sure this next time."

"We should put out a search for the Fern boy," Parker added. "What's his name...John Fern, Junior?"

"Everybody calls him Jack," Flynn replied.

"We'll need to have our people talk to Jack. The boy just might have teamed up with an operation to raise cash and help his dad be mayor. It could be more than a coincidence he's behind in calling home with all this money turning up."

After a pause in the conversation, Parker changed the subject, "The last thing we need to agree about is what do we say and when do we say it."

To this Jones replied, "I suggest we issue a sort of joint release that says from what we know, nothing fits into our ongoing investigations. Right away everyone will want to know if Plain Oak can go ahead and spend the money. Our position should be that it's out of our hands. This'll get them spending away and our donor will start thinking about the next bundle."

"Any problem with returning the anonymous letter? We all have copies."

"Not from Treasury."

"Then we'll return it to the city," Parker advised. "We'll keep the box and wrapping paper for now. I don't think the city will want them unless they're needed in court."

* * *

Two weeks later and just over one mile from Alex Parker's office, Harry Sneed, dressed as a businessman, opened a suitcase in the trunk of his car. From a large number of wallets, he removed the one marked #35. After relocking the trunk, he proceeded toward a nearby branch of the Riggs National Bank. Walking down the sidewalk he reviewed in his own mind, *My name is Phillip Brown. I live in Apartment 4-A, Cranston Apartments in Arlington. My social security number is 204-91-5122.* After repeating this to himself several times, he entered the bank and approached the third window in from the street entrance, one with a young woman teller who seemed to have a trusting face. "I'd like to open a passbook-savings account, Miss."

"Yes sir," she replied. "Do you have another account with this bank?"

"No ma'am."

"Would you please help me fill out this form. I'll need an ID like a driver's license and your social security card."

Sneed reached in the wallet and retrieved a social security card and a Virginia driver's license for a Phillip L. Brown.

"How much do you want to deposit, Mr. Brown?"

"Eight thousand dollars," he answered casually. "Some in cash but mostly by check. Here's a cashier's check from the First National Bank in Roanoke, Virginia. It's for seventy-five hundred made out to me. I also want to deposit five hundred in cash." Four minutes later Sneed was given a passbook showing a deposit of eight thousand dollars.

Certain that no one was following, he returned to his car and exchanged wallets. On the way to another bank, he mused to himself quietly, *My name is Julius Dickson. I live in the Hinton Apartments on Summerville Pike. My social security number is 212-40-4818. My name is Julius Dixon.*

Driving up the Baltimore-Washington Parkway, Sneed reviewed his progress mentally—almost one million deposited in one hundred forty-five separate savings accounts located in cities as far south as Raleigh, North Carolina. In Baltimore the job should prove easier—depositing eighty-five hundred dollars cash in each of forty similar savings accounts opened from two to three weeks earlier.

He began with the Maryland National Bank on Charles Street where he was using wallet #114. *My name is Robert Blake,* he reminded himself. For the second round of deposits he had a canvas banking bag with a top lock. "I'd like to deposit this cash in my account," he declared as the bag and passbook were handed over the counter.

"Certainly, Mr. Blake."

CHAPTER 9
TO SPEND OR NOT TO SPEND

The noteworthy item on the October 30 agenda was whether to spend $350,000 in treasure money, as the mystery cash was now being called, to retain Barton, Callahan and Riley (BCR) to prepare final plans and specifications for the South End project. There were lesser questions of hiring an architect to design the new library and a planning commission recommendation for a consultant to update the city's master plan and capital program. Council action for or against would establish the big precedent, whether to use treasure money at all.

Several things had happened since the visit by federal law enforcement personnel. A few hours before the September 25th meeting of city council, Fern got word from Alex Parker that the probe had produced no connections to other FBI or Treasury Department investigations and there was no evidence of a federal crime. Although any of this might change, Plain Oak was free to deal with the treasure in its own way.

Meanwhile Bill Willy had drafted a legal opinion about the city's rights to the money. This largely dealt with a question of exactly what the package and its monetary contents constituted under the law. Willy reasoned that the money was not a treasure trove because it had not been hidden in a secret place and subsequently lost or forgotten. Since the strange money was clearly intended to become the property of the city and not belong to the first person to find and claim it, the treasure was not "abandoned personal property." This was an important distinction because as "abandoned property" the state government might concoct an arguable claim for it.

The opinion concluded the treasure was technically a gift to the city. While Willy had been bothered by not knowing the donor, the same principle applied to many fund-raising activities where the cash collected could not be traced back to specific givers.

Beginning several weeks before the October 30th meeting, a legal notice had been printed weekly in the Plain Oak Dispatch asserting the city was claiming as a gift the large sum of money discovered on August 28th, and unless convincing evidence was presented challenging Plain Oak's ownership, the council would be seeking to amend its budget and use the money for municipal purposes.

Willy had been hoping the city's ownership of the money could be established in court but the litigation needed to accomplish this would have to be based on a genuine dispute. Lacking a shred of supporting evidence, two crank claims had been easily denied. Fern's fear of professional swindlers proved groundless. In a word, no litigation was filed. The city attorney's opinion stood untested.

After the Pledge of Allegiance and the approval of the minutes of the previous council meeting, the council chairman, Arch Kidd, announced perfunctorily, "There are no resolutions or proclamations tonight so the next item on our agenda is the Mayor's Report and Recommendations. Mister Mayor."

Fern stood and went to the speaker's podium, "Ladies and gentlemen," he began. "I recommend we enter into a contract with Barton, Callahan and Riley to do the final plans, working drawings, right-of-way delineations and general specifications for the South End Project. We've gone through a selection procedure. A number of firms submitted proposals. I suggest BCR because they know our city, their main office is nearby and they've done an assessment and feasibility study for this very project. The firm has engineered a lot of other work in town and we've never been let down by them. The cost will be $350,000. This is a top figure. It could be less but no more than that."

"Question," Julius Hawkins interjected.

"Go ahead, sir," Kidd allowed.

"Mister Mayor, can this money be spent for anything?"

"That's a legal question. One for the city attorney," Fern replied.

"Legally," Hawkins continued after the room was quiet, "can this here money be put to another use, Bill?"

"Mr. Hawkins," Bill Willy answered, "this set of facts has never happened anywhere except in Plain Oak so there's no real precedent to go on. I could make a case, a pretty solid case, that in this situation where there's no clear understanding what our donor wants and the donor is unknown, there's no contract with the city. Even if there were, the mystery man or woman or whoever would have to do the enforcing so this person would need to come forward and prove he or maybe she gave it and then somehow sue us for breach to put a stop to it. What you really have is a policy question."

"If we are taking any kind of gift," Kidd interrupted, "it would be bad public policy for this city not to do what the giver had in mind. Somebody may be thinking about giving us a new stadium. They'd certainly decide against it if they thought we might turn around and use the money for something else because of a legal technicality. If the money's good enough to use, we should honor the wishes of the giver as best we can."

"Oh, I'm with you on that, Arch," Hawkins replied. "I was hoping to get our lawyer to say it had to be spent like that. I came near but I didn't get him all the way there."

"Any other questions by council?" Kidd continued.

"Mister Mayor," Edward Fiske began slowly, "what risk do we have once we've spent the money, someone may establish a rightful claim to it and the city would have to pay it back?"

"There's some risk, Mr. Fiske," Fern replied. "We've taken every reasonable precaution to discover the donor and find out whether it was part of some criminal act. The story about it has been all over this country on the networks and in newspapers and even magazines. You know about our legal notices in the Dispatch. All my lawyer friends say a heavy burden of proof would be required of another claimant to prove it was theirs. Such a person would have to answer the embarrassing questions—Just where did you get all that money? Why didn't you report it when it was missing? We've figured it would be next to impossible for someone to claim it."

"One more question," Fiske added. "Could the city get insurance to guarantee the money for the city? Is there coverage available so the policy would pay off what we've spent if we do get hit with a valid claim and have to give it up?"

"Mr. Fiske," Fern replied, "we've looked carefully into that very thing. We've gotten a quote through an agency that handles Lloyds of London. They'll cover this risk for seven percent of the spent or obligated amount."

"Meaning what?"

"Meaning, let's say we've obligated half of it or spent it or both and a claim is sustained against the city for the whole treasure amount. We would have to return the half we hadn't committed but the insurance would pay off all of what we had spent or obligated or both. The premium would be seven percent of what we obligate as we obligate it."

"In other words, if we let contracts for half a million, the premium would be thirty-five thousand dollars," Fiske stated for clarification.

"That's exactly right," Fern answered.

"Then I move, Mister Chairman, that regardless of what we do with this money, we take out this kind of coverage through a good insurance company," Fiske offered.

"Second," Mr. Hawkins added.

"It's been moved and seconded. Any discussion? Mayor, do you recommend this?"

"As a matter of fact, Mister Chairman, I strongly recommend it. I was going to bring it up but Councilman Fiske beat me to it. We tried every agency in the county. This was the only proposal we could get."

"We have a motion and a second," Kidd repeated. "Can we dispose of this now?"

"It's all right by me," John Fern answered.

"Any other discussion?"

"Question," Williams pressed.

"It's been moved and seconded. There being no further discussion, all in favor say 'aye'."

"Aye," the members replied.

"Any opposed? —Hearing none, the motion passes. Is there any further discussion by the members?"

After a brief silence, Kidd announced to the audience, "All right now, this is an unusual issue and we're going into a public hearing. Any citizen of Plain Oak here who wants to speak to the issues of using up to $350,000 of treasure money to engineer the South End project will be heard. We'll also entertain comments about having an architect design a library and our hiring a planning firm in connection with our capital improvement program. Bear in mind, we've just agreed to get special insurance so the possibility of our having to repay the money shouldn't be at issue. Now, we'll entertain comments."

A young dark-haired man in a short-sleeved shirt stood and was immediately recognized by the chairman. "All right, Mr. Mogena, go ahead. Please state your name and address for the record."

"I'm Al Mogena, Two Oak Place. I'm the current president of the Plain Oak Jaycees and I'm speaking for our chapter. We have a resolution for the record but instead of me reading it, I'd like to tell you what it says. We, the Plain Oak Jaycees, strongly recommend that you go forward with the South End drainage plans. We also favor designing the library and updating our plans in keeping with the donor's letter. We see this as a chance to turn this city around. Thank you."

"Before you sit down, Al, I'd like to ask a question the whole council's probably interested in," Kidd stated. "When your membership voted on the resolution, what was the breakdown of yeas to nays?"

"Just about two to one in favor, Arch. We had a pretty good turnout that night—about fifty showed up—so the vote was something like thirty-three to seventeen."

"Thank you, sir. Reverend Clifford Woodson."

A tall, lean black man in his late fifties, Woodson often used a deep and resonant voice to lend an emotional ring to whatever he was saying. "Mister Mayor, council members, ladies and gentlemen," he began very soberly. "I am Cliff Woodson, pastor of the Mount Zion Baptist Church. I reside at 201 Mabry Drive. I speak—not for our church, not for our board of deacons or for the ministerial alliance here in town. I speak for myself following my own conscience. Now in your hearts, you all know that taking and using this money is wrong!"

With this, a number of persons in the audience politely applauded. This encouragement prompted more tone and energy in Woodson's words and he almost shouted, "In Moses' speech to the children of Israel before they entered the Promised Land, he warned them—and this is from Deuteronomy, chapter 16, verse 19. 'And neither take a gift, for a gift doth blind the eyes of the wise and pervert the words of the righteous...'"

Anticipating scripture being used in the argument against Plain Oak's use of the funds, John Fern had spent time going through his biblical index and reading several translations of every passage mentioning gifts and treasurers. Although not a student of the Bible, he had become familiar with the same verse Woodson was citing. "Reverend Woodson," Fern interrupted, "as I recall this very passage, Moses had in mind judges and officials. A better translation of 'gifts' would be 'bribes.' You may be taking the passage out of context."

"Isn't this a bribe —a bribe of the whole community, Mayor Fern? Aren't we all being bribed?" As a number of persons clapped, the fervor returned to his voice and Woodson continued, "What's the difference—the really true difference or as some of our business friends might put it, the bottom-line difference?"

Having scored a coup in a skirmish with the mayor, Woodson had the good sense to sit down amidst a renewed applause.

The chairman noticed Dexter Snidow standing up and waiving his arm. Deliberately trying to avoid Snidow, Kidd called on a man with a meek sour face who limped forward and announced, "I'm Herman Fowler, 327 College in the South End. I've had water in my house, my garage, and all over my yard many times. I want you to know I'm against all this. I'm opposed to the project and I'm certainly against using Mafia money to pay for it." A burst of applause all but drowned out his "Thank you."

As this speaker began limping back toward his seat, Kidd asked him, "Mr. Fowler, weren't you up here four years ago arguing against the Route 91 By-pass? Am I right?"

"Mr. Kidd, you are quite right," Fowler replied. "I was against it then and I'm against it now even though it's been built."

"I seem to remember your writing a letter to the editor opposing the stadium-lighting project. Are you the same Fowler who wrote that?"

"Mr. Kidd, you have a good memory. I'm also against crime, juvenile delinquency, high taxes and the Mafia."

Councilman Joe Williams next entered the discussion, "Mr. Fowler, when I was a county commissioner, you organized a petition drive against building the new county jail."

"That's right, Mr. Williams," Fowler replied proudly, "because it wasn't needed. Criminals shouldn't be given paid vacations in luxury hotels and country clubs. The old one was fine."

"And you circulated petitions against the airport before it was built. Wasn't that right?"

"That's right, Mr. Williams," Fowler shouted back in obvious annoyance at the ordeal being heaped upon him.

"Tell us, Mr. Fowler," Williams pressed, "what have you ever been for around here?"

"I've been for lots of things."

"Good, name something, Mr. Fowler," Williams continued.

"Listen, I've been for… I've been for… I've been for being against." With this, Herman Fowler sat back down as the crowd laughed and clapped.

The chamber of commerce supported the mayor's recommendation. Separate spokesmen for the policemen, firemen, and other groups of city employees were urging that some of the money be used for a one-time bonus to help them cope with inflation.

A petite lady with a serene face, came to the podium. When things quieted, she announced softly, "I'm Liz Treadnow. I'm a widow and I live at 418 Colonial Way. No one has said what I think. I think it's Communists what give all that money. What have you agreed to do for Communists, Mayor Fern?"

Dexter Snidow could not be ignored. Kidd had been hoping to delay calling on him until after the news reporters had left to meet their deadlines. There was so much media coverage, however, it made no difference. "Okay, Mr. Snidow," the chairman allowed, "try and be brief."

"I'll take as long as I want," he began with a broad grin as he approached the podium. Someone in the back blew a whistle and about a dozen persons stood and cheered. As soon as he reached it, Snidow arranged the speaker's stand to face the audience instead of the council and other officials. Since this gesture was a slap at authority and officialdom, his supporters yelled their approval. "I'm gonna be talking to the people," he explained between bursts of cheers, "not to them fellows up there.

"So our mayor wants to hire BCR using a pile of mystery money. It's so much a mystery, don't nobody know where it come from and it's so mysterious, he's got to take out insurance with a bunch of foreigners to make sure this money belongs to you and me. Now isn't that a …"

Interrupted by the clamor, Snidow held up an arm for silence. When calm was restored, he resumed, "This mayor has made a commitment. He doesn't deny it. He's gonna build his project come hell or what is it? High water? No, it won't be high water, he'll see to that. It'll be hell!" Snidow's supporters in the audience clapped and roared again and the person with the whistle blew it again.

"What kind of deal did you make, Mayor Fern? Are you gonna open us up to gambling? To drugs? How about prostitution? How about all of the above?" Once again Snidow held up his arm to still the applause and cheering. "Remember what the letter said. It read something like, 'Use it for good plans for the South End'—a Fern campaign promise. 'Use it for plans for a new library.' Fern is always talking about wanting a new library. Last and I'm quoting exactly—'Use it for planning whatever the mayor'—note that—'the mayor wants to plan.' Now really, Mayor Fern, don't tell me you aren't mixed up in this! Don't tell me BCR isn't going to contribute to your campaign fund! They did before and they will this next time!" Snidow turned around, starred at Fern and shouted, "Well it won't work. We're onto you! I know you've got the votes here tonight, but you'll get caught at your own little game. Too many people are wise. You can fool some of us all the time and you can fool most of us some of the time. You can't, Mayor, and you won't fool all of us all the time!"

Snidow's ovation continued until after he had sat back down. Someone pulled the light switch reducing the meeting room to total darkness. Arch Kidd shouted at the top of his lungs, "Put those lights back on."

Persons from the South End generally supported hiring the engineers. The head of the local construction workers' union spoke favorably. Apparently divided by the issue, the regulars said nothing. Regardless of the council's decision, Fern expected their eventual opposition.

By ten o'clock, just about everyone had heard enough. Negative groans could be heard whenever a fresh hand was raised for someone to speak. "Just about everything now being said is a repeat of what we've already heard," Kidd announced to the audience. "In the interest of time, I ask any persons wishing to speak, please limit your remarks to things that have not been said already." After this, no one else sought to speak.

Julius Hawkins next asked if he could address the mayor.

"Certainly," Arch Kidd replied.

"Mister Mayor, do you know who or what is behind this money, gift, treasure, abandoned property or whatever it is?"

Fern's answer was slow and cautious. "Mr. Hawkins, I have no idea what the source of this money is. I don't know whether it comes from a crime, criminal act or whatever. It could be from a legitimate business or a wealthy person. I just don't know. The idea that I have made a deal with the Mafia or a bunch of Communists or some criminal or criminal conspiracy is ridiculous. The police have never been held back or tied down by me in any way and never will be."

"One more question, Mayor," Hawkins continued, "and it's a legal one so we'll hear from the city attorney if you don't know the answer. Some folks here are saying that we shouldn't take this money and use it. If we don't spend it and no one makes a legitimate claim that it's theirs, what'll come of it?"

Bill Willy answered for the mayor, "After a long time, it would probably eventually be taken over by the State of West Virginia. The legislature would likely pass a special statute to cover themselves but even if they didn't, sooner or later it would be assumed by the state government. That's the long and the short of it."

Hawkins nodded affirmatively and announced, "Then I move the city enter into a contract with BCR as recommended by the mayor. I also move that the mayor be authorized to negotiate with architects, preferably local, for plans for a new library. Now what was the name of that planning outfit over in Virginia that our planning commission wants to hire, Mister Mayor?"

"They chose Balzer and Associates at no more than $85,000."

"O.K. Balzer and Associates at no more than $85,000, included in my motion," Hawkins concluded.

"I second the motion," stated Councilman Fiske.

"Any further discussion? Call the roll on this one, Mr. Naylor," Arch Kidd instructed.

After polling the council, the city clerk announced, "Five yeas and no nays, Mister Chairman."

CHAPTER 10
PRANKS AND PLANS

In late September a prankish game, "Gift or Treasure," evolved among the social fraternities at West Virginia University and quickly spread to other campuses. The basic idea was to be the first person or team to deliver a wrapped, thirty-pound package to the city clerk's office in Plain Oak without being recognized or caught. The local police, already under orders to intercept the second shipment promised in the letter, had become unwilling participants. City officials had to open a flood of packages only to discover old magazines, heavy rocks, and bric-a-brac. After Thanksgiving these contests halted abruptly.

A few of the legitimate packages destined for city hall had somehow been opened before they arrived. John Fern had ordered a chair for his office. When it came, Allie Eller could tell that the cardboard shipping box had been slashed presumably by someone looking for money. Most delivery persons had become afraid to carry packages to city hall. When the janitor made his regular mail trips to the post office, an armed policeman accompanied him.

Gossip about who had actually sent the treasure swept Plain Oak. Someone started a story it had been a Fort Worth millionaire who happened to own a hunting lodge in an adjacent county. When asked about it by a reporter, for some inexplicable reason the Texan answered, "No comment," causing the rumor to rekindle and spread like wildfire. After a visit from the FBI, the man issued a denial. Even Jay Cuve, a penniless street vendor, was said to be behind the gift. Aside from Margaret, John Fern never heard anyone mention Harry Sneed's name.

There were persistent rumors circulating about a second cash shipment much larger than the first. The several versions of this story shared a theme that the money had been secretly divided among a group of city officials led by the mayor and chief of police. After these rumors became widespread, some of the garbage and street workers grew angry over having been left out of a deal that was said to have included the police and firemen. The mayor received several anonymous letters with messages like, "What did you do with the city's money?" and "Where is it?"

Fern meanwhile had become so immersed in his new role as a master builder, he all but ignored these features of an unfolding civic comedy. Each morning's tasks would be approached with fresh energy. After a full-day's preoccupation with transforming Plain Oak into something much better, he came home for dinner between six-thirty and seven and often went to an evening meeting after that. Margaret was worried her husband might be overdoing it, but he seemed healthier and consumed less alcohol than at any time in years.

The engineers could not work fast enough to suit him. Fern checked every detail of their plans for the South End project and had Bob Ruffy reviewing such things as elevations, underground utility line locations and even storm-water runoff calculations.

The planning consultants especially flamed his passion about the future Plain Oak. The firm's principal asked more than once, "What do you want the city to become?"

Fern would answer, "Show me a good plan. If I like it, that'll be what I want the city to become."

Since the usual financial studies were irrelevant, the principal planner inquired, "How much money should we figure on the city spending?"

"Forget money," the mayor replied. "Do everything right. Most great cities have lots of parks in them. I want Plain Oak to be a park with a city in it. This started an elaboration of Fern's dream of an immense park near the edge of the city.

While they viewed Fern as something of an impractical visionary, the planners enjoyed working with him and quickly began to develop his large-park idea. They gathered maps and aerial photographs of open lands surrounding Plain Oak and took them back to their home office for study. Ten days later the group returned with rough clothes and hiking boots. For the better part of three days, Fern was tromping through woods and meadows and up and down foothills in the company of consultants. By the weekend, they had delineated the site for the dream park.

Thanks to the negotiations of Henry Frei, Millie Frei's brother-in-law, the city soon had options to buy eighteen hundred acres of contiguous land surprisingly near town at a buying price of about four million dollars.

The city contracted with a landscape architect, a recreation specialist, and a golf-course designer. For general advice about the park, Fern went public and set up a large citizens advisory committee. Every church, labor organization, the chamber of commerce, service club and the Plain Oak Jaycees were all asked to name representatives. Seventy-one persons attended the organizational meeting held at the Ramada Inn.

Fern told of the land options and his dreams of the park's becoming the finest recreational facility for a community Plain Oak's size anywhere in the United States. He repeated his list of activities encompassing a large swimming pool, many athletic fields, horseback-riding facilities and trails, and even public gardens. Everything would be skillfully planned and designed to blend in with and to protect the environment.

John Fern had always been looked upon as a safe person who was not especially crusading or imaginative. His talk to this group, however, contained an uncharacteristic fanaticism. News of the land options had been written up in the Dispatch but with little explanation. No one had expected such a sweeping proposal. Bothered by the committee's silence, he asked, "What do you think of all this?"

There was still a long pause broken by a few gentle chuckles which seemed directed at the group's own reticence. Henry Kingery, a respected lawyer in Elliott County, stood and began speaking cautiously, "John, don't you think all this is...I'm trying to think how to put it...Don't you think this is a bit much?"

Fern looked at Kingery and answered quite seriously, "Yes, it certainly is a bit much. But why not? We only live once. We've chosen Plain Oak. Maybe some of us really wanted to live somewhere else but we're here because of our jobs or wives, our family maybe or our friends. Perhaps some of us are here because we don't have the initiative to go and live somewhere else. Since we all do live here and we only live once, why not make Plain Oak into the best place it can possibly be? What better way is there than to develop a huge park? Think of the energy of our young children—many of whom can't seem to find a job anywhere—working to develop the park. We could have our own CCC program to give young kids a first crack at employment. Think of all the opportunities we could give our elderly. Think of…"

"That's all wonderful, John," Kingery interrupted politely, "but aren't you getting this treasure business a little too far out in front? Seriously, where's the money coming from? Dreaming is fun but it'll take millions for what you're talking about. You want to make the South End floodproof. We all do. That alone will run several million, but to buy up and develop all that land…"

"If we hold options and have plans for everyone to see, and we all dream about them like I'm doing, it can happen," the mayor argued. "It may take years but it'll happen, and the best part of the whole thing is getting it all done."

"Mayor," someone asked, "are you banking on another big shipment of money?"

As he looked over the assembly, Fern sensed a range of expressions that varied from amusement to curiosity to disgust. He felt a need to say something and started talking before his thoughts had been put together. "Yes, I suppose I'd like to see us get more money to do all these things," he began. "I do hope it comes. You see, we can't levy enough taxes to pay for this program. Our city tax rates are limited and to float bonds we'll need a favorable vote and the people usually vote 'no' because they don't want to pay any taxes at all. Maybe I am counting on our unknown friend. Of course, it could all be wishful thinking. I don't know."

"Surely, John," Kingery began pleading once again, "you don't think this city will be receiving enough money to do your drainage, build a library and buy up and develop all this land into your park idea?" He then glanced around the room as if seeking support for what he had been saying. "Why to do all these things would cost at least fifteen million dollars."

"Hank," the mayor replied, "these engineers and planning people say we're talking about twenty million!"

"John," Kingery began with a trace of bitterness in tone, "you've always been a man with your feet planted firmly on the ground. I know. We've worked together many times, but I need to say you're getting carried away. Every one of us here will admit that an anonymous box with a million dollars in it is a novelty, but really—twenty million dollars! Seriously every person in this room wants to help our city in any way we reasonably can, but to indulge in pipe dreams…I, for one, have to know the money's going to be there when the city needs it and I need to know where the money's coming from."

"We're going to get all these things designed, Hank," Fern replied projecting his voice over the mumbling within the room. "If we can spend what'll soon be trillions on missiles and submarines, bombs, guns and airplanes—things that get obsolete as fast as they're built—Plain Oak should be able to put a few million into a park that'll be used for centuries."

A program was prepared to pave most of the dirt streets and alleys in town, to resurface one-third of all the streets and to replace many of the worse sidewalks. A few smaller storm drains, including Cherry Corner, were proposed for scattered locations.

The old warehouse area across the railroad tracks was proposed for redevelopment into a medium-sized industrial park. A basic factory building would be constructed, leased or sold, and the revenues used to build another plant in the same area.

The council's preference for a local person to design the new library simplified the selection process because there was only one registered architect in town, Alfred Buonari, the principal partner in a small firm with a good reputation throughout West Virginia. Buonari had started work on Plain Oak's new library on his own initiative long before the mystery money had turned up. John Fern liked the drawings and a contract was signed two days before Thanksgiving.

By late February Fern's plans for Plain Oak were largely done. The drainage projects and the library were ready for construction bids. A master plan for the park was finished, and a logical schedule for the many things to be done was developed. By John Fern's reckoning the entire dream could become a reality for about twenty and one-half million dollars.

* * *

In a tall building overlooking Baltimore's Charles Center, Harry Sneed entered the outer office of J. R. Wysor, a coin dealer. "I'm Preston Perkins," he announced to the receptionist. "The coins I ordered should be in by now."

"Just one moment, sir," the young lady replied. By telephone she announced, "Mr. Wysor, Mr. Preston Perkins is here. He asked if..." Sneed was then told, "You may go back, sir."

Sneed stood in front of a teller's window apparently made of bulletproof glass. "Mr. Wysor," he began, "I would think that by now you've gotten delivery on the Krugerrands."

"Yes, Mr. Perkins," Wysor acknowledged. "We called more than once but the phone must have been out-of-order. You wanted one hundred and fifty. Are you still certain, Mr. Perkins, you want to take these coins with you? If they're lost or stolen, there's little chance of getting them back. We gladly hold them for our customers—perfectly safe, fully insured, and they won't have to be authenticated when you..."

"I know," Sneed replied. "I want them in my own lockbox. It's not that I don't trust you or your firm."

"We understand perfectly," Wysor stated. "Many of our customers feel the same way. I'll need a certified check for $63,150."

"Here's a certified check on the First National for $63,000. I'll have to give you the rest in cash."

"That's fine," Wysor agreed and then excused himself to verify the check.

Ten minutes later Sneed was heading for a lockbox in the Charles Center Branch of the Maryland National Bank. After adding another one hundred and fifty coins, the unit had become so heavy he had difficulty handling it. *One thousand fifty plus one hundred fifty,* he pondered to himself. *Over $480,000 in this box alone.* Arrangements were made for a second lockbox.

As he drove up the Jones Falls Expressway towards Towson, he reviewed one more time the pace of his progress. *I'm lagging behind and gold's been slipping in price. It'll be April or May next year 'fore I'm done.*

CHAPTER 11
A CHRISTMAS VISIT

On a misty evening three days before Christmas, Harry Sneed was caught in heavy traffic moving south on Interstate-81 in Virginia. Although he had been carefully obeying the speed limit, a blue and white rotating light suddenly dominated the rearview mirror. Sneed uttered a brief prayer and brought the car to a halt at the edge of the highway. "I really didn't think I was speeding, officer," he said to the trooper who had stopped him.

"You weren't speeding, mister. May I see your driver's license and vehicle registration?" Sneed reached for his wallet and got out the license. From the glove compartment he produced the registration card. Both were current and in his own name.

"Mr. Sneed, you seem to have a loose connection with your right rear taillight. It's been winking on and off. Would you mind opening the trunk? We might be able to fix it by tightening something."

Sneed's heart began to pound. He said nothing, got out and managed to unlock the trunk without betraying his nervousness. The officer unfastened a plate behind the light. A minor adjustment produced a steady glow. "You should get a shop to check all these connections, Mr. Sneed. How far are you going tonight?"

"Down near Lexington. There'll be places open tomorrow. I'll tend to it."

"I won't summons you or anything," the trooper informed him, "on your word of honor you'll have it checked by a garage."

"It'll be done and thank you, officer."

"And Merry Christmas."

"Same to you, sir."

Twenty-five minutes later, Sneed checked into the Howard Johnson Motel outside Lexington. He continued to wonder whether the encounter was a random happening or part of an orchestrated law enforcement campaign directed at the New Jerusalem. After reviewing everything, he concluded it was a routine matter and meant nothing. Had the officer managed to go through the duffle bags, he would have found nearly seven hundred pounds of gold coins. If there had been a planned operation, everything would have been handled differently.

The next morning Sneed noticed a headline in the Roanoke Times: **RELIGIOUS LEADER SINKS INTO COMA.** According to the article the Reverend Thomas Clair was near death at his family home near Elkins, West Virginia.

Sneed got some change and went to a payphone. After several calls, he finally reached Thomas Clair, Jr. near Beckley. "How long's he got, Tom?"

"Could be days, could be minutes," was the reply. "I'd stay with him but there's nothing anyone can do."

"Is he suffering?"

"I don't think so."

Sneed felt awkward about asking the question that genuinely concerned him, the fate of his request about the insurance. Clair came to his rescue, "You want to know what Dad did about the insurance matter you two talked about?"

"Yep."

"It can't be done."

"That's that then."

"Almost," Clair rebutted. "Dad did decree one thing in a handwritten order to me. It should come about in time and the insurance will help. The faith will contribute one million dollars toward the library. I won't do it if I think it'll get the faith in trouble with the law. That's not what you wanted but changing the beneficiary like you were talking about cannot be done. Dad prayed about it and that's what God told him."

"My name's out of it?"

"Yes, completely. Our records don't show you as being a contributor."

"But I'm from near Plain Oak. There's so few members from Elliott County, they'll tie me in with it."

"Do you want your name purged?"

"Yep, totally. Stop sending me stuff in the mail and take my name off everything—past, present and future." Sneed stated positively, "only I don't want nobody but you a doin' it and no one else can know. No scratchin' out stuff. Burn every piece of paper with muh name on it."

"It's as good as done. Anything else, Harry?"

"Does yuh daddy know anything or anybody?"

"He mainly sleeps. When he comes to, he quotes scripture and says 'amen' a lot. He knows me. That's about all."

"The faith will get it back, Tom."

"I know."

"May God bless you all."

* * *

"We tightened everything, sir, and checked the fuses and connections," the attendant advised. "We don't do complicated auto-electric stuff but everything's okay. With the gas and oil, it'll be thirty-one sixty."

"Merry Christmas, and keep the change," Sneed declared as he handed the man thirty-five dollars.

Sneed was soon driving through Roanoke and onto Route 220. In Boones Mill he stopped to use an outside payphone in front of a convenience store. When certain no one was watching, he dialed a number and asked, "Can I speak to Fred?" After a short delay, he continued, "Was the cheese good? Mine may have some mold on it. See you in a while."

After driving about fifteen miles over back roads, Sneed parked beside a couple of evergreens. He locked the car and walked a few hundred feet to a swinging footbridge spanning a small stream. He sat on the approach steps and began waiting patiently.

About fifteen minutes later, a muddy stake truck driven by a late middle-aged woman, roared up and stopped. A short, somewhat stocky man in his late-sixties got out and slammed the door.

After the truck drove off, the man, dressed in khaki work clothes and wearing a well-beaten black hat, walked over to the bridge. "What say, ole boy," he greeted in a loud huffy voice. After spitting a flow of tobacco juice, he asked, "Whar you been at?"

"Up North sellin' papers."

"Very good, ole boy," the man yelled jovially. "What's this mold?"

"Did you see anything, Albert?"

"No, ain't nobody a followin' as we can see. No strange cars on the roads, no funny talk on the police radio. What's this mold?"

"A smokey stopped me on 81 last night this side of Staunton. Said muh rear light won't right. I opened the trunk and he screwed something what'd come loose with the light. He didn't cite me or nothin'. Muh trunk was full with glitter. When he was done, he went on."

Albert Hoag laughed a hearty chuckle revealing one gold tooth and tobacco stain on the others. After relaxing from his laughter, he took out a package of chewing tobacco, bit off a piece and continued, "You think Smokey mighta put a bug on ya car, ole boy?"

"That's the mold."

"Me and you'll check it out, Harry," Hoag reassured him. "Let's get with it."

After walking back to Sneed's car, Hoag examined the bumpers, the fenders, trunk and rear lights. "Was Smokey alone, ole boy?"

"Yep."

"And he come up to ya on the passenger side and you an' him went back to the trunk. You opened it and Smokey fooled around with one of your rear brake lights and got it ta workin' right. Was it really not working good?"

"The right one was off 'til he screwed something tight."

"What else?"

"He told me to go to a garage an' get it checked."

"Did he tell you any special garage to go to?"

"Nope."

"Don't worry, ole boy. It ain't nothin'," Hoag stated for reassurance. "You was with him all the time. Course it was dark but he couldna done no fancy bug plant on you with you right there. Whar d'ya spend the night?"

"The Howard Johnson up past Lexington."

"You worried somebody come back and stuck on a bug while you was sleep?" Hoag kept quizzing. "Is that it?"

"I ain't exactly figured it like that, Albert," Sneed answered seriously. "Maybe I'm gettin' jittery. I'm tired I guess. I been goin' hard a good spell."

"We'll go to Liz's brother's place and check it over. Carl's got a pit. He gone huntin'. We can look it over good and tell if anybody's been messing with your car but it looks clean to me."

"We best check it good, Albert," Sneed agreed calmly.

The two men got into Sneed's car and drove for about four miles over bumpy roads until they reached a dilapidated mechanic's garage that had once been a filling station. A sign indicated the place was closed but Hoag managed to open the vehicular entrance without a key. Sneed positioned his sedan over the grease pit. For twenty-five minutes, Hoag checked meticulously for any sign of a bugging device or other indication of someone's tampering with the car. When finished, he sought to ease Sneed's worry by saying, "There ain't nothin', Harry. You got the willies like in the old days when me and you'd hear a secret man behind every tree or bush. It's kinda the same. Now what I like about bein' up in here is ain't nobody got no business in these parts 'lessun he lives here or is trading. When a stranger comes a sniffin' about, we know it right off."

Thirty-five minutes later, Harry Sneed was seated in the Hoag living room listening to Albert's talk about tobacco prices. Liz Hoag was waiting patiently for a chance to speak. After several minutes she had an opening. "Mister Harry," she began before taking a few puffs from her short pipe. "Mister Harry, tell us how our new paper moved up North."

"It done perfect, Lizzie," Sneed replied earnestly. "It's better than bureau grade-A prime. Couldn't no banks, no gold bugs—couldn't nobody tell no difference. Yours is the real, Lizzie. Bureau's is counterfeit."

"You jist walked in and put it with banks?" she asked.

"No problem at all. Ain't nothin' by feel and nothin' by looks. Yorn was always perfect specially when it had a little age and some handling."

With this, Liz and Albert Hoag began laughing almost uncontrollably. Sneed would give more details of his walking into banks located from Columbia, South Carolina, as far north as Baltimore, and converting currency for deposits always in amounts less than $1000. Each time he described the ease of passing their money, the Hoags would once again break into laughter as if they had just pulled off an elaborate practical joke and were hearing for the first time how everything had turned out perfectly.

Liz Hoag next repeated her counterfeiting principles, "Perfect engraving, perfect printing, perfect paper and inks, care with the watermark and the numbers and don't never get in no hurry. Check over the bills real good and burn any what ain't right. That'll do it every time, now won't it, Mr. Hoag?"

"You know your business, Lizzie," Albert Hoag said approvingly. "Keep takin' your time. It's all been fuh good. If the gov'ment can print debt money, we can too. Can't we, ole boy?" Hoag then laughed out loud once more.

"Some says 'fittin is stealing," Liz Hoag began reasoning in a serious tone. "To them I says, 'Whar's the theft? Whar's the theft?' Now them what puts out bads is stealin' cause folks'll get stuck with trash paper. Some'll say anybody dumb enough to get stuck with trash don't rate nothin' better cause they took it in the first place, but there's some what don't know no better and can't afford it. But when your paper is cleaner than bureau prime, I says you're a hep to everybody—specially gov'ment. You're a keepin' folks off welfare and stayin' well and feedin' the hungry an' keepin' some workin' and payin' taxes and all such as that."

During Liz Hoag's credo which Sneed had heard before, he sat puffing on his pipe, his eyes glued to the fire warming the simple room. Occasionally he nodded in agreement but said little at all. Finally at a pause in Liz Hoag's discourse, he stated, "Both of you have heard me say it many a time. If high-grade counterfeiting was a sin, the Bible would forbid it. There ain't nothin' again it, so I says have at it so long as it's fuh God's work. Don't hurt nobody. Do good! We all done a lotta good, ain't we?"

Sneed's remarks broke the train of conversation. Albert Hoag next asked, "You want us to melt down them gold coin into something like bricks or bars? It's real easy to melt down gold coin, ole boy."

"Yep," Sneed answered while puffing on his pipe.

"How's them social security cards and driver's licenses working out, Mister Harry?" Liz Hoag asked with concern.

"Real good, Lizzie."

"You sure there ain't nobody on your trail, Mister Harry?"

"Can't never be sure, Lizzie," he answered pensively. "Can't never be sure. At times I think I'm followed but then I know it's in muh head. You see, Lizzie, I'm doin' God's work. I see signs and I know God's with me. Why he chose me, unworthy sinner that I was and maybe still am but try hard not to be no more, I don't know. It's his way though, Lizzie."

"Now don't you worry about a thing, Mister Harry," she assured him serenely. "When you come back after New Year, we's gonna have lotsa nice twenties and fifties and Cs— wont we, Mr. Hoag? Won't we?" Albert Hoag merely grinned affirmatively in reply to the question. "They'll be aged and handled with no fingerprints at all, and won't none of 'em stick together, Mr. Harry. They'll really be a little better than what you been using cause the paper'll be better and we don't have to handle 'em as much. The ink rubs off just right and won't flake at all. It's all worked out, Mr. Harry.

"And don't worry," she continued. "Ain't nobody in no hurry. It's them what gets in a rush what turns out the bads—them what can't wait. Ours is better than bureau prime. Now it's getting' so it don't hardly pay to make twenties no more, but that ain't your worry, Mr. Harry. We'll have 'em here fer ya. All you need."

Chapter 12
Some Good News

Late one afternoon near the end of February, Ted Flynn stopped by city hall to see the mayor. Allie Eller welcomed him in her cheerfully grotesque way, "Hey, Ted, what brings you over here? Are you checking up on the mayor?"

"Hold it, Allie," Flynn protested. "Don't start that talk. No, I would like to see his honor. If he's busy, I can come back but it won't take three minutes."

"You know he's not busy, Ted," she continued. "He's sitting in there thinking—dreaming up great things."

Hearing the exchange outside his office, Fern went to the door to greet the resident agent. "Come on in, Ted. Ignore her the same as if there wasn't anybody there. What can I do for you?"

Flynn entered the private office and sat by the window. "We just had a call from our office out in Fresno, California," he began. "A couple of our people out there have seen your boy, Jack."

"Oh my God!" Fern exclaimed. "Is he in trouble?"

"No, no," Flynn countered, "we were looking for him to question…"

"You wanted to question Jack?" Fern queried while visibly shaken.

"Yes, Mayor, but he's not under suspicion for anything."

"Then what's Jack wanted for questioning about?" Fern pressed with nervous agitation.

"Merely a routine part of this treasure business, Mayor. As you know, we try to be very thorough. Among the many people we wanted to talk with was Jack—I guess to find out if he had any ideas about the treasure. Jack's not…"

"Ted, what the hell would Jack know about the treasure—now really, what could he know?" Fern snapped with continuing anger.

"Mayor, I came here to tell you your boy is in Fresno. He's apparently okay. He's been doing some steady work for an outfit out there that repairs cooling equipment on these big refrigeration trucks that haul produce and stuff. I thought you'd like to know unless you've talked to him lately."

"I'm very glad to learn it and thanks for telling me," Fern replied more tactfully. "You've got to understand when your boy has left and you don't hear from him for months on end and an FBI agent says he's been wanted and picked up for questioning, that's enough to scare the hell out of me. Then too, I really would like to know why Jack's wanted for questioning about the treasure thing. Why him? Cause he's my son, I reckon."

"Merely routine, Mayor," Flynn replied. "No one thinks he or any of his buddies were selling drugs or anything to raise money for your city. The idea is possible but pretty far-fetched. Our wanting to talk to Jack was routine. We thought he might know something... some drug person who'd be the sort to leave a big..."

"And did he know anything, Ted?" Fern asked in a superficially polite tone.

"Mayor, I haven't seen the report and you know I can't discuss bureau business," Flynn explained politely, "but between you and me, I really don't think so."

"Can I reach him?"

Flynn gave Fern an envelope with a telephone number written on it. "Don't ask me where or what the place is. I was told you'd be more apt to get him after nine out there meaning after midnight here."

"Thanks, Ted," Fern expressed solemnly. He then added, "I thought you all were done with this treasure business."

"It's still open but we're not too active in it now," Flynn answered. "As for Jack, we'd been trying to find him for weeks—from back when we were very much into the thing. Only recently did we pick up his trail. Don't worry. Nobody thinks he's done anything wrong."

As Flynn rose to leave, Fern also stood courteously and remarked, "I guess you think this treasure business has criminal ties?"

"You know I can't give an opinion on something like that, Mayor," the resident agent replied when he reached the door. "Off the record and I hope I'm wrong, I do believe somewhere in all this there's something criminal. We'll know though."

As soon as Flynn had left, Fern called his wife and told her the news of Jack. "He's okay and not in any trouble, Margaret. They said he's been doing a little work out there. ...I wanted you to know. There's nothing bad," he gently added before hanging up the telephone.

"It sounds to me like you and Mrs. Fern have just come into some really good news, Mister Mayor," Allie Eller offered cheerfully. "I'm sure glad fer ya both."

"Thanks, Allie," he replied with his eyes noticeably moist. "Almost any news was better than what we'd had."

The mayor returned to his reading. It was a chilling winter day with no unusual crises, problems or complaints. He dialed the number in Fresno two times but there was no answer. Although the office telephone seldom rang, Fern was unable to concentrate on anything.

Having noticed that her boss was lost in thought rather than refuse-disposal technology, Allie stood in the doorway until she caught his eyes with her own. "There's something I been wanting to ask you, Yer Honor."

"Go ahead, Allie, now's a good time."

"You know where all that money come from, now don't you, Mister Mayor? You really know," she pressed in her own persistent way.

Fern was somewhat stunned by the question but managed to remain calm. "Why do you think I know, Allie? What on earth would lead you to believe that?"

"Just something, Mister Mayor—and you don't want to tell because more won't come through fer the good of Plain Oak." Allie was smiling more through the twinkle in her eyes than with her lips and other facial expressions.

"I hope you don't think I made a deal with the Mafia or a drug group or the Communist Party like some of the gossip going around is saying, Allie."

"Of course not, Yer Honor. You'd never do that kinda stuff."

"Allie, seriously, how could poor little me have anything to do with a big package of money getting laid at the door of one Elton Naylor?"

"I don't know, Mayor, but I've gotten to know you pretty good and something's different," she continued as her seriousness of tone clashed with an eye-twinkling smile. "It's the way you keep planning everything like as if a great big boxcar of money is on the way to Plain Oak and you know fer sure it's a coming. You could be spending some of the money fer lots a things that'll cost money this town won't never get its hands on but you keep up with this planning. You could be rebuilding the old Springhouse Bridge. You coulda bought a new garbage packer and even me a file cabinet so I wouldn't have to keep using boxes for the back years' stuff."

"Wherever the money came from, Allie, there was a letter telling how to spend it and saying there would be more," Fern reasoned. "Criminal, goof head or both—I don't know. We decided—and I think it was the right thing—to use the money. When we took it, I felt it was only right to do what the letter said to do. Maybe there'll be more money—maybe not. Plans had to be done for the South End drainage job. We needed a good plan and capital program for this city anyhow. If we don't have a dream to shoot for, we'll never get anywhere. That's true of us as people and it's true of communities of people. Yes, Allie, I'm different now. The treasure had a lot to do with it. It's caused me to think about Plain Oak and the communities we live in—how wretched they are compared with what they could be and how they get caught up in all the little ego games people play. What the treasure has given me is a dream of what Plain Oak can be. Maybe others will get the same sorts of dreams and a new vision of things will get started right here in our little city."

Allie's eyes were still beaming their smile as she quizzed him, "Have you heard the latest one, Mayor—about you and the marijuana seeds?"

"I guess not, Allie," he replied. "I'm usually the last to hear anything they're saying about me."

"It seems you're now the big supplier of marijuana seeds in this country and parts of the whole world. Yer son, Jack, is the lead salesman and buyer. You are giving back some of the profits to the town to keep yer word about the drainage."

"How long has that one been making the rounds?" he asked angrily.

"I heard it at lunch today," she replied, "for the first time."

"One of these days I'm going to start calling in everybody and put them under oath and ask, 'Who did you hear it from?' If they say, 'so and so,' I'll get so and so and if he says, 'I heard it from such and such,' I'll get him and sooner or later…"

"You'd get to Dexter Snidow," she filled in.

"Probably. What really ticks me off is how they're bringing Jack into this. Even the FBI wanted to talk to him. The poor kid's just getting his head screwed on right and they start dragging him through all this."

"That's just to follow up on rumors, Mayor."

"What rumors?"

"Just talk, Mister Mayor, but folks don't believe that stuff. They really don't."

"Allie," Fern began to expound philosophically, "let me tell you something that's very true but it's not in the books. It's not taught in high-school civics or in college political science but I've been around long enough to see it. When you or anyone's in public life, you're part of people's entertainment. They want you to screw up or be crooked or be dumb. It gives them something to talk about and lets them feel superior. You say people don't believe all these rumor stories. Deep down they probably don't, but they want to believe them, Allie. It makes for entertainment. It lets them think they're better than the mayor— not me, not John Fern but the mayor. The mayor's a crook. He's got a boy who's been into drugs and now he's a big time drug-seed dealer. They say to themselves, 'I'm not a crook and my boy turned out better than the mayor's boy.' Then they feel good about themselves and they've had their entertainment. Well, I don't like it, Allie. I'm not in any damned drug business or drug-seed business and Jack certainly didn't send any box of money to his hometown. There hasn't been any deal for me to grant a sanctuary for crime in Plain Oak. Can you see me telling our cops to lay off criminals or drug pushers or communists? Hell, I've been giving them every chewing out because they haven't busted the peddling going on here whether it's little stuff, big stuff, hard stuff or soft stuff. Why if I tried something like that, I'd be run out of town so fast I wouldn't have time to pack my bag!"

"People do like to look down at public officials, Mr. Mayor," Allie agreed, "but you're bigger than that stuff. You'll just have to ignore it. It's what you got into when you filed papers to run. But, Mayor, all this money turning up had to start a lot of rumor talk even if it appeared suddenly and mysteriously out of nowhere on the high altar at St. Luke's Church in plain view of everyone there during a crowded Sunday service."

At five o'clock, Allie covered the typewriter, freshened her make-up, stuffed a few more things into an already hefty pocketbook and left for the day. John Fern watched the arrival of the winter darkness as automobile drivers increasingly used headlights for their short trips home. Learning of the rumors about Jack stunned him initially. He could imagine the persons passing city hall all looking up and laughing at him. As thoughts of being a conversation topic at bridge parties, on the golf links and in barbers' chairs passed through his mind, his smoldering anger began slowly to soften. *What could I do about it if I tried?* he wondered to himself. A public statement might be issued denying each rumor and denouncing what seemed to be widespread calumny. To do this might rekindle gossip which would otherwise fade away as new concerns vied for public attention. He might call in close friends and people who had worked for his election and simply tell them there had been no deal with anyone. As the clock on the wall slid past five-thirty, Fern decided the best action at least for now would be to do nothing. This could always be changed.

As he was leaving, the private telephone on his desk began ringing. "Hello," Fern answered.

Sneed's voice blurted, "John, are you alone and free?"

"More or less. I was just going home."

"I want to buy a gift for Margaret without her knowing about it but I want to make sure she can use it."

After a few seconds, Fern realized Sneed wanted to talk with him on their special telephone. "That sounds nice," he replied.

"Without letting Margaret know it's for her, find out if she'd like a handsome picture frame, twenty-four by sixteen inches, made from real black walnut. I'll give you a ring in a day or so and you can tell me."

"Where are you?"

"I'm traveling. There's a beautiful one in a gift shop in the hotel where I'm at. Find out for me and I'll call you very soon."

Fern thought for a minute and remembered the payphone at the A&P on Cairo Drive. First he telephoned Margaret, "Do we need or want a handsome walnut picture frame, two feet by sixteen inches?"

"No," she answered.

"I didn't think so either. See you soon."

Fern hastened to his car and began driving about town. When certain no one was following him, he drove to the supermarket, parked and entered. He picked out a small bunch of bananas then began examining a few hardware items near the payphones. After several difficult moments of trying to seem occupied, one of the phones began ringing.

"Hello," he answered. "This is a payphone at the A&P."

"Does the coast look clear, perfectly clear?" Sneed asked. "Completely clear?"

Fern looked in all directions. No one seemed to be watching. "Yes, this is a good time. Make it quick."

"Everything's been movin' fine. The deal stands. Keep up the plans. You're hot. Your phones are bugged and that's why I didn't want to talk to you."

"Could be."

"A couple of things. The library—it'll be paid for in a special way. Don't let it to contract 'til you know you got something special. You may have to hold it back a little while."

"I don't understand."

"It's comin' outta some life insurance and the fellow ain't dead yet but he's sinking fast. You'll know. Is the coast still clear?"

"Yes."

"You don't plan no trips away from town ten to twelve weeks from now, do you?"

"No."

"Good. Keep it that way. Figure on something happening in late May or early June. It could be later but it sure ain'ta gonna be no quicker."

"Okay."

"Is there anything I need to know?" Sneed asked.

"Every package coming to city hall is carefully treated and scrutinized," Fern warned. "Folks think they might be full of money."

"I've read about it. Anything else?"

"No," Fern replied, "except the FBI and Secret Service are big into this."

"God's with us," Sneed stated confidently. "If you get afeared, remember you're doin' his will. Don't say nothin' ta nobody. That includes Margaret. Good-by."

* * *

John Fern was so lost in thought he scarcely recalled the drive home. After he was relaxed with a fresh cigar and a drink of bourbon, Margaret asked in her strong but quiet way, "What's so important about nine o'clock in California? Why don't we give that number a ring?"

Fern rocked with a nervous steadiness. After a few seconds he handed her the envelope. "You dial it. I've tried twice already. Go ahead, Margaret. You'll get through if anybody can."

"All right," Margaret concurred and reached for the telephone. A few seconds later she was listening anxiously to the ringing while her husband feigned calmness.

A familiar voice answered and Margaret Fern sobbed, "Oh Jack, Jack, it's your mother!"

"Hello, Mamma," Jack Fern answered.

"How are you? Tell us," she exclaimed while weeping.

"I'm fine. Everything's cool. I'm working and before too long, I'll be coming home and..."

"Oh John," she cried out, "he's fine and he's coming home!"

John Fern hastened to the kitchen and picked up the extension phone. "Hey boy," he opened, "how's everything?"

"Fine, Dad?" their son answered. "When I get some more money saved up, I want to start a repair business for refrigerator trucks back home."

"Wonderful, Jack!" John Fern exclaimed in a jubilant voice. "If I can help, I certainly will but if you want it to be all your own doings, that'll be fine too."

"And I've figured out a lot about life and why we're here and how a lot of things all fit together. I'm clean and I'll never be on drugs again. Honest."

"That's so wonderful, Jack," Margaret Fern added in a struggle to hide her quiet sobbing.

"Do you need anything, son?" John Fern continued. "Are you well?"

"Oh I'm fine, really fine and I don't need a thing," the youth answered. "I've read about all that money. That was really something. An FBI man thought I might have known who sent it but I certainly didn't know."

"Of course not," his father agreed.

"Mom, I'm sorry I haven't been in touch but I've been busy thinking and learning a lot about refrigeration."

"We're glad we know where you are and that you're safe and well. We worried about you, Jack. We worried a lot," Margaret Fern explained solemnly. "That's all behind us now."

CHAPTER 13
A LOAD OF GRAVEL

Plain Oak's city hall was a T-shaped edifice located on a large corner lot downtown. The top of the "T" faced Elliott Boulevard while the rear, housing the council chamber in the basement and a few offices on the first floor, almost extended to a back alley. The left corner of the building was landscaped with some parking next to the street. The other side, a make-shift work area known as the city yard, was used to store pipe, bricks, piles of sand and gravel, street signs, a small shed for rock salt, and general odds and ends. Earlier complaints about the city yard being an eyesore ceased after the Temple Theater got built on the right side of the building making the area difficult to see from either street.

At quarter past nine on a Friday evening in mid-June, a large dump truck, marked with the decals of an S & J Construction Company from a nearby town, pulled into the city yard from the rear alley. A thin elderly man got out of the cab and gave hand signals to the driver. "Come on back. Come on back," he shouted with authority. "Hold it right there." After the dump body was fully hoisted, the tailgate was unlatched. Gravel quickly fell against the side of the building forming a pile. "Ease her ahead a little," the man yelled and the truck moved forward about six more feet. "Pull on ahead," the man shouted. The truck next eased forward and its dump bed began to lower back into place.

Albert Hoag got out of the cab carrying an electric lantern. After making a quick inspection of the stone pile, he uttered softly, "You was right, ole boy. It come out real good!" Satisfied the gravel completely covered whatever had been buried in the pile, the two men remounted the truck and quickly drove off. From the time they had first arrived until their vehicle was moving down Elliott Boulevard, less than two minutes had elapsed.

The next stop was the front of the main post office. Wearing gloves, Harry Sneed mailed a letter in the box marked Plain Oak and Vicinity. Once the truck was driving on, Sneed remarked, "It said on the box that the pickup is 10 p.m. on Fridays. John might get it in tomorrow's mail."

As they moved on out of town, Sneed muttered, "I'm still bothered about that gravel. Them laboratory cops might trace the quarry and get to you and Lizzie."

"Ain't no way, ole boy," Hoag answered in a tone that seemed on the verge of a laughter that never developed. "You gotta quit worrying so much."

"Tell me about that load again," Sneed pressed nervously. "You sure you ain't signed nothin'?"

"I ain't signed a damned thing," Hoag replied emphatically. "Like I done said already, I went to the weigh house, weighed in, and told 'em I wanted eight ton a crusher run. An ole boy said, 'Will what's in that pile do you?' and it was a great big pile. He tole me how they had a good deal on account of somebody done backed out of a big order and they wanted that pile ta git gone. It looked plenty good to me. He loaded me up with a payloader, and I pulled up and got weighed plum full. We settled on forty-five dollars. I give it to him in genuine bureau prime. He wrote a little something on a slip. I ain't signed a thing. Folks go there all the time to get gravel rock. I seen a lotta trucks leaving plumb full. Ain't nobody paid no mind to an ole boy like me pullin' in, gettin' weighed empty, gettin' loaded up and bein' weighed plum full. Didn't nobody know it was Hoag. Didn't nobody take no license number and if'n they had, they was old plates only the same color with a new sticker. I had six days of beard on me and all of this was what...five weeks back. Ain't no way. If'n they tie the rock to a quarry clean down in Georgia, who's gonna think of Hoag? I ain't never seen nobody down in thar and ain't nobody never seen me. Quit worrying, ole boy."

"Sounds solid," Sneed observed seriously. "Be sure and wash the whole truck real good. We'll trust the Almighty."

"I think we be getting some rain, Harry," Hoag remarked as the truck passed the city-limits line.

"Yep," Sneed observed flatly, "be a good thing too. It'll wash away all tracks. God's doin' it."

Hoag burst into a heavy deep-throated laugh, "What d'ya think all that gift'll bring, ole boy?"

"I don't rightly know."

"Bet it'll be right smart," Hoag continued as he drove. Laughing again, he added, "It's sure gonna cause a stew in your old home town! Man, I wish I could see all them faces when they get to fishing around in that gravel pile!"

At what used to be Shorty's Drive-In several miles outside town, Liz Hoag was waiting in her brother's car. As soon as the two men pulled into the abandoned parking lot, the S & J decals were peeled from the truck and burned. "The coast was clean as a whistle," she advised. "Won't nobody payin' no 'tention ta nothin'."

"Looks like we're home free, ole boy," Hoag said jovially. "Anything else we gotta do?"

"Nope," Sneed answered, "just stick to the plan. Get back the roundabout way. Wash the truck real good first thing. Make sure to change them tires and get good and shed of 'em. Shave and lay low. No calls. Remember, we been doin' the Lord's will. God bless ya and get goin'."

The images of the two vehicles fading from view marked Sneed's inevitable return to solitude. He forced himself to recall the accomplishments of the past nine and one-half months, but his exercise of will did little to shake off a surge of desolation now sweeping over him.

Sneed had previously experienced this intense loneliness only a few times in his life: It happened first when his uncle's farm had to be sold and his parents had taken him back for one final visit. He had been happiest there and he recalled their departure in his father's Model T Ford. As it had passed through the gate he, only eleven and knowing he would never return, turned around for one last look through the trail of dust behind the car. Next there was the senior-class picnic which, having just lost Mildred Fox to Richard Frei, he chose to avoid and, having avoided it, brooded all alone about the fun his classmates were having without him. Finally, as his mother's coffin was lowered into her grave and he witnessed the clumps of earth pounding the wooden box, this same unbearable isolation returned once again.

Before getting into his car, he breathed deeply hoping to soften the agony. A soft, moist breeze caressed his face and he paused briefly to enjoy it. The wind grew stronger and became gusty. Sneed started his car and headed straight for his garden paradise. Soon there were flashes of lightning with thunder rumbling in the distance.

After Sneed had pulled beneath his gate and the loud bell had sounded, it began raining gently. *It's coming on strong*, he was thinking to himself. *God wants the tracks good and muddied up and another washing of them gravel.*

Sitting alone on his porch, he watched the rainfall becoming intense. A spray came through the screen and moistened his face. Deep in thought, Sneed turned over an idea that was frightening—something deep within his soul was causing him to want to be caught. *Why?* He wondered. Was it punishment for earlier sins, known and unknown? *No*, his innermost being answered. *God had forgiven everything.* Had he committed more sins? *No*, because he had constantly begged God to lead him away from temptation and sin. As he searched deep inside his innermost self, Sneed stared at the wilderness lit sporadically by lightning, and he listened to the rain's soft percussion as it fell upon the roof and the leaves and water. Soon the downpour was bringing forth a steady roar from the earth itself.

Almost mesmerized by this harmony and splendor all around him, Sneed came to understand his faint compulsion—the sin of pride. Unless he were caught, no one would know how he had succeeded in his clever undertaking. Millie would also never comprehend his persistence and ingenuity and how stupid the bankers had been. Even if Richard Frei were still alive, Lizzie Hoag's currency would be passing through the First National with ease.

Sneed vowed his arrest must never happen. These thoughts, this sinful pride, were the work of Satan to obstruct God's plan for the New Jerusalem. The secret must remain with the chosen few. There must be no Sneed memorials in the city.

As for Millie, Sneed could only imagine her adulation if she were as she should have been and could be told what she must never learn. The slightest change in the order of things would have made a totally different world for him and for many. This had once been so close only Richard Frei, older and a returning doughboy from the trenches of France, had bewitched Millie's heart.

Sneed smiled as he recalled Frei, the prohibitionist, land speculator, banker and community leader in Plain Oak. For Frei's temperance crusades, Sneed had offered the finest moonshine in abundance at low prices. For his real-estate development, Sneed's massive garden paradise had effectively choked off a major land-sales operation his rival had been striving to achieve for years. As for Frei, the banker or "moneychanger" as Harry Sneed labeled him, there was now being produced an exceptionally high-grade counterfeit currency in the service of Almighty God. For this civic leader's many intrusions into the affairs of the city, Sneed was aiding Plain Oak's transformation into the New Jerusalem thereby eclipsing every vestige of Frei's legacy as a civic leader.

Richard Frei was the Antichrist, Sneed reminded himself.

CHAPTER 14
METICULOUS EXCAVATION

The mail delivered Saturday morning to 327 Oak View Drive included a letter in a typed business envelope with no return address. John Fern knew at once it pertained to the treasure. Two shiny pennies had been taped to the bottom of the letter. The text was:

> John Fern, Mayor
> Plain Oak, West Virginia
> Dear Mayor Fern:
> Peace and blessings from God and His Son, Jesus Christ, Savior of Mankind, through a humble servant. You and the city have spent the first gift wisely on plans to make Plain Oak great. Behind the city hall in the city yard sits a pile of gravel. Beneath this pile is a gift which like all gifts comes from God Almighty. Use it to achieve the plans. If it is spent right, there will be more. If it is squandered, there will be no more.
> A Friend of Plain Oak

John Fern immediately went to his telephone and called police headquarters. "Where the chief?" he asked.

"Probably at home," the desk sergeant replied.

"Do everything you can to get him. Send a car out looking if he's gone somewhere. Have him call me here at my home right away."

"Yes sir, Mister Mayor."

"Next he telephoned Albert Triere and Bill Willy and asked them to meet him at his city hall office as soon as possible. Elmer Naylor had gone out-of-town for the weekend. Chief Sacker then telephoned. "Your line's been busy, Mayor. What's up?"

"Chief," Fern instructed, "you and three of your best men get down to my office at city hall right away. I'll explain when I get there. Try and get Ted Flynn there too."

"I'll be there in ten minutes."

"And chief," Fern added, "Keep it quiet. I don't want a mob scene."

"Is it what I think?"

"Wait and see. Remember, not a word."

John Fern yelled to Margaret that he was going to city hall and might be late. At seven until eleven, he pulled into his reserved parking space. Once inside, he ambled over to a window on the south side of the building. A few yards from where he stood, there was a large pile of gravel. A shudder went down Fern's spine. *We'll be back in the news again*, he mumbled to himself before mounting the two flights of stairs that led to his office. Al Triere, dressed casually in a green-knit sport shirt, was standing in the hall outside the entrance. As Fern unlocked the door, Triere asked, "Will this be a long or a short one?"

"A long one, Al."

"Did our friend strike again?" the treasurer continued.

"Let's wait 'til the clan gathers, Al."

Several minutes later Bill Willy and Chief Sacker arrived. "Ted should be here by now, Mayor," the chief advised.

"Where are your three men, Chief?" the mayor inquired.

"Downstairs, if you want 'em up here…"

"Not now, Chief," Fern answered. "I hope all us coming in like this didn't attract attention."

"There could be a little buzzing among the men," Sacker acknowledged, "but they're under orders to keep their mouths shut."

Two minutes later, Ted Flynn walked in carrying a paper cup of coffee. "Good morning, gentlemen," he opened. "What's this about?"

Fern looked at everyone and began slowly, "This letter came in the morning mail to my place on Oak View. I got it about a half hour ago. I opened and read it. Now some of my fingerprints are on it. Two copper pennies, new shiny ones, are taped to the bottom. Let me read…"

"Don't touch it anymore," Flynn cautioned immediately. "Lay it flat on the desk, Mayor. Same with the envelope. We can all read it that way."

"Certainly," Fern assented and cautiously placed the letter in an opened position on the corner of his desk.

After everyone had digested the contents, Fern began excitedly, "Now there's a pile of gravel out there! I saw it when I came in just now!"

"Couldn't it be there for patching city streets or something like that?" Flynn inquired.

"Sure," Fern agreed, "and maybe it's another one of these practical jokes. But nobody knew about the two pennies before. That was a well-kept secret. Sure, there might be only a pile of rock out there, but maybe there's a box of money buried in it!"

"You've had a lot of college kids' games here, Mayor," the resident agent continued. "What makes you think it could be the real thing this time?"

Flynn's question made Fern nervous. He sensed the FBI and maybe his own police chief believed he was conspiring with criminals and had inside information. His mind began imagining how a genuinely innocent person might respond. His nervousness also made him feel he gave an appearance of guilt and, believing so, Fern's anxiety was all the more intense. "The coins!" he answered. "The tone of the letter! No one knew about the pennies, and all that talk written there about greetings from the Lord Jesus Christ! As for college kids' pranks, we haven't had one in months. That's why I think this time it really could…"

"What do you want to do, Mayor?" Bill Willy asked pointedly.

"I...I...I want us to dig up...to dig up whatever's in that pile," Fern replied.

"You are the mayor," Willy advised in a slow calm manner. "The gravel's on city property. It may cover up some money or it may be a simple heap of pebble. You of all people certainly have every right to dig it up. And from a legal standpoint, you should exercise and maintain city control over it. If there's money out there, we don't want other folks making claims to it."

"But you may be destroying evidence of a federal crime," Flynn objected.

"Ted," Willy continued, "if you have any evidence of a federal crime, you can take jurisdiction over the whole thing. I'll give anybody ten to one there's nothing out there but a pile of gravel. There's almost always some gravel laying around out there."

"Then let's dig it carefully," Fern decided, "and preserve any evidence."

"First we secure city hall and keep everybody out but the police," Sacker suggested. "Next we'll fence off the side yard. We'll need to check thoroughly for tire tracks and footprints and measure the pile itself. We'll take complete photography of everything we do." Sacker looked at Ted Flynn and declared, "This is our job, Ted. We welcome any help or suggestions you or anyone from the FBI wants to make. Frankly I don't see there's much to it. It rained long and hard last night. If the stuff was dumped before it started raining, there probably won't be any tracks or prints or anything to go on. Trucks and cars and street equipment and things go in and out of there all the time. If it got dumped after the rain stopped, we might have some real good evidence."

"All the same, I'd like to have an FBI team dig it up."

"That would take a couple of days and we'd soon be dealing with a mob scene out there," Willy reasoned. "We ought to get on with it. Chief's well trained. If there are any special tricks to digging up a pile of gravel, let us know so it'll be done right. Chief'll have a police photographer take a picture of every shovelful if that's what's needed. We'll sift through the whole pile, almost pebble by pebble if that's the right way to go about it."

"Let's get on with it," Fern ordered. "Keep the whole thing quiet. Let's see if we can keep this away from the news people so we won't have a mob of people all over us."

"Chief's got the right plan, Mayor," Willy reasoned. "Secure the building, barricade the yard, check for tire prints and footprints. It's important the men are in uniform and are being paid by the city. Anybody working on this is doing it for the city. That's got to be understood up front."

"Okay Chief," Fern instructed. "We'll do your plan. Call out what men you need. Make sure they're in uniform and understand they're getting paid. There'll be no volunteer stuff on this. Get that camera going. I want a thorough photographic record of everything we do."

"Who's going to dig, Mayor?" Sacker asked.

"We all will but only one of us at a time," he answered.

* * *

The temperature outside was hot and steamy. Ted Flynn sought direction from Alex Parker but learned he was away sailing off Annapolis and would not be home until that evening.

Chief Sacker tried to pick up tracks of any kind but concluded the load had been dumped before the rain had started. The pile had also been placed in a low spot causing the surface water to immerse the soil around and beneath the gravel. Even Ted Flynn agreed that between the extra hard surface and the clay soil, swollen with moisture, there was no hope of identifying tire prints.

Sacker arranged for one of his men to take a number of pictures of the gravel pile each from a different angle. A yardstick was placed in all of the photographs to aid with later measurements and computations. "This may become the world's most studied pile of rock," Willy remarked casually.

Twenty-five minutes later, the chief advised, "We've got about all the evidence we'll ever get without actually digging. What do you say we get started?"

"Let me have the first shot," Fern directed. He picked up a spade and used it to remove several modest amounts of gravel. These were all placed in a wheelbarrow for movement across the yard to a designated spot. At first a photographer carefully took a separate picture of each shovelful. Just as the wheelbarrow had almost been filled with its first load, Fern's spade hit a hard object buried in the stone. His eyes made contact with Chief Sacker's and both men began digging with their bare hands. Fern soon grabbed something almost the size of an ordinary brick and extremely heavy. After Sacker had wiped it off, there was a dull golden shine.

"Lock it in the vault in your office, Al," Fern instructed soberly. "It's the heaviest stuff I've ever picked up in my life. I've never seen gold bullion before but I'm guessing that's what we got!"

CHAPTER 15
THE GOLDFINGER AFFAIR

Seven months before "Plain Oak Treasure Two" exploded into the national and even international news, the Central Intelligence Agency had lost just over a ton of gold coin destined for an insurgent group in Libya. A navy submarine was to have transferred this cargo to a seaplane at a rendezvous point west of Sardinia. An aircraft made contact, landed at sea, received the shipment and then disappeared. When the legitimate plane showed up eight minutes later, the mission's leaders realized pirates had taken the coin. In a very few minutes, about twenty-two million dollars worth of gold had vanished.

Within the CIA this episode, "the Goldfinger affair," had been so uniquely classified no one except the highest officials and a few trusted investigators knew what had happened. The investigation to follow was as complete as these embarrassing and super-secret circumstances would permit. A few speculative leads were advanced in top-secret, special-clearance memoranda. These hypothesized that the disappearance might be traceable to several named terrorist groups, a small band of Israeli ex-intelligence officers who had evolved into a criminal organization and finally an international relief agency whose mission was to assist displaced refugees in Southeast Asia. Neither a communist nation nor any domestic criminal organization was blamed.

When the president of the United States was briefed about Goldfinger, he became furious. The fact that a pirate group, whatever its origins or goals, had sufficiently penetrated the CIA to discover a sensitive rendezvous time and location, had learned of a submarine carrying gold for transfer (something even the sub's captain and crew had not been told), had gotten access to infrared signal codes and was able to forge important documents, meant that there was insider involvement. Until such persons were ferreted out, similar operations could be in jeopardy. The president and his chief-of-staff also feared an even worse hypothesis—Goldfinger was an internal CIA operation "to raise a flower fund to benefit certain agency employees," as the president himself occasionally phrased it. Word might leak out and become big news. This could precipitate a scandal at home and disgrace the United States in the eyes of other nations.

As soon as Plain Oak Treasure Two hit the news media late on a Saturday afternoon near the middle of June, the president immediately summoned the deputy director of the CIA and the director of the FBI to Camp David. The unusual meeting to follow lasted about two minutes. At its conclusion the president announced firmly, "I want to know if there is a connection between Plain Oak and the Goldfinger thing and I want to know who it is, what it is and I want to know it quick!"

As the FBI director listened, he felt quite uneasy because he had never heard of the Goldfinger affair and did not to want to admit his ignorance fearing the president might think him incompetent for being uninformed about an important national-security matter. While they were walking toward their awaiting limousines, he asked his colleague from the CIA, "What in the hell is Goldfinger?"

"You don't know about it?"

"I've never heard of it in my life. Should I have? If so, why wasn't I told?"

"It's a highly classified matter," the CIA official answered. "Several months ago something more than twenty million in gold coin was stolen from us during an important operation, a super-secret and sensitive mission overseas. No one must know anything about it. Frankly we don't know who or what to blame. There must have been at least two insiders. The boss seems to think there might be a Plain Oak connection. He tends to put two and two together in his own unique way."

The FBI director stared pensively into the trees. "We weren't told because we didn't have a need to know," he remarked. "Now, by God, I need to know."

"True," the deputy director agreed nervously. "You and your top man on the Plain Oak case. No one else. I cannot stress adequately how frightfully sensitive this thing is and how very political it would become if word got out."

"We'll have to work out another joint strategy," the FBI director remarked. "We'll have to move a team into Plain Oak." As the two men paused for a moment, he concluded by asking, "How much will I be told about Goldfinger?"

"Only what you absolutely need to know."

"Could there really be a Plain Oak connection?"

"I'm completely unfamiliar with the first Plain Oak episode and the second just broke. They're in your sphere. We had an overseas mission where lots of gold was essential. A brilliant act of piracy was pulled off last November with great skill. There's no trace of the gold. Today a large quantity turns up in West Virginia in a highly unusual way. Who can say if there's a connection? We use gold in our work because it's a currency anyone will take anywhere. Often we can't account for a few pieces here or there. In this case we lost around a ton of it in coin. Aside from what the mission was and where it was, we can tell you the rest.

"You can readily see where the president's coming from and why we are so very concerned. The whole thing had to be investigated and there's no good way to keep something this damned secret and still investigate it all over the world. We did a complete inside probe. A few people were sent around to look for unusual things. There's nothing solid to go on. A Plain Oak connection is pure speculation. We'll turn the agency upside down to see if anyone having a remote connection to Goldfinger has any sort of ties to the Plain Oak area. If a name pops up, we'll grill him.

"We won't be sending any counterintelligence people out there to sniff around. We'll trust your people for that. We'll want to know what the bureau comes to know if it could be relevant to our problem."

The FBI director sat on a low rock wall near the awaiting limousines. He seemed lost in thought amid the Maryland woods that had just thickened into summer opulence. "Our head man on the Plain Oak case is Alex Parker," he advised. "We'll be assigning him full time. There has been some Treasury and Secret Service involvement that Parker knows about. I haven't been briefed on the Plain Oak situation in several months. There were no really good leads. A few of our people seem to think the mayor is in it somehow but they haven't been able to put anything together about that."

The CIA deputy nervously lit a cigarette, puffed a few times and snuffed it out carefully. When a loud signal buzzed from his limousine fifty feet away, he advised, "Our man will be Ronald Craig. He'll contact you tomorrow through the duty officer. I can't be in on the briefing. Craig will tell you everything about Goldfinger except the nature and background of our mission that led to it. Craig's okay. He knows more about Goldfinger than I do. If you absolutely need information Craig won't divulge, contact me personally. Anything we may do in Plain Oak will be cleared through you and Parker.

"Naturally no one but the two of you must know Central has an interest in the Plain Oak thing. Even the boss made a mistake calling us both out here a few minutes after the story broke. Goldfinger is a ticking time bomb about to explode into Newsweek or the Washington Post. We've got to defuse it before this happens. Plain Oak could be a detonator whether there's a connection or not."

CHAPTER 16
NEW WEALTH

Although about twenty times more valuable and offering the added excitement associated with gold, Treasure Two was taken more calmly in Plain Oak than Treasure One. The same sorts of rumors about the donor and his or her motivation recirculated but in a more matter-of-fact way.

Curiosity nationwide, however, was epidemic. Network television coverage was extensive especially in the beginning. Newspapers and magazines featured articles about Elliott County and the two treasure episodes. A Chicago newspaper offered a $25,000 prize to the first person to identify the mysterious giver with absolute proof.

Amateur sleuths who came to be known as "Plain Oak Treasurer Watchers" began cropping up all over the United States. Many visited Plain Oak and went door-to-door in search of clues, folklore and even county history.

A few people spent countless hours examining the extensive police photography of the gold's discovery. This review substantiated the city's inventory of one hundred and sixty-seven bars. Even Fern's most caustic critics had to admit, albeit reluctantly, that the gold was all present and accounted for.

Since there were no solid leads, most hypotheses involved the mayor because he had been mentioned in the first letter and was the addressee to the second. Reporters and the watchers alike were continually trying to arrange meetings with him. After several of these ordeals, Fern began to tire of them and often became uncooperative. As he refused interviews, terminated telephone conversations with abruptness and gave no-comment answers, the mayor became increasingly suspect and all the more newsworthy.

The more sensational press recycled the old rumors and launched a few new ones: Fern was offering a base for communist activity; Fern was working with one or more big-time drug dealers; Fern was secretly allowing toxic wastes to be dumped near the town; Fern had developed a lucrative business in marijuana, coca and opium-poppy seeds; Fern was working on a deal to bring gambling to Plain Oak; Fern was linked to some organized-crime syndicate and Fern once had a rich mistress whom he had rejected and who was seeking to rekindle his affection by bailing him out of a campaign promise with financial assistance which, for reasons of discretion, needed to be given secretly. Ties were also fabricated between Plain Oak and a number of super-wealthy Americans. Whatever the speculation, not a shred of evidence was ever produced to back up any of these stories.

Capitalizing on the publicity, the chamber of commerce began a campaign to boost tourism and business development. Ads captioning **Join the New Gold Rush to Plain Oak** were placed in industrial-development magazines and other publications. Bus tours were chartered from places like Pittsburgh, Norfolk and Cleveland. For about two weeks the location of the gravel pile was something of an attraction, and an enterprising businessman tried to market "Gold Dust Gravel" in little souvenir bags. The same person opened a passably good restaurant named "The Treasure Trove." Another sought to start up a brewery and sell "Plain Oak Gold," a beer, but he was unable to arrange financing.

On the Monday following Treasure Two, an impressive team of FBI agents, crime-lab personnel and other specialists arrived in Plain Oak. Once again the unofficial explanation was that by unlocking the town's mystery, other federal crimes might also be solved.

The West Virginia State Police also had a brief but conspicuous involvement. Governor Burns summoned "Jimmy" Snellings, the superintendent, to the Governor's Mansion just after the breaking news of Treasure Two reached the media. "Jimmy," he instructed, "find out where in the hell Plain Oak got all that money." Snellings, who had political ambitions of his own, personally set out for Plain Oak early the next week leading a caravan of three plainly marked police vehicles. With flashing lights and sirens blaring, the cars traveled all the way from Charleston at high speeds. Once in Plain Oak, Snellings was televised, photographed, interviewed and seen by the public. Two days later he and his team quietly departed having accomplished absolutely nothing.

FBI laboratory specialists went through the gravel pile almost pebble by pebble and kept samples for laboratory analysis. Their attempt to identify tire prints was unsuccessful. With the city's formal permission, a carefully weighed sample of gold was taken from each of the bars. The envelope and letter to John Fern was sent away for a complete laboratory evaluation.

By the end of June only Alex Parker and five additional agents on special assignment actually remained in Elliott County. Nevertheless there was a public perception that the Plain Oak area was swarming with undercover investigators. Routine criminal activity declined almost to nothing. Pot and other illegal drugs virtually disappeared countywide.

A rumor also got started that John Fern and Chief Sacker were about to be arrested. There was no hint as to what the charges would be. While they might wreck the city's claim to more than twenty million dollars, the community's mental state had reached a point that the arrests would have been welcomed news.

John Fern withstood a lengthy interrogation that seemed to consist of the same questions being asked over and over. As time went on Parker and another agent would often stop in to see the mayor at city hall. On one of these visits they put him in an awkward posture by requesting an interview with his wife, Margaret Fern.

"Certainly," John Fern answered, "I'll take you over there."

"Mayor," Parker continued, "we'd like to talk with her without you being present."

Fern was disturbed by the request. If he refused, he would clearly be a suspect. Margaret might unwittingly lead them to her uncle. He thought for a moment and answered, "It's up to Mrs. Fern."

"We realize, Mayor, this may seem unorthodox to you," Parker continued. "Certainly a wife cannot be made to testify against her husband and, indeed, we have no suspicion of your involvement in any crime. Quite frankly we believe only one thing—you know more than you're telling us. Maybe your wife has some idea where all this gold came from—maybe not. If she wants a lawyer present, she certainly may have one. If she refuses the interview, we'll drop the matter. As a courtesy to you, if you object, we won't pursue it."

John Fern was striving to maintain his composure. He felt his face might be a little flushed and he experienced a slight dizziness. "Whatever she says is all right by me," he mumbled.

"Do you want to call her or do you want us to do that, Mayor?" Parker persisted as both men stared intently at him.

"Maybe I'd better," was the answer. "You men might scare her or, more likely, she'll scare the hell out of you." He reached for his private telephone, dialed a number and in a few seconds was talking with his wife. "I'm sitting here with the FBI," he began. "They want to talk with you alone." There was a noticeable delay before Fern resumed, "And if you want our lawyer to be with you, you can have him present."

"John, I don't know anything," she answered.

"I know that," he continued, "and if you don't want to talk to them, you don't have to. They made that clear to me."

"Tell them I don't know anything," she requested.

"Mr. Parker," Fern repeated with the phone positioned so his wife could hear what he was saying, "Mrs. Fern asked me to tell you she doesn't know anything."

Parker asked if he might speak with her directly and the mayor assented by yielding the telephone to him. "Mrs. Fern, I'm Alex Parker. We met by phone almost a year ago. I'm certain you believe you don't know anything about this treasure business but oftentimes we'll ask questions which as you answer them you'll help us. You may know something without suspecting how important it really is."

This discussion went on for several minutes and John Fern could see a dogged persistence by Parker to talk with his wife. The niceties of the opening conversation about either John or Margaret Fern being able to decline the interview had been intended to overcome a refusal. Parker desperately wanted to talk with Margaret Fern and was not about to give up trying. What Alex Parker did not know was Margaret could be stubborn in ways only those who knew her quite well could understand. When she got an idea someone was trying to work psychology or to pressure her, she would cause the effort to fail.

Parker began to argue that by cooperating fully with the FBI she could help clear her husband's name of the rumors, suspicion and innuendo circulating throughout the United States. This line of reasoning infuriated Margaret Fern. She fired back, "Mr. Parker, John hasn't done anything wrong. I've never known anyone who had twenty million dollars to give away and I don't think I'll ever get to know such a person as long as I live.

"One thing you ought to know is that Plain Oak is a small place and everyone here knows everything about everybody else. Ever since John became mayor, there have been a lot of people who are down on him about one thing or another. They'd love to be able to prove he's done something bad or gotten mixed up with some criminal or Communist or whatever. He's an honorable man and that's why no one can back up any of the crazy rumors about him that they got started. If he had done even some little thing wrong, they would love to smear him. That's the way it is with being a mayor. I've got to go now. A pot's about to boil over. Good day, sir." With this, the telephone clicked.

Stung by the rebuke and suffering with the July heat, Parker began questioning Fern aggressively, "You were a naval aviator, weren't you?"

"In World War Two, yes."

"Do you still fly?"

"I'm way out of practice now, Mr. Parker."

"Did you ever fly seaplanes, Mayor?"

"No, I can't say that I did," Fern replied calmly.

"Never a seaplane," Parker continued as if he were an attorney cross-examining a witness, "are you sure about that? Never?" Parker's tone suggested he believed the mayor was lying about his lack of experience with seaplanes.

Fern thought the nature and thrust of the questions were unusual. He looked at Parker and replied softly, "I've never really flown a seaplane. I've certainly never had a rating or logged any hours in one. Now once I hopped a flight from Pearl to San Diego in a PBY and sat most of the way in the co-pilot seat. The pilot checked me out a little and let me have the controls for a few minutes. That's one of the few times in my life I was ever inside a seaplane."

"Where were you in early November?" Parker continued with some arrogance.

"What do you mean, where was I?"

"Were you here in Plain Oak? You didn't go away on some kind of business or something say around the 5th of November?"

John Fern reached into one of his desk drawers and pulled out the filler pages from last year's calendar. After leafing through late October and the first week in November, he announced, "Mr. Parker, I was right here on November the 5th and during the days before and after November the 5th. If anybody tells you I was away from here the first week or so in November or says I've flown seaplanes, he's a damned liar and I'll tell it to his face."

Alex Parker realized that for a few moments he had succumbed to a burst of anger brought on by high-level pressure to produce results. With no good leads or promising suspects, his temporary assignment in Plain Oak had become slow and frustrating compared with the routine at headquarters where his overseeing a number of operations created an impression of rapid progress.

As soon as the two agents had excused themselves, Allie Eller entered to deliver a couple of callback messages. Although the door was closed, she had been able to overhear most of the conversation. "I heard him bringing up the 5th of November, Mister Mayor. That other one—that Cy something or other—was asking me about your comings and goings from the middle of October on up to December. Heck fire! You didn't even go to that HUD meeting up in Pittsburgh on the 3rd of December. I had told it all to that Cy, but I guess Mister Alex Parker had to hear it straight from you."

"Something must have happened early in November, Allie."

"Somebody robbed the stagecoach of twenty million in gold and made a clean getaway in a seaplane—somebody fittin' your description, Mister Mayor!"

CHAPTER 17
WHEELING AND DEALING

On a hot Sunday afternoon in July the local lodge of the Fraternal Order of Police hosted a meeting with off-duty firemen to devise a joint strategy for sharing the bounty of Treasure Two. The younger men argued for a flat twenty-thousand dollars per person. Those with more longevity wanted twenty-five hundred dollars per year of service. A compromise was developed and accepted—ten thousand dollars per man plus another thousand for each full year with the city. The two groups retained Melvin Horness, an ex-police judge, to press their demands. After accepting, Horness persuaded everyone to support building the flood project in the South End. Since this was Fern's highest priority, the gesture might secure the mayor's backing for the bonuses the men were seeking.

Horness drafted a petition which was quickly signed by every policeman and fireman in Plain Oak. A reporter got wind of what was going on and an article about the meeting appeared on the front page of a Monday Dispatch.

As soon as he read it, Horness telephoned the mayor. "John," he began, "I want to apologize about the story coming out like it did before you and the council knew about the petition itself."

"That's all right, Judge," Fern reacted. "Was the story correct?"

"As far as it went but what wasn't mentioned were the other petitions being circulated—the ones to show citizen support for their demands."

"Demands?"

"What they want," Horness added for clarification. "Naturally we all hope you will be supportive. The men have been underpaid for years. This would…"

"I'm sure a case can be made," Fern scoffed.

"We'll be presenting all the petitions to council before long," Horness advised. "Incidentally we've figured up the cost. It all comes to nine hundred and two thousand dollars as of right now."

"And if we give the police and firemen what they're after," Fern reasoned, "the city will get requests—demands as you put it—from the street workers, the garbage crew, our water and sewer people and everyone else."

"I can't speak to that, John. I only represent the policemen and firemen. The firemen always want parity with the police in wages and fringe benefits. On this one issue, the police are in full accord. As for the others, you'll probably be seeing more resolutions and petitions about that money than Carter ever had pills."

"I expect you're right, Judge."

"Seriously, John," the attorney continued, "we want you to understand that the lodge and the firehall are both in full support of your Southside drainage program with an even higher priority than their own bonuses. After that, they feel their petition should be honored, and then both the lodge and the firehall will be one hundred percent in support of your program—park, library and all. They'll both be *amicus* with the city if you run into a snag in court over the city's legal right to the gold. Think about it, John. Think about it."

"I understand, Judge. I understand perfectly."

* * *

Two weeks later Fern got a belated call asking him to attend a meeting in progress at the chamber of commerce. After arriving, he soon became annoyed at the discussion then underway. The Brown Brothers, owners of Elliott County Asphalt, were urging the chamber to advocate hard topping every dirt street and alley in town and resurfacing most of the other streets. When the executive board called on the mayor to comment, Fern managed to control his temper and described the city's program which also included lots of street work. He argued that what the Browns were seeking would use up so much of the treasure money, the city could not accomplish what was already planned. Fern used this opportunity to elaborate once again about the library, an industrial area, the drainage works and his park concept—a multipurpose program that ironically had been endorsed earlier by the Plain Oak Chamber of Commerce. The yawns and occasional glances between fidgety members gave him an uneasy impression that the chamber's leadership had other ideas.

Later that day, Fern called Henry Kingery to find out what had really been going on inside the organization. "They're trying to work up their own program for your money," the attorney informed him. "Don't worry. They can't agree on a damned thing."

A week or so later, Fern found out the school superintendent, Bill Harrison, was behind a grass-roots campaign to use almost ten million dollars of treasure money to help pay for a new junior high school. Proponents were saying that by using these funds, this badly needed facility could be built with no increase in taxes.

New proposals for treasure funding were being generated almost daily. By August, most factions in Plain Oak seemed to be aligned behind one project or another. This state of affairs was described succinctly in a front-page, center-column editorial written personally for a Sunday Dispatch by Henry Edwards Robert Stauffer, its principal stockholder, publisher and occasional editor:

OUR GOLDEN CALF

Two treasurers have been given to us by an unknown donor who writes in the style of a religious person. Treasure One was said to be for engineering design and planning. Treasurer Two is supposed to pay for carrying out the plans.

Now whether expected or unexpected, gold fever has smitten our citizens and we are losing civic unity. The chamber of commerce has become so embroiled with dissension over what to recommend to the city, some of its members are not speaking with one another.

Since most of the new ideas are different from the ones developed by the mayor and his advisors, our municipal government is headed on a collision course with some of its citizenry: The Plain Oak Arts Society, divided for several weeks over whether to restore the old Bixler Theater or to construct a building, now wants a new fine-arts museum with an auditorium wing for the performing arts. Our fire department is seeking a new pumper truck. The trustees of Plain Oak Community Hospital are about to submit to the city council a wish list of five pieces of modern equipment said to be essential to cutting-edge medicine. Our school board and its superintendent have instigated a pressure campaign by teachers and PTA members for a new junior high-school building. City employee groups are once again petitioning for salary bonuses.

These are only a few of the items. The reporters, staff and managers of this newspaper all labor to stay informed about what is going on in Plain Oak. New schemes for this strange money are being generated so rapidly, however, we cannot keep up with them.

In the last two weeks we have been contacted by spokespersons seeking the backing of this newspaper for and occasionally against some of the proposals. The arguments being advanced are so overpowering we wonder how plain old Plain Oak has managed to survive for one hundred years without these things.

We have decided not to editorialize in favor or against any specific proposal. We will, however, support wise planning and good sense and will not tolerate poor judgment or petty politics guiding any program. If this gold is proven to have criminal origins, we trust it will not be spent at all.

Our hands-off policy stems partly from the fact that there are probably one-hundred million dollars in ideas floating around but only about twenty-one million dollars with which to achieve them. Also, we refuse to fan the fires of community discord which are already spinning out of control.

Lots of people are going to be disappointed. We do not envy the job of the city council. Also, we do not know how seriously to take the sentences, "Use it to fulfill the plans. If it is spent correct [*sic*], there will be more." This implies our unknown patron supports the planning done by Mayor John Fern and his people and is suggesting that if these funds are used to implement his program, more money will be forthcoming.

Now if this person or these persons would come forward and identify themselves, our town would feel better about using the money in the first place, and the purposes to which it is put could be legitimized sparing the widespread agony and civic dissention we do not like to witness here. We at this paper have always thought Plain Oak was a nice place. We still do and will continue to think so even if none of these ideas materialize.

HERS

P.S. Among the countless rumors on the subject, there is a story that this newspaper was behind Treasure One and Treasure Two. To the best of my knowledge, no one connected with the Dispatch had anything to do with either of them, and I do not know who the person or persons are or where he, she, or they got the money or the gold.

HERS

* * *

Early the next day Arch Kidd and Bill Willy stopped by the mayor's office and closed the door for privacy. "Mayor," Kidd began, "this treasure thing is tearing our town to pieces."

"What now, Arch?" Fern asked as he removed the wrapping from a fresh cigar.

"Everybody's wiggling for some of the damned money. You've heard the stories and saw what Stauffer wrote yesterday. I just heard the Red Cross has started to dream about getting the city to make a multi-million dollar grant for a new building. One idea leads to another. Soon the fever will start getting to the council and each member will be coming up with a pet project of his own. What I'm guessing is we might not be able to hold the council in line. It's a shame because the park and library are both great ideas and are well planned. There's enough momentum behind the South End job to carry it through but that's the only one, Mayor."

"Unless…" the city attorney began.

"Unless what, Bill?" Fern asked.

"Unless our donor comes out of hiding, identifies himself or maybe herself and says, 'This is what I meant the money to be used for.' We would then have a clearly stipulated gift, and the giver can dictate how a lawful gift to a municipality will be used if it's to be used at all."

John Fern stared solemnly at a fixed spot on the wall and stated cautiously, "Bill, I don't know how to bring about what you're saying because I don't know the source."

After this remark, Kidd and Willy exchanged glances in a way that revealed there was an understanding between them. Almost on cue, Kidd began, "John, we've been through a lot of battles together for the good of Plain Oak. On most things we see eye-to-eye. I've never once doubted your integrity or your sincere desire to do what's right for this city. But, John, I believe you know more about this treasure business than what you're letting on. Probably you're keeping quiet because that's the only way the city will get the money. I understand this perfectly. I'd keep quiet too. We all want Plain Oak to get the money. All we're asking you to do is go to whoever it was, try to talk him or maybe her into identifying himself or maybe herself, and like Bill says, have him tell us how to spend it."

"I can't do what I can't do, Arch."

"Try to understand ...The public—they don't know you," Kidd continued. "They'll believe any damned thing. There's never been a really popular mayor here—certainly not after they've been in office long enough to tell a person or two they can't have every cock-and-bull thing they want. John, you were once a fairly popular mayor. Hell, after all this treasure stuff and what people are saying, you'd be lucky to carry Country Club Hill in a runoff election against Dexter Snidow."

"Arch, seriously," Fern replied, "the only reason I ran for mayor last time was to keep Dexter from sitting behind this desk. That's all. I don't like the dad-burned job. As for popularity, I really don't care. My customers are mostly farmers. They don't even live here in town."

"But John, you've been around," Kidd continued. "Of all people, you should know that as your popularity falls off, your ability to persuade the council to go along with the program also dries up. We all want to see the things done—the two drainage projects, a library building, the industrial area, the big park—all for the good of Plain Oak. I really want to see them happen, John. What we're getting at is can't you get this Mr. Treasure guy to come out of the closet? Hell, a gift to Plain Oak is tax-deductible."

"Why me, Arch?"

"Because your name is part of both letters," he replied. "I'm seriously worried the twenty-one million is going to get blown away on the silliest program anyone could ever dream up."

"Okay Arch," Fern agreed, "if I ever get to know who this person is, I'll tote your message."

"Including," Kidd added, "if you already know right now who it is. You see, we think you do."

CHAPTER 18
AN ARAB SHEIK

Although repeated searches failed to turn up a single snooping device, Fern remained suspicious his phones were being bugged, someone was x-raying personal mail, and electronic spying devices were in widespread use in Plain Oak. This explained his constantly uttering things to convince unseen listeners he was not involved with either treasure and had no idea who was responsible for them.

There was no doubt about his being followed. For several weeks amateur sleuths took turns tailing him during the daytime. After work, someone would follow him home, wait around outside for fifteen minutes and then leave. Another would trail him to work the next morning. The fact that no one stood all-night duty outside 327 Oak View Drive added to Fern's conviction his residence and car were bugged. Were he to rendezvous with the mysterious donor after hours, the watchers would not be around to take note but might learn of it electronically.

After several weeks of this "cloak and dagger stuff," as Fern called it, he arrived home one evening, poured a gin and tonic and went to the dining-room window to view his pursuer, a quiet-looking middle-aged man with blondish-red hair. Angered at the man's being there, Fern complained to Margaret, "I wish those bastards would get the hell on back to where they came from and leave me alone. I ought to have that one arrested for disturbing the peace."

Margaret merely continued knitting a gift blanket but suggested in a matter-of-fact way, "Why don't you invite him in? You might get to like him."

Fern gave an understanding look, lit a cigar and chuckled briefly, "You might have something there, honey. Maybe he can tell me who's been giving all this money and gold to our city." After placing his drink on a side table, he went out the front door and shouted, "Hey, you over there! Aren't you getting hot standing out here all by yourself? Come on in. I'll fix you a good cold gin and tonic and might even now put a sprig of peppermint in it. Then you can tell me what you're finding out."

The man seemed instantly stunned by Fern's invitation. His face turned crimson. Offering no reply, he hastened to an automobile parked nearby and drove away. "Why do you suppose he retreated like that, Margaret? Those bastards have been wanting to talk to me. I invite that one in and he flees in total panic."

"You frightened him, John," she advised slowly without once removing her eyes from the knitting. "You don't realize what an overpowering personality you have. You obviously scared the poor fellow almost to death. Also, he might not drink. Some people don't, you know."

"Whatever the true explanation, my dear, he left a little early. As it turned out, you put forth a pretty good idea."

Fern continued to sit in his rocking chair puffing on a cigar. He was bothered by what Bill Willy and Arch Kidd had been saying. For years whenever there was so much as a modest surplus in the general fund, the policemen and firemen initiated a strategy to convert it into wage and fringe-benefit increases for themselves. This would lead to similar requests from other groups of city employees. Most councilmen would also come up with a pet project or two. After endless haggling, everyone would be dissatisfied with whatever decisions finally got made. The same kind of thing was happening again but this time there were big dollars at stake. *If only the money could be used to carry out the plans*, he reflected to himself, *and the drainage works, big park, library and industrial-area project all got built so the public was accustomed to their being there, the people would never let Plain Oak be without them regardless of the cost.*

He could certainly see the wisdom of getting Snead to acknowledge his being the donor thereby enabling him to dictate Plain Oak's program. This might avoid litigation and permit earlier use of the money. While it would clear up the mystery, he knew Sneed would never reconsider. Even making the contact was risky. The FBI, state police or the amateurs might pick up Sneed's trail and ruin everything.

An "either/or" seemed inevitable. Either Sneed becomes discovered in which case the whole thing is probably over, or he does not get caught and eventually the treasure is spent through the appropriation process of the city council. As mayor, Fern might persuade, pressure, cajole and beg to get his way, but the final decisions were the responsibility of the council. While he was on good terms with all five members, if they believed he was mixed-up in some sort of mischief, his credibility with them would be non-existent.

As he sipped the cold drink, Fern reviewed the options: turn in Harry; do nothing and wait it out; take another fishing trip with his cousin and beg him to assume responsibility for the whole thing. No alternative guaranteed success. He might work the bonus deal with the police and firemen to secure their backing of everything else. If their dependability could be assured, their support would be persuasive with council because whenever the lodge and fire hall managed to stick together on an issue, the men plus their families and friends were a strong lobby. Indeed Fern reminded himself how some past mayors had chosen recruits, not for agility on a ladder or an ability to wear the shiny badge and carry a stick, but because of the size and unity within their families who lived, paid taxes and voted in Plain Oak.

As he snuffed out the cigar and drained the last of his gin drink, he had another idea, a devious one: Suppose, for example, a rumor got planted that he had saved someone's life in the Pacific during the war and this same somebody had subsequently gotten to be quite rich and wanted to do something for Fern in return but he, as mayor, wanted the favor to go to Plain Oak and not to him personally. Pondering this scenario, Fern knew any such deception was destined to fail. The FBI and the watchers would probe deeply, and he had already stated he did not know the source of either treasurer.

* * *

Ironically the very next day, through the only noteworthy hoax in months, six summer-session students, all members of a social fraternity at Washington and Lee University in Virginia, almost gave Fern what he wanted. To meet expenses the students raised several thousand dollars. Two Cadillac limousines, each with a uniformed chauffeur, were rented. A member of the group with a dark complexion donned the robes of a wealthy Arab sheik. Another posed as his interpreter and personal secretary. The remaining four served as bodyguards and wore bulletproof vests and shoulder holsters. After days of practice, the "sheik" and "interpreter" could perform their skit with rapid Arabic-like sounds. Their rehearsals had even included someone standing in for Allie Eller and John Fern. Contingencies were anticipated in advance. The "sheik" and "interpreter-secretary" were both fine student actors and impersonators. The one thing all six students feared was uncontrollable laughter.

About ten o'clock on that workday morning, the two limousines paraded down Elliott Boulevard and parked boldly in front of city hall. When one of the bodyguards opened the door for the sheik, townspeople were stunned. A few treasure watchers began using their cameras and taking notes. Too frightened to giggle, the troupe entered the building, mounted the stairs and passed into the mayor's outer office. "Sheik Abdu Aurenz to see Mayor John Fern," the interpreter announced boldly.

Allie Eller was dumbfounded. "Sure, Mister Sheik!" she replied excitedly. She next opened Fern's office door and announced nervously, "Mister Mayor, there's some kinda sheik feller out there with several people and he wants to see you. One of 'em is a real A-Arab, you know, like live in the desert and have money and camels and lots a wives. It's fer real, Mayor!"

Fern remained stoical for a few moments. "The hell you say," he remarked.

"It's true, Mister Mayor, and he's got bodyguards or something like that!"

"My goodness! I guess you'd better show 'em in, Allie," Fern instructed as he stood up.

After the sheik and the interpreter had entered the office, Allie attempted the introductions, "Mayor, this is Sheik... and I'm sorry I didn't exactly get the last name."

"Abdu Aurenz," the interpreter supplied. "I am Oliver Smith-Hauser, his personal secretary and translator for English."

"Be seated, gentlemen," Fern offered. Allie excused herself and closed the office door as she left.

The sheik smiled politely and nodded to Fern before uttering a stream of exotic gibberish. He next paused for a translation.

"Sheik Abdu Aurenz says you have a beautiful oasis with green trees and lots of water. He sees Plain Oak as heaven on earth."

"Thank you, thank you," Fern acknowledged slowly. "We're proud of our town and like it here."

The sheik recognized the "thank you" and repeated with an Arabic accent, "Ah shank you," then smiled warmly. He resumed his strange sounds even more rapidly with the interpreter offering a simultaneous translation: "Sheik Abdu Aurenz wants to know if you have gotten your plans made so the gold and other gifts can make Plain Oak into the place it deserves to be, the finest oasis of all."

Listening to the babble and streams of translation to follow and thinking of Alex Parker, Fern immediately concluded that this "sheik" appearance was an FBI production. He instantly resolved to play the role of true believer, grateful at last to know the identity of the city's benefactor. Fern replied with a hearty conviction, "Oh, the plans are done and I'm happy, ever so happy, to learn who this wonderful person is that gave all the money and gold to our city—to our oasis. Oh, thank you Sheik Abdu Aurenz! On behalf of our citizens, I want to thank you!"

Before the interpreter could cast Fern's words into exotic gibberish, the sheik again smiled warmly and repeated, "Shank you," several times.

"We must show you our city—our oasis," Fern offered heartily. "We must do you honor! You will be our honored guest!"

After the interpreter rattled on with his sounds, the sheik answered almost reverently in broken English, "Ah no. Sorry, sorry. Must goes." He then continued with his rapid babble. Next he stood, smiled warmly at Fern and bowed respectfully.

The interpreter opened the door to the outer office where a press photographer, a television crew and Marion Walk went into action. When various questions like, "Did you give the money and gold to the city?" and "Why all the secrecy, Sheik?" and "How did you happen to choose Plain Oak?" were asked, the sheik merely stretched out his arms in a universal gesture that means, I do not understand.

He next uttered more babble to the interpreter who translated, "Sheik Abdu Aurenz says spend wisely and follow the plans and there will be more." The bodyguards took their place and escorted the sheik out of the mayor's office and down to the sidewalk in front of city hall where the group disappeared into the two limousines. As the big cars pulled away from the curb, the sheik was smiling and waving through the window at a throng of viewers that had gathered on the sidewalk in front of city hall. From their arrival to departure, the production had taken about ten minutes.

After the troupe had descended the stairs and departed from the building, Fern's shock wore off and he was all the more convinced that the visit had been instigated by Parker and the FBI. *The play's the thing wherein they'll catch the conscience of the mayor*, he mused to himself while resolving to perform perfectly a grateful-mayor, official-thanksgiver role.

With a television camera aimed at him and a microphone in his face, Fern had no way to avoid an interview with Mary Taylor, a local TV reporter. "Mayor Fern, are you convinced this Sheik Abdu Aurenz is the true source of Plain Oak's two treasures?"

"He said he was, Mary. That's all I know about him."

"Did he give any reason for choosing Plain Oak for the donations? Why us, Mayor?"

"Mary, the only thing he said about that was Plain Oak is an oasis and he said it was a great oasis and he wanted it to be, I think he said, the greatest oasis in the world. He asked about the plans and when I told him they were done, he was pleased. It seemed like he knew a lot about them from somewhere and he liked them."

"Had you been in contact with this sheik or any of his people before they came here, Mayor Fern?"

"No, Mary, not at all."

"Did you have any hint or even a slight indication he might have been coming here?"

"No, Mary, until he showed up, I'd never heard of him or even knew he existed."

"Did he say where he was from or where he was going?"

"Not that I could make out. Of course, I don't speak a word of Arabic," Fern continued. "I told him we wanted to show him around town and make him an honored guest worthy of someone like that but he said he had to be off. I thanked him on behalf of our citizens for all his kindness and he thanked me for something in a sort of broken English. You see, Mary, he couldn't talk English very good—almost couldn't speak English at all. That's what that other fellow was for, to translate for him."

"Didn't it seem strange, Mayor Fern, that this sheik and his party would come in so rapidly, have a brief visit and not even let you know how to contact him?"

"It would seem that way, Mary, but I really don't know. You have to put yourself in the place of someone like this sheik. He's got to be really rich and we might figure he got rich probably by oil, I guess. Then he remembers his country sells a lot of oil over here so he, being a good man, thinks about how he can do something good in return. Well, he can't do nice things for all us Americans. The twenty million dollars he gave here couldn't even buy a candy bar for every American so he wants to give it to a city and—God knows why—he picked our little place. If he had left his calling card, he'd get people after him all the time asking for money about something so he was secretive about it. Now, for the record, Mary, he didn't tell me any of what I just said. I sort of figured it out. I can't speak for him but to answer your question about it being so strange to come and go so quicklike and not tell us how to contact him, what I said is one way to look at it."

"One last question, Mayor Fern," she continued. "Did you know any Arab sheik, including this one, had given the money and gold to the city?"

"No, I did not," Fern stated convincingly, "but it's nice to know now."

The interview concluded with, "Thank you, Mayor John Fern. As we captured earlier, the spokesman for Sheik Abdu Aurenz said, 'Carry out the plans and there will be more.' This is Mary Taylor, Channel Six's On-the-Spot News, at the mayor's office in Plain Oak, West Virginia."

Meanwhile Alex Parker and two other agents had entered. When Mary Taylor sought to interview them, they refused immediately. "What time will your story be telecast, Mary?" he asked.

"Six," she replied, "unless the boss wants to run a special."

"Did you get any good shots of this sheik and his crowd?"

"We should have," she replied. "So did Henry Adamson."

"Who's he?"

"A freelance photographer," she informed him. "He does good work. He's under contract with the paper, but his stuff's for sale so long as the paper gets the break."

"Thanks, Mary."

The FBI agents departed without saying anything to John Fern.

CHAPTER 19
THE MAYOR CAN'T WIN

Fern's high hopes that his stellar performance as "appreciative mayor" might shake the FBI off his trail came quickly to nothing. The hoax was short-lived. NBC Nightly News featured some of Mary Taylor's material. Arabic-speaking persons identified the "sheik's" utterances as contrived gibberish. The parents of the "interpreter" recognized their son and his college friends. While amused, they contacted their lawyer whose advice was for them to explain the prank immediately to the public. A joint statement was quickly released and the fun was over.

The hoax-admission story broke the day of a city council meeting. By seven that evening, a rumor was buzzing around town that Fern had instigated the spectacle to build support and credibility for his capital-improvement program. While few people in Plain Oak seriously believed their mayor would contrive such a thing, Dexter Snidow had signed up to speak.

After working through a dull agenda of budgetary transfers and subtle word changes to a littering ordinance, Arch Kidd called upon Snidow. Snidow's presentation was again preceded by his rearranging the speaker's podium to face the audience.

"Citizens and taxpayers," he began. "Our dear Plain Oak is once more splashed all over the news—not just in this country but all over the world! We've had a prank—a hoax. We've been tricked by a bunch of college kids. Now I ask everybody here, do you believe six kids going to college over in Virginia could think up this kind of Arab stuff? Do you?" he shouted.

At this point the dozen or so persons who had accompanied Snidow to the meeting shouted, "No," and "Ain't no way!"

Louder and even more forceful, Snidow continued, "I'll tell you who put them kids up to this thing—that mayor sitting there, John Fern!"

Snidow's claque cheered. One member yelled, "Tell 'em, Dex," forcing Kidd to tap his gavel and demand order.

"You know why he wanted to fool me and you?" Snidow harangued. "You know why? Cause he wants to spend the money all by hisself in his own special way. That phony on TV—what did he say? We all saw it. He said, 'Spend wisely and follow the plans and there will be more.' Whose plans? Whose plans? I'll tell you whose plans—John Fern's that's who.

"He knew our police and firemen were pressing to get a little money to make up for years of being underpaid. He knew other workers would follow the lead of the police and firemen. He didn't want that! No. He wanted to control it all. He wanted his park and his fat-cat industrial place. He was thinking about him cutting at a ribbon with his picture getting took. He knew everyone of you would have ideas how to spend the money. He didn't want that. No! He wanted to do it all! That's what the talk of plans is all about.

"So he puts on a show for us. He tries to fool you and me—the people of Plain Oak. He has a phony sheik come up here and play like he give the money and starts asking how the plans is coming. He talks something like, 'Do the plans right and be sure and follow them and I'll send you some more money!' Well, citizens of Plain Oak, officials of Plain Oak—you, John Fern, you're not fooling us anymore!"

As he returned to his seat, Snidow's group applauded vigorously and there were shrill whistling noises.

The chairman pounded the gavel and called for order several times. He yelled even louder than Snidow had been doing, "Mr. Snidow, you're accusing our mayor of dreaming up a hoax and bringing a bunch of college kids in here to play rich Arab sheik as the treasure donor to Plain Oak. Is that what you're saying?"

"I sure am."

Kidd became more subdued and logical. "Nothing in the statements made by those college boys would substantiate such a charge, Mr. Snidow," he argued. "They all said they cooked up the whole thing themselves. What proof do you offer that John Fern put them up to pulling off a stunt like we had here?"

"I don't need no proof," Snidow replied bluntly. "The whole thing speaks for itself."

"I think you do need proof, Mr. Snidow," Kidd argued sternly. "You're trying to discredit our mayor for political gain. You make up a crack-brained story and spread it all over town, then come in here with a bunch of cheerleaders and accuse John Fern of pulling off a hoax! Before you make charges like that, you need proof."

Arch Kidd turned to Fern and continued, "Mayor, we as council have the right to put you under oath. Do you deny Dexter Snidow's accusation?"

"Mr. Chairman, I never saw any of those kids before in my life. I certainly never put them or anyone else up to any kind of trick, prank or hoax. I thought the sheik was for real and finally we knew who was giving all the riches to our city. You can put me under oath or I'll give it to you in an affidavit. I can't speak for those kids but I doubt if any of them would say I or anyone connected with me put them up to any kind of hoax."

To quell the sounds beginning to come from the audience, Kidd begged for order. "Mayor, to clear the air, I'm asking you to make a complete sworn statement about the Arab hoax and your role or lack of role in it. The statement will be on file with the city clerk who will read it at our next meeting. I also request the city clerk to contact the students who put on that show and ask them to state in writing, preferably through sworn affidavits, whether our mayor or any of his representatives had anything to do with getting them to do it—either in dreaming up the idea or approving or encouraging it. Can you do this, Mr. Naylor? Feel free to call on the city attorney for help. Is there any objection to this by the council?"

After all members nodded their approval, Kidd announced, "There being no objection, that's how we'll proceed." Kidd next looked at Snidow and challenged him, "Included in this, Mr. Snidow, is your proof the mayor had something to do with the hoax. You need to prove what you're saying with hard evidence—not a bunch of headline-fetching assaults on a man whose job you're trying to get—hard evidence. Bring it in if you've got it. Forget it if you don't."

Kidd next asked of the council, "Is there any other business to come before this body? Anything else? Hearing none, I entertain a motion for adjournment."

CHAPTER 20
GENEALOGY IN ACTION

Top federal investigators overseeing the Plain Oak case eventually developed an assumption that if the mayor had a role in the treasures which Parker strongly believed, any co-conspirators were probably related by blood or through marriage. A consulting genealogist was retained to develop a family tree for both John and Margaret Fern. After it was finished, federal agents began paying a call on everyone whose name was on a long list. Those making the visits would be seeking a person having some semblance of the personality profile developed by psychologists at headquarters for the treasure donor—a young to middle-aged white male or possibly a female, intelligent, maybe or maybe not a religious fanatic, superstitious and a loner. They were also on the lookout for someone who at any time in his or her life might have been in a position to embezzle lots of money.

Mrs. Margaret Rogers, "Miz Margie" as she was affectionately called, became frightened after talking with Cy Cvenski on the telephone. "Lord, a special police agent coming to this very house!" she announced out loud. This was overheard by her maid, a robust black woman of sixty who weighed about two hundred and twenty pounds and, being slightly deaf, tended to shout everything she said. "Why would a law officer want to see me, Babsey? Why me?"

An hour later, there was a knock at the door. Mrs. Rogers got her cane, limped to a parlor chair and sat down. "And don't forget the tea, Babsey," she advised. "Now go and let the gentleman in."

Babsey hobbled to the front door and opened it. Cy Cvenski removed his hat, showed his identification and announced, "I'm Cy Cvenski from the Federal Bureau of Investigation. I'm here to see Mrs. Margaret Rogers."

"Show him in, Babsey," Margaret Rogers commanded in a loud voice.

"He don't look too mean, Miz Marge," Babsey added.

"Show him in and don't talk about people who've come to call, Babsey." Cvenski seem amused at the conversation. "And don't forget the tea."

"You wants tea, Mr. Swinski?" Babsey asked politely.

"No thank you."

At this Babsey exclaimed, "The doctor say you can't have no tea, Miz Marge, and he don't want none. Ain't no use in…"

"You go on now, Babsey," Margaret Rogers reacted. After the maid had left the room, the conversation continued, "Please be seated, Mister…"

"Cvenski."

"Mr. Cvenski, what would the F.B.I. want with an old widow woman like me?"

"Mrs. Rogers, for reasons long and complex, we're investigating the two treasures that turned up here in Plain Oak at the city hall. We have no reason to believe you know who's behind them, but if you would give us any thoughts about who you think the person might have been, we would welcome whatever you want to say."

"My heavens above, what would I know?"

"Like I said, Mrs. Rogers, we had no reason…"

"Mr. Cvenski," she interrupted, "you should talk to Johnny Fern. He'll know all about it."

"We have talked with him, Mrs. Rogers," Cvenski advised. "What reason do you have for saying John Fern would know what we want to find out?"

"Because, you see, Mr. Cvenski," she replied innocently, "he's our mayor and I don't think he's crooked like other… like other…"

"You mean like some politicians, Mrs. Rogers?"

"Yes, I guess that's what I mean," she answered. "Johnny loves this town."

"Mrs. Rogers, we have already talked with the mayor many times and he either doesn't know or doesn't tell us who might be responsible," he explained. "When so much money and gold suddenly turn up mysteriously, we have a concern it might have come from a criminal act."

"Mr. Cvenski," she said, "I simply don't know about that."

"We didn't think you would, Mrs. Rogers. We thought by some chance you might have an idea who around here could have done this."

"Giving away so much money all secretively," she stated wistfully. "I'm sorry, Mr. Cvenski. Most people I know would hang onto big money if they had it. A few might steal to get it so long as they figured they wouldn't get caught. But giving away so much money like that—why you wouldn't even get a tax deduction, would you?"

* * *

The directive from headquarters to contact Jack Fern and prepare a special report about him seemed such a waste of time, Steve Browning telephoned his supervisor to make sure there had been no mistake. The mayor's son had already been interrogated by FBI agents three separate times including a hastily arranged visit late the afternoon of Treasure Two. Alex Parker was asked to return the call. "We want you to see the kid again and do the full report—all the questions," he insisted. "This case has White House attention, and I don't mean from some name-dropping, eager-beaver file clerk who works under the press secretary."

Browning managed to find Jack Fern eating alone at a pizza parlor not far from his truck-repair work. "Do you care if I join you, Jack? I'm Steve Browning. Remember?"

"Yeah man. Sure, sit on down. You guys must still think I know something. Go ahead and ask away, but keep me being out here in Fresno to yourselves. Every reporter in the United States is after me and a friend of mine advised me to be careful. Somebody might want to kidnap me as ransom for a few pieces of that gold."

"When are you heading back home, Jack?"

"I don't know. That whole town's turned into one big nuthouse. Everybody's playing cops and robbers. Probably whoever did it wants to pin it on me and the others think I can help them get the newspaper reward. Dad's afraid all the pressure might get me back into drugs. It won't but I really don't want to see anybody.

"Dad and Mom have been telling people I'm down in Texas. My boss is great. He won't tell anyone John Fern's my father or that I'm from Plain Oak. I don't mind you federal fellows because I believe you when you promised me you won't blow my cover."

"So you grew the beard?"

"Yeah, and lost fifteen pounds."

"What does all this do for you starting a refrigeration business?"

"Dad's done a lot of checking for me. I asked him to. He got some people at West Virginia Tech to do a study about it, and they said nobody in Elliott County could make a go at fixing refrigeration units on tractor-trailer trucks. There wouldn't even be enough business to keep a small shop going."

"Too bad."

"Not really. When I showed the report to my boss, he started talking about me buying him out in a way so when he retires four years from now, the business would eventually belong to me. We're drawing up the papers. He's got a gold mine."

"A gold mine?" Browning exclaimed.

"Not like that. Not like the kind you're looking for, Steve. You know what I mean."

"Tell me about Harry Sneed, Jack."

"Momma's Uncle Harry? He's a hermit nut. I don't think he's your man if that's what you're after."

"Why not?"

"He's too old for one thing. He used to be a moonshiner—real big—but that was long, long ago. He lives all by himself and hardly ever sees a soul. He's too crazy, Steve. He can't be the person you're looking for."

* * *

Travis Schnellerman was chosen to call on Billy McCoy whose farm was a few miles outside Abington, Virginia. The McCoys were Fern's mother's people. The FBI had pieced together a history of bad feelings between some of the McCoys and John Fern stemming from the acquisition of his uncle's business.

When Schnellerman arrived at the farmhouse and asked for Billy McCoy, an elderly woman pointed to the road, giving a clear indication he could be found by driving on. Schnellerman eased his car over a winding farm road until he heard a loud engine and saw two men using a conveyor machine to move hay into the upper part of a large barn. When one of the men saw Schnellerman, he turned off the motor, "Howdy, Mister," he began.

"I'm Travis Schnellerman, Federal Bureau of Investigation," he announced while showing his identification. "If you don't mind, I'm looking for a William McCoy, Jr. I understand he's called Billy. Nothing serious. I want to ask some routine questions."

The more elderly man replied, "I'm Billy McCoy. This here is Joe Stuart, my son-in-law."

"We're checking into the treasures that turned up in Plain Oak, West Virginia. We thought you might have some idea who could be behind all the money and gold turning up over there," Schnellerman explained in a fake folksy manner.

McCoy smiled and blushed slightly as he declared, "I sure don't, mister. What in the world would bring you to me about something like that?"

"No special reason," the agent answered. "We heard you were John Fern's kin and thought you might have some idea."

"Whoever it was, I wisht they'd left some of it to me," McCoy added with a soft chuckle. "Is Johnny Fern in any kind of trouble?"

"Oh, no, no," Schnellerman assured him. "We're just trying to make sure the gold and currency didn't come from a bank job or some other case we haven't cracked yet. If we knew for sure who gave it, we'd feel better, that's all."

"I wisht I could help you, mister," McCoy declared sincerely, "but really, I ain't got no idea at all. The way we heard it, there was over twenty million dollars. Money like that ain't around my kinda people."

* * *

As he read through the files of material about him, Parker became intrigued with the possibility that Harry Sneed might be the person they were seeking. While a suspect, no legal proof was ever developed of earlier moonshining. A lengthy memorandum summarized the issues in an involved 1946 and 1947 lawsuit over income taxes.

Discreet inquiry had also produced a lot of confusing opinions about him: Sneed was for all practical purposes a hermit. Some people were afraid of him. Two women said he was senile. A member of Fern's family told how Sneed read Civil War history by the hours and would spend days visiting battlefields in Virginia, Tennessee and Maryland. He was also said to be well-versed in the Bible and could quote many passages from memory.

One afternoon Parker stopped in at the Crossroads Store located about two miles east of the only entrance to the Sneed property. The place sold everything from soft drinks, beer and chewing tobacco to groceries, work clothes and gasoline and motor oil. Crossroads produced its own sausage and sold a popular water-ground cornmeal. A crude sign on the inside wall read:

If We Ain't Got It, We'll Get It, and If We Can't Get It, It Either Ain't Worth Having or You Couldn't Afford To Buy It Nohow.

Parker purchased a quart of local honey. As he made payment, he tried to communicate with the storekeeper, an elderly white-haired man. "Is this stuff as good for you as people says it is?"

"Some says it's good for you. Some says it ain't nothin' but honey."

"What do you think, sir?"

"Me? I ain't no doctor. Anything else, mister?"

"No, I guess not," Parker replied casually, "unless you can tell me how to get in touch with a man named Sneed who lives around here, a Harry Sneed."

"Right across the road's his place, mister. It goes fer miles. His gate's a couple miles down the road."

"I guess he comes in here a lot?" Parker probed.

"From time to time."

"Do you know him?"

"I know who he is."

"A man with lots of land like that, thousands and thousands of acres, must be mighty rich?" Parker pressed.

"Maybe so, maybe not."

"You ever been hunting over there?" Parker pressed.

"I ain't much fuh huntin'."

"I hear he doesn't like hunting on his place. Does...?"

At this the elderly storekeeper excused himself abruptly and went outside to tend to an automobile customer. Parker knew of the local custom never to divulge information to strangers about anyone in the area. The storekeeper had probably sensed that Parker was either an investigator or perhaps a bill collector. This would account for the progressively vague answers.

Behind the meat counter stood a man of dark complexion, rugged appearance and medium height. His face seemed to smile all the time and when he laughed, one noticed two missing teeth. While mixing ground sausage, the butcher had been listening to the questions about Sneed. When no one else was around, he asked, "Are you some kinda police or detective askin' 'bout Harry Sneed?"

"I'm Alex Parker, FBI."

"What do you wanna know?"

"Merely routine," Parker replied factually. "We're checking out a few leads having to do with this treasure case in Plain Oak. There's nothing against Sneed and we've got no reason to suspect him. We're trying to find out who might know something—nothing more."

"How important is it to ya to learn somethin' about Harry Sneed?"

"That depends on what you might know, Mr...."

"Dillon. Pat Dillon. Folks calls me Pat. I tell you, mister," Dillon continued, "I don't claim to know nothin' 'bout no treasure ova in town. I heard tell about it and I seen it on TV—that's all. But I know as much about Harry Sneed as any that'll talk. Him and me, we don't get on good nowadays. You come across with a clean one hundred bucks in talkin' money, and I'll tell ya anything I reckon you'll ever get to know about old Harry. Won't nobody else do that. Some's scared of him cause he's peculiar. Others won't talk cause he done 'em favors. Me and him had a fallin' out a time back."

"What about?"

"One of his big cats kept getting' outta his place and was getting' into muh goats. One night I got it in a trap and shot it. Ole Harry, he find out it was me what done it and he was steamin' mad. He tole me no more fishin' at his place. I tole him if any more of his damned mountain lions got into muh animals, I'd kill them too. Now ole Harry, he don't like nothin' botherin' them cats. 'I'll pay fer the animals,' he was a tellin' but that ain't the point. Them big cats're dangerous. Now mostly they'd stay on his place but some seasons they'd jump the fence and roam around at night. Ya don't hear 'em no more but they used to sound like a baby yellin' only real loud. Could a been I kilt the last one."

"You know a lot about Sneed but nothing about the treasures," Parker stated. "Are you saying there's no connection between Sneed and the treasures?"

"I ain't never said that, Mr. Parker," Dillon replied. "There might be some tie in but I ain't gonna lie about it. I sure can't link him in with it. I know a lot about ole Harry, and maybe there could be some tie back to him; but I'll have to level with ya and say it ain't in keepin' with Harry Sneed to be givin' nothin' away, little or big, to nobody specially to some town like Plain Oak."

"One hundred dollars," Parker stated to reassure himself.

"Ten tens," Dillon instructed. "Five when we start and five more when we's done."

"When and where?"

"Why not tonight at my trailer? Follow the road that leads off on behind the store. Take the right fork about a mile on up. It's another half mile from there at the very tail end of that road. Wait 'til it's good and dark."

"It's a deal but there'll be another agent with me."

"Don't ya go a tellin' nobody," Dillon insisted, "and come in a different car."

"Don't worry, Pat. This stays confidential. We'll see you around nine-thirty."

* * *

At six-o'clock, Pat Dillon closed the meat counter, changed clothes and drove away in a dusty pickup truck.

Once the truck's sounds had faded, the elderly storekeeper went to a wall telephone, dialed a number and paused a long while. Finally he spoke loudly into the telephone, "Harry, this is Abe Dillon over at the store…Not too bad, Harry…Yes, there is. There was a man in here askin' a lot of questions about you like he was the law or something… He was sneaky-like, askin' all around what he was a wantin' then getting' to it… He had some words with Pat. I don't know what that boy mighta told… Sure I'll let you know… You don't owe me nothin'."

* * *

In a rented pickup truck, Parker and Cvenski turned off the main highway at the Crossroads Store and proceeded over a dark and bumpy road with only a few isolated dwellings. "This could be a waste of time," Parker admitted, "but what the heck, this old guy's interesting. We might learn something."

Just after they took the right fork, the vehicle encountered deep ruts in the road. Several minutes later the lights from Dillon's house trailer were seen. A few junked cars were nearby. Before the engine was turned off, several dogs began howling aggressively. A voice yelled, "Quiet, Henry! Hush it. Hush." It was Pat Dillon. "Don't mind them, Mr. Parker. They's all bark."

Cvenski and Parker were startled by the dogs but the harsh, aggressive barking soon softened into an eager, more friendly whimper.

"Come on in," Dillon entreated. "Muh wife's done left me again but she'll be back. She ain't but eighteen and ain't growed up yet."

Parker introduced Cvenski to Dillon and advised, "We picked up some cold beer, Pat. Have a can."

"Now you're talkin'," Dillon began cheerfully. "Come across with five tens and soon I'll be talking."

Parker removed an envelope from his coat pocket and counted five ten-dollar bills. "When we leave, I expect you'll get five more. This all stays among ourselves. Anything you say will remain confidential and we'd just as soon you keep our being here the same way."

"First, the things I know about ole Harry, I've heard tell of. I pro'bly couldn't be no witness or nothing in court."

"We aren't after witnesses right now, Pat," Parker explained. "We need to be pointed so we'll know where to look."

"Harry was a big moonshiner, did you know that?"

"Was or is?" Cvenski asked.

"Was."

"When?"

"Years back, 'fore I was born. He made a lotta money."

"What did he do with it—the money, that is?" Cvenski queried.

"Bought up his place and fenced it off. He got tax-sale lands and old boom-time tracts and traded around to get it all together. Muh mamma, she didn't wanna sell so he traded her a place near muh aunt. It had a better house and was better land than what she had, and he give her some cash on toppa that. He'd do anything to get all that land together. He wanted it wild like 'fore white man come. If there was a road, he'd plow it up and plant trees where it had been. He only wanted native animals. He even went after the mineral rights cause he didn't want no mining. At first he'd let some of his liquor buyers hunt but soon he put a stop to it. The wilder it was, the better he liked it. Said it was God's way.

"Then come a time he blowed up his stills. Nobody knowed why he done it but they say it was 'boom' and they was all gone. Then they say he started keepin' to hisself. He'll fish and kill snakes and any animals what ain't native. I used to go frog giggin' and I could fish whenever I wanted but when I kilt that big cat, he broked a promise he'd made to muh family how we could fish forever only it won't in writing. He was so sore about that big cat, he backed down off from his word.

"He cried over that cat—sat on the ground and cried. He even wrapped the damned thing up in sheets and buried it on his place. He wouldn't even now let nobody mount it or take the hide. He's peculiar, Mr. Parker."

"Did he use up all his moonshine money to buy the land or has he still got some of it left?"

"Don't nobody know," Dillon answered, "but there's something peculiar about that."

"What?"

"Occasionally along he needs money mainly fer to pay taxes. He'd sell a corner piece, pay the taxes and after a while he'd go and buy it back. I even heard tell that once he give cash money to old man Earl Sanders who turned around and bought up the corner piece. Sneed paid his taxes and then bought it all back. I can't prove it and Earl's dead."

"What sources of money has he got?" Cvenski continued.

"Some says he was borned with money," Dillon answered, "but I ain't got no way a tellin'. He sells snakeskins and gets a little for bees rights, but there ain't no money in that."

"Bees rights?" Cvenski repeated.

"Some folks'll pay him a little to leave their hives on his place for honey."

"Sounds like he'd have to have some money somewhere, Pat," Parker concluded.

"Could be,' Dillon agreed. "Now the one guy who had him shook up was Richard Frei. They hated each other."

"Who's Frei?" Parker asked.

"Who was Frei?" Dillon corrected. "He was a banker and a big shot over in Plain Oak who'd died something like ten or twelve years back. He wanted some of Harry's land for development. He told how he was gonna drain the swamp and put in houses and factories. He told how our store and all up in here would go up in price and we'd all get rich."

"I guess Harry wouldn't sell," Parker surmised.

"Right you are," Dillon agreed as he sipped the last swig from his first can of beer and opened another. "But it didn't end with that. You see, Harry had Frei's scheme all choked off so Frei tried to get the State Road Commission to condemn a right-of-way for a road through Harry's place and bust it up; but ole Harry, he had a smart lawyer a fightin' it and he come up with a plan for Harry to will it all to the state fer a nature preserve. The talk was the state didn't wanna build no road through there noway so Frei got stopped dead in his tracks.

"All of us knew if Frei hadda got a road put down through Harry's place, wouldn't no cars much come up to the store on account of it wouldda been off the main road. Frei was lying about it hepin' us. Anyhow, after Harry's lawyer struck the deal, the state wasn't gonna take nothin'. Frei still kept going around drumming up backing but old Harry had him beat. That was mainly the end of it."

"When was all this going on?" Parker asked.

"It brewed for years, but the big feudin' was on when I come back from Korea—I guess maybe thirty years back.

"You see," Dillon continued, "ole Frei was mean. You didn't cross him. He was used ta gettin' his way. He tried to get Harry arrested for his old moonshining. Wouldn't nobody say nothin'. Powerful as Frei was, them what knowed somethin' didn't wanna tell it. He started putting pressure on people. They didn't like it neither. Some even switched their business to other banks."

Seeking to refocus the conversation, Parker stated, "Pat, you know we're trying to get to the bottom of this treasure thing."

"I never said I knowed nothin' about that."

"Okay, fair enough," Parker agreed. "Do you know anything illegal Sneed's into nowadays?"

As he drained a lengthy swig from the beer can, Dillon seemed deep in thought. "Like what?" he asked.

"Let's start with illegal drugs. What about smuggling them in from Mexico or South America. He's got a huge place. Could anyone be using it or airplanes be going in there?"

Pat Dillon listened soberly and remarked, "Well now, I ain't never heard nothin' such as that. There ain't no landin' strip in there. It's too rough and steep."

"Do people go in and out of his place? Who does he hang around with?" Cvenski probed.

"Nobody. Ole Harry keeps to hisself. Now and then you'll see him talkin' to somebody around here but not fa' long. Folks don't stop by to see him as I know about."

"So he lives on that big place all alone?" Parker restated. "And you don't see traffic going in and out?"

"That's right," Dillon confirmed. "Folks say that years ago there was an Indian ova thar with him what had the run of the place but he's..."

"Let's stick to drugs and drug smuggling," Parker insisted.

"I ain't never heard nothin' about no drugs and Harry Sneed, honest. Folks hereabouts is honest. They may poach game but I don't know nothing about no drugs or smuggling 'em."

"What about bootlegging cigarettes?" Cvenski suggested.

"Like shippin' 'em in and around from North Carolina?" Dillon stated for clarification.

"Right."

"I'd know about it. We could trade 'em in the store if we wanted to gamble but ole Harry wouldn't be having nothin' to do with it."

"What about a laboratory for processing illegal drugs?"

"I ain't never heard it. I don't see how that could be."

"Could he be into gambling or prostitution?"

"Ain't no way."

"He wouldn't be raising marijuana on his place, would he?" Cvenski probed.

"Not as I've ever heard tell about. He ain't got no help and Harry's got some age on him, but he is strong and healthy."

"What about counterfeiting money?" Parker continued.

"I ain't never heard of that and I don't see how ole Harry could be a doin' it."

"Fraud, beating people out of things, flim-flam, bonko?"

"Not his style."

"What is his style, Pat? If he were into something illegal, what kind of thing might it be?" Parker quizzed.

"Honest, Mr. Parker," Dillon replied, "like I said, moonshining was his thing, and he's been out of it since pro'bly 'fore I was born. Now if he's into somethin' what's again the law, I don't know about it but he's a smart one. He could be back into liquor but the word is he ain't. Now if anything's his style, moonshining would be it."

"Let's change the subject again, Pat," Parker suggested as he opened a fresh can of beer. "Suppose Harry made it big, real big, back in moonshining times, and he put away a big amount in different banks under a false name. Let's assume the amount grew with interest over many years and got to be huge. He's John Fern's wife's uncle and he's some distant kin with the mayor himself..."

"I didn't know that."

"Yes he is." Parker confirmed. "Now he's getting old. He's leaving all his land to the state. Wouldn't it make sense for him to be giving a big slice of money to the city?"

"It might," Dillon agreed, "but why all the big secret? He's giving his land to the state and everybody around here knows all about it. What would he be makin' it such a secret thing for?"

"Because originally it came from moonshining and maybe he owes a lot of taxes."

"I can't be one to argue with you, Mr. Parker," Dillon acknowledged, "but ole Harry ain't the sort to be a givin' nothin' ta nobody. Why the state people was tryin' to work it out with Harry for him to sign away the deed and they'd let him live on that big place all his life, all alone if he wanted it like that, the same as if it was hissun. He wouldn't have to pay no taxes and that whole big place would stay the same. He couldn't bring hisself to do it even though the talk was his lawyer told him it was the smartest thing to do. No, it just ain't like ole Harry to be givin' away nothin'—specially money."

"We've heard it said Harry scares people," Cvenski stated. "What scares them?"

Dillon paused a moment and began to answer thoughtfully, "I don't know fer sure, mister. It's just he's strange. Lots a times he goes around with a sour look about him. Mainly he carries a gun when he walks around his place. Maybe it's just cause he stays alone and is peculiar what scares 'em. Some says he's crazy, but he ain't crazy and he won't hurt nobody."

"What's his religion?" Parker asked. "We understand he knows the Bible inside out and quotes it a lot."

"Yeah," Dillon agreed, "he's all the time quoting the Bible. When I kilt that cat I says to him, 'Where in the Bible do it say I can't kill no big cat to keep it from muh goats?' He say somethin' about Sampson a killin'a lion with his bare hands. I told him I warn't no Sampson, and he said like that was fuh sure."

"Where does he go to church?" Parker asked.

"Dogged if I know," Dillon answered, "I know it ain't around here. Might be ova in town."

"Are you sure he goes to church at all?" Cvenski asked.

"I don't know for dead sure, mister," Dillon replied. "Seems like he would but come to think of it, he ain't no more dressed up on Sunday than any other day if that tells anything."

"Does he stay over at his place all the time or does he travel around?" Parker inquired. "Does he visit anyone?"

"I reckon nobody keeps up with him," Dillon explained. "Sometimes he be gone fuh days at a time but it's hard to know cause he keeps to hisself so much. You can't hardly tell if he's gone. 'Fore last Christmas he was away a lot. I don't know whar he goes to but he puts an awfully lot of miles on that car of hissun. I seen his speedometer. That car ain't that old. He rolls up big miles."

CHAPTER 21
A HIGH COURT DECISION

As part of a strategy to get cash bonuses for his police and firemen clients, Bob Horness filed a petition in the Circuit Court of Elliott County pleading that Treasure Two was "abandoned personal property" and not a "gift" to the city. As such, a claim to part of its ownership was being made by a few of the persons who had helped find it, some seven police officers. Horness knew he had a weak case at best but was hoping the litigation, by putting at risk the city's claim to the entire twenty-plus million, would improve his bargaining position to negotiate a settlement for his clients.

Bill Willy's reply argued that the gold, like the box of currency, had been placed on city property expressly for the City of Plain Oak. This was a continuation of Treasure One which had promised more of the same after engineering design and general planning had been completed. While the letter pinpointing the gold's whereabouts was unsigned, one would logically assume it had been sent by the person or persons who had deposited both treasures. The bullion, Willy reasoned, had certainly not been "relinquished without reference to a particular person or purpose," the essential ingredient under the law for its being "abandoned personal property." Willy's reply ended with five pages of legal argument which asserted that the gold was a gift, and even if it were somehow declared to be an abandonment, the policemen and other city officials recovering it were agents of the city working under the mayor's direction on city property and they all knew they were being paid by the city at that time.

After studying the petition and the city's reply, Judge Morton Wambler asked Willy to step down as attorney for Plain Oak because his personal involvement with the gold's recovery might be viewed as a conflict of interest. The judge next scheduled an evidentiary hearing to establish a complete record of testimony and other materials about the gold.

The mayor and council retained Henry Kingery to represent the city. Several weeks later the courtroom was packed with spectators and lawyers for banks and insurance companies trying to claim that Plain Oak's treasure was the fruit of earlier crimes against their clients. The state of West Virginia through its attorney general intervened as a party but filed no brief with the court and took no part in the hearing.

The letter to John Fern was presented as evidence. The mayor took the stand and told of telephoning Chief Sacker. Fern described the meeting in his office and explained how the city had exercised unusual control over the gravel pile by sealing off both the city hall and the public works yard. He told of personally uncovering the first bar of gold and ordering it stored in the treasurer's vault. Fourteen other witnesses also covered these events in great detail. A policeman explained the photography, prints of which were then placed in the record. It was established that 53,570.12 ounces of gold had been uncovered and moved into the city's vault for safekeeping. Each witness, including the mayor, had to swear he did not know where the gold had come from. Fern felt cheap about this but reasoned that what was best for Plain Oak was more important than the state of his own conscience.

After the scheduled witnesses had all given testimony, the judge did an unusual thing. He gazed over the courtroom audience and announced, "If anyone here knows anything about this, you may step forward and testify. You'll be under oath and may be cross-examined but you may speak." Wambler spent at least a minute making eye contact with all spectators. "The record will show that everyone here was given an opportunity to testify and none chose to do so," he announced to the court reporter. "I'll hear oral arguments from the attorneys-of-record at 9:30 a.m. Monday after next. This hearing is over."

Twenty-seven days later, Wambler rendered a decision that surprised many lawyers. The gold, he concluded, was neither a gift nor abandoned personal property but was a treasure trove because it had been hidden and the owner was not known. Furthermore the gold belonged to Plain Oak City because of the mayor's supervision of the discovery and having it secured in the city treasurer's vault. There had been no discussion among the finders about splitting the bullion among themselves. Wambler rejected the gift argument because there was no evidence the donor had owned what was given. He also cited an old legal maxim that a clandestine gift is always open to suspicion.

Horness appealed the decision to the West Virginia Supreme Court. Seven months after it was first rendered, Wambler's decision was upheld. The seven policemen accepted Horness' advice not to attempt an appeal through the federal courts.

A few weeks later, arrangements were made to market the gold. Amid television cameras and curiosity seekers, the bullion was shipped to Washington, D. C. in an armored car with a police escort. Two weeks later, Al Triere, the city treasurer, was investing almost twenty-one million dollars into treasury bills.

Chapter 22
An FBI Visit

"Sneed's muh name. Call me Harry," he announced while extending his hand cordially.

"Mr. Sneed…Harry, this is Cy Cvenski. Call him Cy. Travis Schnellerman—we call him Travis or Trav. I'm Alex Parker. As you know, we're all from the FBI."

"We best go in, men," Sneed advised as he pushed open the screen door. "We'll be eat alive by mosquitoes if we stand around out here." When everyone was seated on the porch, Sneed volunteered, "Now what can I do for you men?"

"Mr. Sneed…"

"Harry."

"Harry, we're investigating the two treasures that turned up in Plain Oak—at the city hall in both instances," Parker began. "We thought since you were John Fern's wife's uncle, you might have some idea who gave the money and the gold to the city."

Harry Sneed stared stoically through the porch screen and tapped his pipe which he methodically filled with tobacco. Next he took a large wooden match from his reading table and without removing his eyes from a fixation on something dead ahead of him, he struck it on the wall behind his chair and lit the pipe. The style and originality of this simple chore caused the conversation to cease for several seconds. Parker repeated, "As I said, we thought you might know who left the two treasures at city hall."

Sneed puffed his pipe a few times, stared briefly at each of the three agents and replied seriously, "Well, I don't."

"I see," Parker reiterated, "you don't."

"Right."

"Harry," Parker continued, "what do you do for a living?"

"Why do you ask?"

"It's part of our inquiries in this matter," Parker replied. "It's merely routine."

"It may be routine for you…what was it, Alex? But it's not routine for me."

"Why would you object to our knowing what you do for a living, Mr. Sneed?" Parker continued. "Why does it bother you?"

"Please call me Harry, Alex. It makes me feel younger and it really doesn't bother me, Alex."

"Then why don't you want to tell us what you do for a living?"

"It's very simple, Alex. It's my private business. If from time to time I sell a rattlesnake skin, someone may think that old fellow sells rattlesnake skins. If I sell land here and there, someone may think how awful it is to sell land. Now if they don't know what I do, they can't think these things about me, can they?"

"But if you sell snakeskins and I want to buy a snakeskin, how would I know to ask you to sell me one?"

"You won't."

"I guess, Harry, I don't understand," Parker tried to reason. "I would think you would want to sell them to lots of people. The more you sell, the better for you."

"Are you men here investigating something, Alex, or are you buying snakeskins? You see I can sell all the skins I'll ever get."

"We're here investigating the Plain Oak treasures," Parker replied with exasperation.

"Well, how can I help you men?"

With this, the three visitors exchanged glances at one another as Sneed puffed on his pipe and gazed into the distance through the screen.

"Mr. Sneed…"

"Harry."

"Harry, you have a large place here," Travis Schnellerman began questioning. "What do you do with it?"

"I keep it."

"For what?"

"I live here."

"Do you need almost seventeen thousand acres to live on, Harry?" Schnellerman probed.

"How large a place do you have, Travis?" Sneed fired back in a calm but slightly strained tone.

"We have six acres," was the reply, "for the five of us."

"Six acres! Do you need six acres?" Sneed asked in mockery.

"We certainly don't need six acres just for us but we have horses, Harry. It takes a place as big as ours for that, but your place is almost three thousand times the size of ours. Why do you need so much land to live on all alone?"

"You have horses," Sneed resumed logically. "I understand. Six acres at the least would be needed for horses. Here there are lots of animals and bears and mountain lions. They need a large tract to roam on. No, muh place ain't too big. The truth is it ain't big enough."

"Harry, there's a lot of talk around that says you were a major moonshiner," Schnellerman stated. "Was this so?"

"Now listen," Sneed quipped instantly, "if you're gettin' into that, you'd better bring in ya witnesses! I've had revenuers after me since the twenties a tryin' ta lay them charges on me. If you're bringin' charges, you'd better bring witnesses."

"We're not out here to charge you with moonshining, Harry," Parker interjected.

"Then what do you want?"

"We want to know about the treasures."

"I done told ya," Sneed answered with antagonism, "I don't know nothin' about no treasures. If somebody says I give the town anything, tell him ta swear to that."

"How well do you know John Fern, Harry?" Travis Schnellerman inquired.

"He's muh niece's husband and I'm supposen ta be some kin—don't ask me what," Sneed replied. "Why do you ask?"

"How often do you see him?" Parker added.

"I see John when I got somethin' ta see him about."

"How often is that?"

"Oh, I don't know, Alex," Sneed answered thoughtfully. "Every oncest in a while. I don't keep no logbook 'bout what I do. Living on this place, lots a times I don't even now know what day it is."

"When did you see him last?" Parker continued.

The question caught Sneed off-guard because he did not know what Fern might have told the agents already. After thinking for a few moments. He replied, "It's been a pretty good while...maybe a year or so...maybe more. I don't rightly remember."

"What was the occasion?"

"I don't recollect, Alex."

"Was it out here?"

"Pro'bly," Sneed replied. "Seems he come a fishin' and that coulda been the last time I seen John."

"And you say it was a year or so ago?"

"More or less. It coulda been eighteen month. I don't keep no records and time's started movin' right speedy fuh me. A year nowdays seems 'bout like a month used to seem."

"Do you ever phone him?"

"I don't recollect a callin' John on the phone."

"Does he call you?"

"I'm sure he has but I don't remember no time he called me."

"Harry, could somebody be using your place without your knowing it?" Schnellerman inquired.

"Like who?" Sneed asked almost in rebuttal. "Fuh what?"

"Drug smuggling," Schnellerman explained. "Opium, heroin, hashish. Cocaine from South America."

"I'd know it," Sneed replied emphatically. "Ain't nothin' like that goin' on out in here. You fellers can look the whole place over as much as you want just so you leave the animals and plants alone. If ya take a notion, tromp all ova. Fly ova it in a plane if ya want."

"Thank you, Harry," Parker acknowledged. "We might do that very thing."

"Getting back to the treasures, Harry," Cy Cvenski spoke up, "you've lived in Elliott County all your life. You were born and raised in Plain Oak. We'd like to hear your views—your ideas—about who you think might have given the money to Plain Oak and why the person did it."

"Now mister..."

"Cy."

"I ain't got no idea, Cy," Sneed replied showing some visible uneasiness with the question.

"You mean you don't know anybody who might have left the city a pile of money without letting it be known who it was?" Travis Schnellerman continued.

"I don't," Sneed answered with a nervous quickness.

"Wouldn't you think such a person would have had a lot of money?"

"They'd have to."

"Wouldn't it be likely the person lived in Plain Oak or maybe near Plain Oak?" Schnellerman queried.

"That don't follow," Sneed countered.

"Why not?"

"Might be somebody what'd moved away. Might be they wanted ta do somethin' good fuh the town. Might be they didn't want nobody ta know who it was," Sneed speculated.

"Might be," Schnellerman agreed, "but it might be someone living in or near Plain Oak, don't you agree?"

"Might be," Sneed acknowledged, "but it coulda been some stranger what come in and done it fuh kicks."

"For kicks! For kicks!" Schnellerman almost shouted. "Harry, who in the hell would go around giving away twenty or more million dollars for kicks?"

Sneed puffed on his pipe soberly and nodded affirmatively, "I didn't never say I knowed anybody, but it coulda been a feller like that."

"Do you know anybody, Harry, who moved away that might have given Plain Oak twenty million dollars?" Schnellerman asked.

"There's hundreds, Travis,…no thousands what had moved out of Elliott County in my lifetime. Why I don't know even so much as a fraction of 'em."

"So what you're saying," Schnellerman continued, "is you don't know anyone who moved away that might be the sort to have given this treasure. You don't know anyone in these parts who might have done it and you don't know anyone who might have done it for kicks?"

Sneed made eye contact with each agent and tapped the burned tobacco from his pipe into an ashtray. "That's exactly right," he announced after a pause. "'Tain't no reason I gotta know who done it for 'em ta do it."

"We may as well be frank, Harry," Alex Parker declared. "You're kin to the mayor. You were a moonshiner. You made a lot of money moonshining. You probably stuck it away—God knows where or how—earning a lot of interest or something. You're giving this place to the state. Doesn't it make sense that you'd give all or some of your millions to your hometown?"

Sneed's face flushed slightly. He rocked nervously a few times in his chair, then asserted, "Now, Mister…Alex, there's been a lot of revenuers spent time back in Prohibition and since a figurin' me to be running a moonshine business. One of them men, since dead, stayed out in here a long time checkin' around. Didn't nobody bring no charges then and I ain't figurin' nobody gonna bring no charges now. Folklore and rumor had me a moonshiner. I've heard all that. I know a thing or two about who was into moonshining—I mean really in it and big. They's in the grave and I ain't stirring up no ghosts and spoilin' names fuh grandchildren and great-grandchildren.

"Now as fuh me a givin' this land to the state, that's true and it's a long story. It's fixed so it'll stay as it is with no huntin'. There's some wildlife bunch around what's all mad about the no-huntin' part, but they'll just have to stay mad or get over it.

"Now as to me bein' kin to Johnny Fern, there's lots what's kin ta him same as me. Some's in Elliott County. Some's done gone.

"As for me havin' millions from wherever or whatever, maybe you can help me find out whar I got it hid at so I'll know too. Then I can use it. I'd like ta buy up some more land cause what's here really ain't enough.

"Now as fuh me a bein' the man you're lookin' for, you get yuh witnesses an' come on after me. Even at that, what crime is it? What crime? You're all here—lawman—accusin' at me and you don't even now know what crime somebody done. Dope smugglin'—I ain't got time fuh no dope smugglin'. Them what does it is low-down, common trash. If I was into moonshining—which I ain't—there ain't nothin' awrong with it. It's jist the gov'ment aint a gettin' its licenses and taxes; and the big liquor boys—they don't want no competition; and Prohibition was a deal cooked up by the devil himself but that's all another story. You boys wasn't even borned back then so you don't know nothin' about it 'cep what you read in books and hear tell about.

"Yeah, file yuh charges," Sneed concluded as he stared through the screen. "Bring in yuh witnesses. Look this place ova all ya want fuh muh stills an' muh dope smugglin' an' muh buried treasure or whatever else you think I got out heah or whatever else you think I might be doin'. But if ya don't find nothin' an' you ain't got no witnesses, you'll have to take muh word, won't you? So what I'm a sayin' is satisfy yuhselves, then leave me alone. Ain't that fair enough?"

"You're right about one thing, Harry," Alex Parker agreed thoughtfully. "We don't have a crime as yet and we're speculating. We're really trying to clear the case. Tell us, have you ever been outside the United States?"

"Never in my life."

"Where were you in November?"

"Around."

"Around where?"

"Here, there, all over."

"Doing what, Harry?"

"Retracing my great, great uncle in the war. I been followin' his time fightin' mostly with Pete Longstreet. I been tracin' his steps day-by-day all through right on up almost to Appomattox. So I drive around a lot, follow old maps, take walks and look around. I check old records and stuff such as that. I come across a bundle of his letters and this started me off. It's interesting."

"I bet," Parker offered in facetious agreement. "Do you do this all alone?"

"All by muhself."

"Is this what you were doing in October and November?" Parker continued.

"Like I say, I don't pay no 'tention to days and months like you fellers but back along about that time, I was up in the Shenandoah Valley and over at Fredericksburg and around and sometime back in there I was into Maryland. I was at Baltimore for a spell to see if I could see the place Lee lived at when he built Fort Carroll."

"Did you see it?"

"Nope, it's been tore out."

"Do you ever let anyone know when you're going away and where you're going?" Parker continued.

"No suh," Sneed answered positively. "When I take a notion ta get goin', I hop in the car and I'm gone. You see, I'm free—really free."

"Who takes care of this place when you're away like that?"

"Nature takes care of itself, Alex," Sneed explained. "Alls I gotta do is get the phone and the co-op paid so they won't cut me off. I stay paid ahead four months all the time and everything's okay here when I'm out."

"Harry, we understand you're a deeply religious man," Parker asserted. "Where do you go to church?"

"Right here," Sneed replied emphatically.

"What church is right here?"

"God's all around us here and I got muh Bible. As fuh me, this is muh church. Now I'll go here and there from time ta time. I's born a Presbyterian but muh mother was Baptist so we went to two churches. I reckon I'm a borned-again Baptist, some Presbyterian, a trace of Episcopal, and from time to time a spot of Methodist. I go to a lotta churches when I take a notion to be goin' but right now I ain't on the roles of no church."

"What you're saying is you're not a member of any church, Harry, but you have your own religion and call this cabin your church," Cvenski added for clarification.

" Now you been sittin' there mostly quiet-like, Mister..."

"Cvenski, call me Cy."

"Cy, you been all quiet-like and you got it almost. I admit it's confusin' the way I put what had ta do with this place a bein' muh church. Muh church is with me wherever I go at. You see, muh church ain't no buildin' whar somebody signs up an' then he's a member. I can pray and read muh Bible wherever I'm at."

* * *

Little was said as the men drove back to Plain Oak. The extended fence by the edge of the road helped lock Sneed's image into Parker's mind as thoughts shifted from Goldfinger to Sneed and back to Goldfinger again. As much as he wanted it to be so, there could be no connection. Even his dictum of expecting the unexpected would not allow a thin ray of light into the murky darkness of the Goldfinger affair. As for investigating and perhaps prosecuting a legendary moonshiner who had abandoned the trade forty-five years earlier, this would be the last thing he would attempt. Even if a good case were made and the U. S. Attorney somehow agreed to prosecute, what good would come of it? Sneed would be such a colorful and generous character, the bureau would be seen as an army of demons in a front-page trial.

Why did he suspect Sneed at all, he wondered to himself. It was probably his religious fanaticism plus his kinship to both John Fern and his wife. Sneed was also the loneliest hermit Parker had encountered in over twenty years with the FBI. Of all the relatives only Sneed, albeit remotely, resembled some of the features of the personality profile. Near the outskirts of Plain Oak, Parker asked, "What do you guys think of Sneed?"

"I don't think he's our man," Cvenski volunteered.

"Why not?"

"I can't see him doing all that stuff alone, and he's not the sort to team up with anyone else," Cvenski explained.

After Cvenski was dropped off at his motel, Schnellerman continued discussing the case. "I don't see a Goldfinger connection here. That's why the boss assigned me to this case.

After we've turned in all the reports on the family-interview visits, if we still don't see a link to Goldfinger, the boss will probably take me off of it."

As they walked from their parking lot toward the hotel, Schnellerman suggested, "Alex, we ought to fly all over the Sneed place at low level in a plane with an underslung fuselage. If anything looks fishy, we should take pictures of it and come back maybe in a chopper or on foot. We should also try and find out more about Sneed's movements in the fall and winter. He flipped a little on the question about when he'd last seen John Fern. He is getting on up in years so that might not mean anything. We'll try to get the phone people to see if there are still records of any long-distance calls between Sneed and Fern. I also suggest we sneak a photo of this guy and have our field staff drop in on some gold-coin and jewelry people. In spite of what Cy thinks, Sneed could be mixed up in this. I wouldn't rule him out."

"I don't rule him out, Trav. Brother Sneed might have graduated from moonshining school and gone onto something else. I wonder what."

CHAPTER 23
THE MAYOR'S PROGRAM

A sense of urgency was thrust into the Plain Oak treasure question when a prominent state senator introduced legislation giving the State of West Virginia clear ownership to any treasure trove or abandoned personal property found on publicly-owned land. Also a gift from a completely unknown donor to a city, town, county or school district would be instantly appropriated to the state of West Virginia. Although the initial draft had excluded the Plain Oak treasures, there was concern that this provision might be deleted as the bill underwent committee hearings in Charleston. Since the state had financial problems of its own and no legislator wanted to raise taxes, a "shot in the arm' of almost twenty-one million dollars would be useful to the state-government's coffers. The sponsoring senator stated that his legislation was intended to discourage counties, cities, towns and county school boards from "making questionable deals with the underworld in exchange for creative public financing."

As soon as the legislation got introduced, the mayor and council were being urged to "get on with it." The two-member delegation from Elliott County would be outvoted in Charleston, the state capital. Moreover the two representatives were seeking to avoid a no-win showdown which might very well cause their constituents to judge them ineffective. Wearying of the national publicity, Plain Oak's citizens likewise wanted to put the treasure episodes behind them as soon as possible.

For these and other reasons, the city council quickly put the treasure questions on its agenda as ordinances to amend the city's capital improvement program and annual budget. The action required legal notices in the local newspaper, a public hearing and formal enactment by the city council.

This intensified the lobbying, arm-twisting and power politics already underway. Petitions began flooding the city clerk's office once again. Soon there was a document with a long string of signatures for every project ever discussed in Plain Oak. As instruments for helping the council choose which among the competing proposals to select for funding, the petitions cancelled out one another and were useless.

There also developed an epidemic of different groups calling on prominent citizens and important political campaign contributors to "put in a good word" with different councilmen or with John Fern in support of one or the other of the projects.

While the change seemed sudden, the people of Plain Oak began siding with John Fern. The best explanation for this had to do with economics. By the end of the year, eighteen percent of Elliott County's labor force was unemployed because of the recession. Criticizing a mayor who wanted to spend over twenty million dollars and put hundreds of people to work had grown out-of-fashion.

One afternoon Arch Kidd happened to meet John Fern in the post office and they began discussing city business. "I never thought it would happen, John," Kidd opened, "but we'll see most of our plan come into being."

"How's that, Arch?"

"We're all getting so much pressure from so many factions, and one person is getting another to call the council, and so it goes on and on. Everybody's bringing in a petition about one thing or another. Members are ready to throw up their hands and say, 'Let's go with the original program.' That way if it flops, they'll blame you. If it's good, they'll take a lot of the credit."

"Interesting," Fern observed.

"There's something else," Kidd continued. "The big mouth in town against John Fern has been Dexter. People are getting sick of him. They think he's a redneck rabble-rouser."

"I'm glad to hear I'm not all alone about that, Arch."

"I hear the FBI's been paying calls on your kin, John."

"That's what they're doing, Arch. The whole thing's a personal slap at me. They're even calling on guys from my old naval squadron and air group. Kin are turning up I never even knew I had. The FBI must think the Fern family fortune is behind the treasures. I hope they find it. Some of it might belong to me."

* * *

Compared to other public hearings this one seemed dull. Only a few more persons attended than came to most sessions with a routine agenda. The national media seemed to have lost interest in Plain Oak, and the treasure watchers had all gone home. On the back row sat three rugged-looking members of a construction workers' union. John Fern had never seen any of them before. Each held a placard of his own that read: **THE MAYOR'S PROGRAM MEANS JOBS.**

After Fern gave the planning commission's recommendations, heavy applause engulfed the council chamber. The persons holding placards raised them. Television cameramen took shots of the construction workers. After purposely allowing the demonstration to go on for almost a minute, Kidd rapped his gavel and the audience quickly quieted. "Are you finished, Mister Mayor?"

"Yes, Mister Chairman."

"Any one else whether speaking for oneself or for an organization?"

A black nurse, Lavinia Frank, gave a statement for the local NAACP, a group that had strongly endorsed the mayor's program. The organization had reached an understanding with Fern that minorities would be hired to work on the projects in proportion to their numbers among the unemployed.

Blanche Singleton, president of the local League of Women's Voters, presented a written report to each council member and to representatives of the press. She summarized its contents and commented that the mayor's program had the league's support because it met civic needs, promoted community progress and would do a lot to stimulate the local economy because the projects were designed and ready for quick implementation.

As nine o'clock approached, Arch Kidd began bracing himself for the challenge of chairing a meeting of motions, substitute motions, points of order, amendments and the like. Councilman "Hawk" Hawkins, however, surprised a few people with his motion. "Mister Chairman," he announced, "I move we adopt the planning commission's report as recommended by the mayor and we introduce the ordinances necessary to do all this. Final passage would be taken up two weeks from tonight. Included in this motion is doing all the legal stuff to make it right."

"Second," two members shouted.

"Seconded by Councilman Black," Kidd declared. "Any discussion? Any discussion? No discussion at all?"

"Just a minute," Hawkins exclaimed. "I made that motion and I want to tell the people what I'm thinking.

"Sure I'd like to see the hospital get a lot of fancy equipment. All of us up here would. But how would that add jobs or make us really better off as a city?

"Sure if we put a lot of this money into a new junior high school, jobs might get started sooner or later; but it would go straight to court over whether we can use city money to build something like a school. Some says we can. Others say we can't. Isn't that right, Bill?" the councilman asked as he made eye contact with the city attorney.

"There's a question, Mr. Hawkins," Willy replied.

"It could hold everything up six months to a year," Hawkins resumed, "before you could even now start drawing up a set of plans. I says let the school board build their schools. Some says if we don't appropriate this money for a new junior high, the school board will do it and raise taxes three mills countywide to pay for it. To them I says if the school board would cut out all their waste and extravagance, they could build the school and lower our taxes.

"As for this arts center and museum and all, I'm for it someday but not with this money. To them that are for it, I ask, 'Where's the money coming from to run it once it's built?' I'm thinking they'll be looking to the city government, that's where.

"Now about this drainage, it's needed, folks. If we don't build those two projects, we're going to lose another kid to drowning in high water just as sure as I'm sitting here tonight.

"Now, I'm a workingman, and I understand the need for a wage bonus. But how is that going to cause more people have a job in this recession? How's it going to do that?

"So all this is why I'm thinking along the lines of the mayor's recommendations. Now I'm not for John Fern and I'm not against John Fern. If I see something that I think is right, I'll back it. If I think it's wrong, I'll be against it.

"I've given all this my best thinking. I've talked to lots and lots a folks. Some will agree. Some won't. Some'll agree partway. That's how I've made up my mind and why I made this motion, Mister Chairman and ladies and gentlemen."

"Thank you, Hawk...Mr. Hawkins. Any other discussion? Any other? Now's your chance. Any other? There being none, call the roll, Mr.. Naylor."

* * *

Two weeks later, the council conducted a quiet businesslike meeting attended by very few people. Within thirty-two minutes, John Fern was authorized to execute the purchase contracts for the land that would become the Greater Plain Oak Park and to acquire easements and schedule public bidding for both the Cherry Corner and South End drainage projects. He was to devise a jobs program as part of developing the park. Construction was to get underway on everything as soon as possible.

CHAPTER 24
FUNNY MONEY

As part of an investigation into labor racketeering in New York City, a strike force against organized crime had been using marked currency in an elaborate sting operation. The serial numbers on all the bills were entered into the memory of a dedicated police computer. In an affiliated action, eighty-two thousand dollars in cash was seized in a narcotics raid. The serial numbers for all this currency were also processed through the same computer.

When the numbers on the first set of bills were crosschecked against those on the second, there was a duplication. An initial excitement turned into confusion when it was learned that one of the bills was in a bank vault under strike-force custody while the other had been seized in the raid.

At first everyone believed there had been a coding error or computer malfunction. Both bills were located and carefully examined. Since neither appeared counterfeit, treasury investigators contacted the Bureau of Printing and Engraving to see if two bills bearing identical serial numbers and other markings could have been issued somehow by mistake. The answer came back that any such duplication was impossible and at least one of the two bills had to be a fake.

After careful analysis, crime lab experts determined that in both cases new genuine one-dollar bills had undergone an unusual process through which the ink had been removed, recycled chemically and used with the blank paper to turn out new fifty dollar bills. Both were so authentic, trained tellers with sensitive fingers and keen eyes were unable to judge them counterfeit.

Three months later, a young bank executive attending an afternoon wedding reception at the Sunnehanna Country Club near Johnstown, Pennsylvania, happened to be strolling past the swimming pool. When he saw a young girl struggling to stay afloat while gasping for air, he jumped into the water fully clothed to retrieve her. Later what he had thought was a fifty dollar bill showed signs of losing its green ink and appeared to be different from the other soaked currency in his wallet. After examining this bill the next morning, the bank executive's boss, the bank president, contacted the FBI. The currency investigator who examined it concluded that the bill was another product of the "one-dollar gang," the code name assigned to this counterfeiting operation. The chlorine in the water had reacted chemically with the green ink causing it to change color and to leach.

Throughout the year, eight more converted bills surfaced usually in accidental ways. By identifying the serial numbers of the former one-dollar bills through a sophisticated crime-lab process, it was concluded that the "one-dollar gang" had procured the fresh currency in Virginia where it had first gone into circulation. This information was disseminated to bankers and state and local law enforcement agencies throughout Virginia, West Virginia, North Carolina, Maryland, Tennessee and the District of Columbia.

As soon as he had learned of the one-dollar operation, a teller working for a bank in Martinsville, Virginia, suspected an elderly couple who had visited his branch, always separately, seeking quantities of crisp new one-dollar bills. What had caught his attention was the man would first make an exchange and the woman would usually do the same thing about an hour later.

The bank's manager contacted the FBI and had all the tellers relate everything they could remember about the couple. Soon bank employees were looking over several hundred photographs of known counterfeiters, embezzlers and other criminal types. No identification was made. Several of the tellers assisted a police artist who prepared a sketch of the two persons.

* * *

While listening to the police bands, Lizzie Hoag heard reference to an elderly man and woman living in or near Martinsville who had been collecting large numbers of new one-dollar bills. This couple was wanted for questioning in connection with the "one-dollar" counterfeit operation. It was announced that artist sketches of the couple were being distributed among banks and law enforcement agencies.

"Mister Hoag, Mister Hoag!" Lizzie shouted. "They's a gettin' onto us, Mister Hoag!"

"Don't you pay 'em no 'tention, Lizzie. We best change all we been doin'. We'll stay away from them places we been doin' business, and we ain't goin' nowhar near to Martinsville."

* * *

That weekend Albert and Lizzie Hoag saw the police artist's identification sketches.

"That supposen to be me? That thar is you?" Lizzie jested confidently. "Them pictures is too good lookin' fer me and ain't good enough lookin' fer you, Mister Hoag. Won't nobody tell nothin' from this Dick Tracy stuff."

CHAPTER 25
A NEW CITY FROM AN OLD ONE

Mayor John Fern soon became engrossed with expediting his program. The irksome chores of listening to complaints and taking care of the Plain Oak routine fell upon Allie Eller. His sense of urgency was rooted in a persistent feeling that Sneed soon would be caught bringing everything to a sudden halt.

Fern's workday almost always began at the South End drainage project where ironically some of the persons being benefited the most by the improvement seemed to complain the loudest about the nuisance problems caused by its construction—occasional blasting, traffic detours, dawn-to-dusk noise from pumps and other machinery, streets that were either muddy or dusty and occasional interruptions in water supply. Fern ducked these complaints with a tactless lack of sympathy. "It'll be over someday," he told one lady, "and you'll be a thousand times better off. One big rain down here would cause you more trouble than all you little gripes put together a hundred times." His indifference led some to say they would just as soon have the floodwaters as the temporary inconveniences. Fern would then give a stern look and answer, "You didn't talk like that two summers ago when a lot of the people out here had a few inches of water in their houses."

From these irritants he would escape to the massive park undertaking. Because of its isolation, there were few complaints and progress was visibly rapid. Every detail received Fern's scrutiny—access roads, a golf-course architect's layout for an eighteen-hole championship facility, water and sewer lines, countless trails, children's playground equipment, picnic areas, shelters, public toilets, two small lakes, a large community swimming pool, and on and on.

The park was becoming a source of community cohesion and pride. Every civic club had at least one project. The Rotary Club was buying a diesel bus to make scheduled runs between parts of town and the park. The Black Alliance furnished labor and materials for a handsome stone picnic pavilion. Nine garden clubs each agreed to care for designated portions of a four-acre public garden. Every Boy Scout troop and Cub Scout pack had its own contribution ranging from an outdoor grill to a complete softball field.

The U. S. Forestry Service furnished two professionals who spent ten weeks examining almost every tree on the entire tract. Unusual species were labeled and the ages of the very old trees were estimated. Detailed recommendations were made for selective cutting and some money was recouped from the timber.

The Soil Conservation Service mapped all the soil types and installed drain tile in a few low-lying areas to keep them from becoming marshy in wet seasons. An elevated walkway was constructed through a small swamp. Three and one-half miles of roads and ten parking lots were located and constructed throughout the park.

One-half a mile from city hall, several old warehouses were bought and demolished to provide an eighty-acre site for an in-town industrial park. Four months later a simple shell building was completed and the development committee of the chamber of commerce began advertising for a tenant. Eventually a manufacturer of modern office furniture began operations in the building putting fifty persons to work. The rents paid by the firm were used to finance a similar building on another part of the site.

Elliott County Asphalt was low bidder on a contract to pave many of the remaining dirt streets and alleys in Plain Oak. Twenty of the city's most deteriorated streets were resurfaced.

Because of Harry Sneed's earlier telephone conversation about a library bequest, Fern deliberately deferred construction of the new building. His inaction was judged to be strange by supporters because he had been such a strong library advocate and was pursuing the rest of his program so aggressively. The excuse Fern used was he wanted to spend a lot of time personally supervising the job and until the other work was completed he was overextended, an explanation that made no sense. The architect being paid for this very thing had such a reputation as a taskmaster, some contractors were reluctant to bid projects he had designed.

After several months had gone by with nothing happening, library supporters talked Fern into advertising for construction bids. After the city had gotten a reasonable proposal from a reputable contractor, Fern could delay no longer and the city awarded the contract to the Thor Construction Company of Roanoke, Virginia.

* * *

After Harry Sneed had read about the library being under contract, he undertook elaborate arrangements through a cryptic exchange of messages for a booth-to-booth telephone conversation with John Fern. After satisfying himself that no one could be bugging either phone, he asked, "Why didn't you wait up the library 'til you got the other money?"

"Harry," Fern replied, "we got kids that need to use the building. People were wondering why I'd been holding it up. I couldn't drag my feet any longer. I figured if anything else was coming, it should have gotten here by now."

"All right. Let me see to it."

* * *

Driving to another rendezvous with Tom Clair, Sneed sensed that he was being followed. After a few quick detours near Galax, Virginia, he managed to convince himself the pursuers were imaginary. Two hours later, Sneed again had a vivid feeling that someone was tracking all his movements by means of an orbiting satellite or high-altitude airplane.

Several minutes later he pulled off the road and drove beneath a spreading oak tree. *This'll lose them. God, give me a sign,* he muttered to himself.

It was Sneed's custom to arrive for any appointment an hour early. His antics to escape anyone following or watching had used up at least forty minutes of this lead time. Sitting in his car, he prayed, *O Lord, give me strength in my hour of need and show me a sign that my path is right and safe from mine enemies.*

Some fifty yards ahead there was a wrought-iron fence partly hidden by the grounded branch of another oak tree. He shut off the ignition, got out of his car and approached a small overgrown cemetery marked with a simple monument: CANFIELD.

Sneed removed his hat and read from one tombstone:

Ida Sullivan Nelson Canfield
Born Amherst, Virginia, April 3, 1876
Died December 7th, 1941

*Blessed are they which are persecuted for righteousness'
sake for theirs is the Kingdom of Heaven*

Matthew 5:10, Sneed whispered out loud. *Thanks be and praise to Almighty God,* he shouted and then rushed to the car saying to himself, *Let them persecute me*!

* * *

When he got to the Church of Prayer Prophesy and Revelation, no one was around. Sneed was bothered by the church being locked. While waiting for Tom Clair, he began weighing the merits of deeding his property over to the state. If the police and the others managed to trap him, his land might get attached or its title somehow be called into question. In state ownership there would be an army of officialdom and legal experts to fight off the hunters and greedy speculators who would enjoy seeing him in trouble.

Eventually a large new Lincoln coated with a light layer of dust pulled up next to Sneed's Pontiac. Tom Clair, Jr. got out, nodded coolly at Sneed, mounted the three wooden steps and unlocked the entrance door. "It'll be hot and musty inside, Harry," he advised.

"Why's the door locked, Tom?" Sneed questioned as they entered.

"To stop vandalism."

"Trust in God, Tom." Sneed lectured sternly.

"We do trust in God, Harry. All the same, we're locking the doors."

"What if somebody wants to pray and can't get in, Tom?"

"They can pray anywhere. You don't got to be inside here to pray, Harry. Besides, most members got keys."

"I ain't got no key, Tom."

"You asked to be purged," Clair answered indignantly. "Your name was removed from all our records. This was done by me in person at your request. Remember?"

"My name's supposen to be purged, Tom, that's right; but I sure am a member and I ain't got no key. There's others whether joined up or not, can't get in if they feel a need to be inside."

"There has been vandalism, Harry, and the doors are stayin' locked except when the churches are being used. That's the way it is and that's the way it's gonna stay."

"Okay, Tom, okay," Sneed replied in a soft jeering tone clearly portraying his disgust about the church's new policy.

Clair kneeled in silence at the altar for a few minutes while Sneed sat on a bench waiting patiently. Clair next turned toward him and stated, "Well, I reckon you're wondering about the money for that library. Is that it, Harry?"

"It's being built. The money's needed."

"If they can pay for it without money from the Church of Prayer, Prophesy and Revelation, Harry, why should the church give its funds to that city?"

"Cause yuh daddy prayed about it, and God told him to get it done. There ain't nothin' more to it. Yuh daddy was a prophet. God talked to him all the time."

"God hasn't told me to give over any money, Harry."

"Oh, yes he has, Tom," Sneed countered unequivocally. "He speaks through the prophets and yuh daddy was a prophet. When you refuse ta do what yuh daddy told you God said ta do, you're a refusin' to obey the voice of Almighty God! You best get on your knees and beg for God's mercy and forgiveness! You ain't no prophet. That's the plain truth,"

"Dad was sick, Harry."

"Do you think God would abandon yuh daddy when he was dyin', Tom? Do you really think such as that? Do you think he'd let Satan a come in and whisper in his ear ta tell you to give Plain Oak that money? Why Satan couldn't come nowhar near to yuh daddy. You should know that, Tom—you of all people."

Saying nothing for a few moments, Tom Clair stood up, walked down the aisle and returned then stared at Sneed. "Harry," Clair stated, "you've had the law all over Plain Oak. I seen it in the papers. They're getting onto your money. Just as soon as we give that town a library, we'll have police checking all over the faith and it'll be on TV too."

"Trust in the Lord, Tom," Sneed admonished sternly as he pointed his finger at Clair. "Trust in Almighty God. You're a tryin' ta trust in yuhself. God's a testin' you. You're a lockin' the doors of churches. That's trustin' in a man-made lock. Keep the doors open like your daddy done and be a trustin' in Almighty God! So you get a church tore up here or there. God'll either punish 'em or turn their hearts to true repentance like he done the Apostle Paul. What's a lock? A child can bust open a lock. When he gets inside what's he gonna do? He's a gonna desecrate the house of God cause he don't know no better. If'n he walks in through an open door, what'll he do? Well, he jist might feel Almighty God's presence like Isaiah done the year Uzziah died. Locked churches! You best get on yuh knees and beg the one true God ta lead ya. It ain't a gonna be easy, Tom. It warn't easy fuh Moses. It warn't easy fuh Jesus Christ. It warn't easy fuh Peter and Paul. It warn't easy fuh yuh daddy, and it sure ain't a gonna be easy fuh you. Trust in God, Tom. You got church money in yuh head. It ain't fuh yuh own use, I know, but the money's in yuh head all the same, and it'll take the place of faith in Almighty God. Open them locked doors, Tom," Sneed exclaimed, "and obey the word of God as spoke through a prophet who just happened ta be yuh own daddy."

Tom Clair broke into a visible sweat. He mopped his forehead with a handkerchief and tried fanning himself with a magazine.

This pause was broken by rapid footsteps leading into the church. Once inside, a black lad, five or six years old, looked around curiously and reverently.

"Can I help you, son?" Clair asked politely.

"Is dis heah de house uh God?" the child inquired seriously.

"That's right," Clair replied.

"I come in cause I wanna see what God look like."

"We can't see God, sonny," Clair explained. "He is all around us but we can't see him with our eyes."

"Yes suh," the boy agreed politely. "Dat's what muh mommy say. Do he stay shut up in heah?"

"Who?"

"God."

"Oh no," Clair answered with a maudlin smile. "He's everywhere."

With a perplexed look on his face, the youngster uttered, "Yes, suh," and turned and left the church. From the sound of his footsteps, Sneed could tell the youth had jumped over the front three stairs and had landed directly on the ground outside.

"You best pray on it, Tom," Sneed admonished. "You best ask for God's merciful forgiveness. You best ask yuhself why the Almighty sent that boy in here."

"God didn't send that little kid in here for any special reason, Harry," Clair tried to explain with a slightly condescending smile. "He's just a young fellow who lives near here and plays around. He saw the door open and came in. Like a lot of children he asked about God."

"Tom," Sneed countered forcefully with a harsh look on his face. "I'm a gonna pray fuh ya to rescue ya from the clutches of Satan. Whoever's been advisin' ya must've been sent by the Antichrist. God's sending signs and you ain't seeing. He's been sending words and you ain't hearing."

"I'm not in any clutches of the devil," Clair protested with his face perspiring.

"God help ya, Tom. You're on yuh way down into the pit."

"Harry, that was just a little neighborhood kid," Clair tried to reason as he shook his head negatively.

Sneed stood and looked over the small empty church. He continued with a look of sour disgust, "You're a slippin', Tom. I'll be praying fuh ya."

Tom Clair was now becoming visibly angry and he attempted to restrain himself by speaking slowly and deliberately. "Now Harry," he began somewhat bitterly, "we don't want no more bogus money coming into the Church of Prayer, Prophesy and Revelation."

"So now you've stopped taking up collections," Sneed retorted sarcastically.

"No, no," Clair countered. "Your money's gotten hot now. There are ways they've been telling it."

"There you go again," Sneed answered back. "You ain't trustin' in God, are ya? Well my money's as good as any. All you need is faith. You could have the finest bill what ever come from the Bureau of Printin' and Engravin' and if you ain't got no faith, you ain't a gonna spend it, are ya? You might as well not even own it. I'm sorry fuh ya, Tom. I'm sorry fuh God's church but it'll get straightened out. The library'll get built and the church'll be pure again."

Sneed walked to the rear door and turned around toward Clair who, seated facing the altar, was mopping his forehead and fanning himself. A thin beam of sunlight cast through a small window above the altar caught Sneed's attention. He then uttered just loud enough for Clair to hear, "And a little child shall lead them."

Clair continued staring ahead silently as Sneed turned and went out of the church.

CHAPTER 26
A FINAL CAPER

Seven weeks later, the state of West Virginia accepted a fully executed deed to the garden. Harry Sneed and his wife, if he should ever marry, would have full use of the land exactly as if it were their own for as long as either would live. Should he decide to be buried on the place, there was provision for one family plot. Any tax liability was forgiven. Strong language against hunting or trapping was written into the deed. The only exception related to getting rid of non-native species and diseased animals. Timbering was forbidden as were mining and gas and oil exploration except during grave national emergencies.

There was some publicity. A bill whisked through the state legislature naming the property the Sneed Wildlife and Nature Preserve.

Sneed had been expecting things to seem different when the title to the acreage no longer bore his name. Nothing had changed, however. The accustomed lonely beauty pervaded the tract as did the ceaseless whirring sounds, changing parades of birds and strange animal cries in the night.

The altercation with Tom Clair preoccupied him. If the church's new leader was being manipulated by Satan, he might inform the FBI and the others. Such a thing would be illogical, but to Sneed there was no greater madness than disobeying the word of God. A man in such a yoke was capable of wild destruction. If Judas could betray Jesus, certainly Clair might turn against Sneed. If not being done already, the FBI soon would be bugging his telephone, and a spy satellite or special airplane would be tracking his car wherever he went.

Plain Oak still needed enough money to finish the library and other projects. Sneed had made a promise. His pledge would be kept.

One night about a month after the deed transfer, Sneed was sitting deep in thought about Clair's treachery. *His car, full of currency, was being chased by the police. With each quick turn to escape, his pursuers always knew the exact road to take. When he realized they were being directed by a spy satellite, he escaped into a rainstorm. Millie was smiling proudly and a rainbow appeared.* He awakened sitting in a rocking chair on the screened porch.

Sneed's dream was an instruction from God! A spy satellite or high-flying aircraft could not keep track of him through the rain. God's message had been sealed by the rainbow and Millie's smile. Before going to the Hoags for more cash, he would stay put until there was an extended rainfall to conceal his movements. God would tell him what else to do.

At long last the weather reports called for a lengthy period of gentle rain to cover most of the Middle Atlantic States. Sneed patiently awaited its arrival. Eventually strong winds swayed the taller trees around the cabin. At dusk a gentle but steady rain began falling.

Sneed checked one more time for a bugging device hidden on his car and just before 8 p.m. he turned off the switch to his entrance bell and motored away from his paradise toward Rocky Mount, Virginia. Driving ever so carefully, he took short detours over backcountry roads to be certain no one was following. Twice he stopped to check the rear brake lights.

After about four hours of circuitous nighttime driving, he reached a familiar filling station with an outside payphone in Boones Mill, Virginia. Next he made contact with the Hoags. After a few cryptic remarks about mold on cheese, Sneed drove to an abandoned sawmill three miles from Ferrum. Meanwhile the rainfall had softened into a misty drizzle. Sneed put on his raincoat and removed a suitcase from the trunk. Next he changed his car's license plate.

Thirty minutes later, Hoag drove up and Sneed, carrying his suitcase, got into the pickup. "What say, ole boy," Hoag greeted jovially.

"God sent this rain, Albert," Sneed began seriously.

Hoag laughed heartily, rolled down the window and spat a flow of tobacco juice. "Well, ole boy, I sure didn't think it wuz a sent by no Baal."

"No," Sneed continued seriously, "you don't follow what I mean. What I'm sayin' is God sent this here rain sos I could get away from a spy satellite or airplane what's up thar a keepin' track of whar I'm at and whar I'm goin' to. I got away from 'em but you gotta make sure ain't nobody put no bug on muh car."

"I see," Hoag observed. "You done got the willys again."

"Tom Clair's done turned. Satan's got him hooked. Satan'll make him squeal. Might be it's already happened. God told me to get away in rain. I need big money to finish the work."

"How much, ole boy?"

"One million."

"Bureau prime?"

"Grade A choice—aged."

"You'll have to turn it ova, ole boy," Hoag stated solemnly. "They're onto it all around in here at banks. They been running bills through some kinda chlorine gas tank thing and can tell if'n it come from us. They got a Dick Tracy drawin' supposen to be me and Lizzie. They says we been swappin' big bills fuh lotsa fresh ones. Them pictures ain't like me an' Lizzie at all but bank people hereabouts will remember us. We ain't goin' nowhar near to banks in these parts. You're a gonna have to turn it ova a fer piece from here. Maybe Chicago or out West. Maybe New York."

"I don't like New Yawk."

"Lizzie's pretty well sure she got the chlorine gas thing whipped."

"God's with us, Albert," he advised Hoag confidently. "I had a dream and in the dream comest a rain ta hide me from them."

"Who's them, ole boy?"

"The evil ones who're after us," Sneed replied seriously. "They don't want no New Jerusalem to come outta Plain Oak. After I hid in rain, comest a rainbow and I knowed I'd been visited by Almighty God."

"I see," Hoag commented seriously.

"But if'n I go away, like out West a turning" ova bills, I gotta have me another car. Mine may be bugged. Anyhow they know what it looks like and can follow it oncest they pick up muh trail. I can't stay in no rainsquall fuhever."

As they crept through the thick night fog that lay in the lowlands adjacent a creek, Hoag seemed sad and remained silent. Finally the road led up a hill where the mist disappeared.

"Tommy Clair ain't a gonna turn on you, ole boy. He ain't that dumb. He don't know nothing about me and Lizzie. If'n he turned and ratted on you, he'd be a cuttin' off his nose to spite his face. He's in it as much as me and you."

Sneed looked at Hoag and replied, "You're only seeing the sensible part of it, Albert. What you ain't figurin' on is how Tom Junior's bein' led around by Satan. He's lockin' up churches. He don't see signs when they're right before his very eyes. He don't obey the revealed word of Almighty God. A man what's in the clutches of Satan'll do anything. Bein' sensible ain't got nothin' ta do with it," Sneed continued. "His own daddy tole me how Tom Junior wuz a getting' church money in his brain. He loves money and the love of money brings forth evil. Me and you and Lizzie, we make money. We sure don't love it fuh itself. He done got to lovin' money same as me and you love God."

Hoag drove Harry Sneed silently over back roads to reassure themselves no one had been following. Soon Sneed felt confident he had escaped whatever forces were pursuing him and at least for the moment he was safe.

The next day Hoag spent two hours examining every inch of Sneed's Pontiac. Although no bugging devices were found, Harry Sneed, fearing a device might have been so skillfully planted it could not be detected, remained uneasy. After removing identification markers and filing down engine numbers, they drove the car that afternoon during a drizzling rain to an abandoned rock quarry with water fifty-five feet deep. The Pontiac, carefully mined with dynamite, was driven over the edge where it splashed and eventually sank to the bottom. Hoag pushed a plunger and a sharp, loud booming clap was followed by a big splash of water.

That evening in their subbasement, the Hoags and Sneed counted out one million dollars in fake fifty and one-hundred dollar bills. Wearing rubber gloves, Sneed examined a sample with a magnifying glass. "These are perfect, Lizzie—better than genuine." The currency was next sorted into four piles, each set being free of serial-number duplications. The bills were next arranged into envelope boxes and placed in a new canvas suitcase.

At noon the next day, Albert Hoag and Harry Sneed reached the Charlotte, North Carolina, airport. Using an assumed name and a credit card to go with it, one that Harry Sneed had labored to keep current by using a Beckley, West Virginia, post office box address and paid by money orders, Sneed rented a car for an extended period. Soon he was motoring towards New Orleans and Texas where Hoag currency would be exchanged for "bureau prime."

CHAPTER 27
A FAKE FIFTY

───────────

Bill Sizemore, a teller with a Roanoke bank, had waited on the "one dollar" man and woman several times. He remembered their thick rural accent and knew that the sketches done by the police artist scarcely resembled the couple at all. After a reward of $50,000 had been offered "for information leading to the arrest and conviction of the 'one-dollar gang,'" Sizemore decided to play detective and comb the countryside around Roanoke hoping for a chance encounter.

After several fruitless weeks of visiting rural stores, attending country churches and taking in county fairs and other events, he became discouraged and thought of concentrating his search in areas where the local banks had not been frequented by the couple. His theory was that the man and woman would never exchange currency near their homes or in places where they might be known.

Sizemore told his bank's president what he was doing and asked him for help in contacting area banks. Struck by the shrewdness of his idea, the banker was enthusiastic. "Let's give it a try," he offered. That afternoon the two of them telephoned every bank with branches in an eight-county area around Roanoke. When the survey results were in, a number of the institutions had reported no employee recollections of the couple at all. This narrowed the areas somewhat but there was much territory to cover.

The bank president suggested to Sizemore, "Why don't you take a few days off with pay and nose around. You can be surveying potential branch locations. You might do some real good and if you manage to catch the couple, we could use the publicity too."

The few days turned out to be two weeks but Sizemore remained unsuccessful. He continued his search after hours and on weekends before deciding to call off his quest.

Returning to Roanoke one Sunday from a weekend on Smith Mountain Lake, he stopped to buy gasoline near Rocky Mount, Virginia. Since this was one of the places where no one had remembered the couple, Sizemore almost instinctively began looking for them. The driver of a mid-seventies Dodge which was just pulling away from the service station resembled the man. Since Sizemore could not get the license number, he asked the cashier if she knew the driver.

"No sir," she answered in a soft southern accent.

"Did he pay with a credit card?"

"No sir," she replied. "He paid with a fifty dollar bill. He wanted as many ones in change as we could spare."

"Does he come in here a lot?"

"Seems like I've seen him around before but I can't be sure."

Sizemore filled up with gasoline and noted that the road taken by the man led toward Ferrum. When he was paying for his gas, he asked of the cashier. "Would you save that fifty dollar bill, miss? If I had fifty bucks on me, I'd trade for it but I'm short."

"Are you some kind of policeman, mister?"

"No, but the police may be interested in that fifty. Don't touch it. Put it in an envelope and someone will get it and pay for it tomorrow."

"I'll have to talk to the owner."

"Certainly. Just put that bill in a special place where you'll be sure it's the one you got when the man paid for the gas."

"The boss doesn't like to get mixed up in things."

"I understand. Do you work here tomorrow?"

"After four in the afternoon," she advised. "Do you mind telling me what this is all about?"

"That fifty is probably a counterfeit," Sizemore informed her. "I'm with a bank over in Roanoke. I'm into this but I'm not a policeman."

"Okay, I'll set it aside but I did touch it."

"Of course you did. You had to touch it."

"Come to think of it, he handled that bill funny—sort of by the edges. It seemed funny but I wasn't paying all that much attention."

* * *

After a police crime laboratory determined that the fifty was counterfeit and had previously been a one-dollar bill, Sizemore was given another month for his search. He concentrated in the Rocky Mount, Ferrum and Callaway areas of Franklin County. He wore old clothes, grew a beard and set about selling magazines and Bibles to masquerade what he was really doing.

Twelve days after he started his renewed search, he knocked on a farmhouse door. When Lizzie Hoag answered it, Sizemore recognized her instantly. Shortly afterwards, he caught sight of Albert Hoag driving an old pickup over a road nearby.

* * *

Secret Service agents were amazed at the sophisticated photoengraving and related equipment discovered in the subbasement of the Hoag premises.

As it turned out, Elizabeth or Lizzie Smith had been trained as a cartographer, and in the late nineteen thirties she had worked for the U. S. Interior Department drafting topographic maps. In 1941, the Office of Strategic Services recruited her for mapmaking. Fifteen months later she was assigned to a unit responsible for producing counterfeit Italian lira and afterwards a high-quality scrip currency for the postwar military occupation of Germany and other parts of Europe. Through these assignments, she learned all about currency design and production. Because some of her projects were classified top secret, her name and skills never came to the attention of the Secret Service.

In 1947, Lizzie Smith returned to the family farm in Franklin County, Virginia, and married Albert Hoag, a farmer, preacher and a chemist of sorts who had once worked with several moonshiners to improve the quality of their liquor and to make certain it was safe to drink.

After their capture, the Hoags made no comments or public statements, and they absolutely refused to answer questions about their work. Despite promises for better treatment and shorter sentences, the couple repeatedly pleaded the Fifth Amendment.

CHAPTER 28
A VISIT WITH MILLIE

When he read about the Hoags' arrest, Sneed was at a motel near Phoenix, Arizona. While shaken and saddened, he accepted the news calmly. Nothing could link him with the one-dollar couple. All their old moonshine friends were now dead. Sneed had been careful to leave nothing, especially fingerprints, in the Hoag household or their vehicles. A gnawing sense persisted, however, that Satan might have caused him to have done something foolish in a moment of weakness.

His mission was now clear. In several more weeks, he must deliver the final gift to Plain Oak, about eight hundred thousand dollars in genuine U. S. currency. He prayed for the Hoags, the New Jerusalem, the Church of Prayer Prophesy and Revelation and for his own worthiness as a servant of Almighty God.

At the beginning of a leisurely return east, Sneed felt free from surveillance. Every two or three days, he changed rental cars at major airports by turning in a Hertz and picking up an Avis, and settling every bill and drop-off charge in cash. No one seemed to be watching, following or hovering above.

This confidence was short lived, however. For no apparent reason, he suddenly felt repeated compulsions to double-check the car trunk for reassurance the currency he had been amassing was still there.

After eating something that had made him sick, Sneed felt certain he was a victim of a plot. Following two days of recuperation in a motel outside Dallas, he was surprised to discover that the nearly eight thousand currency bills he had been carrying were still intact in his rental car. He next became so concerned that someone might have substituted counterfeit for his genuine currency that he spent most of an entire day carefully checking all the bills again.

Late Thursday evening about one week later, Sneed took an exit from the interstate near Bristol, Tennessee, and checked into a motel for a few hours' rest. He remembered nothing about falling asleep but *his friends were laughing and chasing. Millie was there, beautiful and dressed in white. Holding her closely, they kissed passionately. The schoolmates were catching up so they ran away by mounting a tall obstacle. He was ashamed because she was a more agile climber. Millie laughed, and he wondered whether she meant affection or ridicule of his clumsiness. He wanted to kiss her again but she had gone. When the friends got closer, he jumped down the rest of the way and hurried to the church. Millie was waiting outside. The little black boy opened the door and cheerfully he beckoned them to enter. Smiling, she nodded a refusal and went away. When the friends appeared again, he went inside but Millie was not there. He tried to leave but the door was locked. His mother and father, dressed in formal attire, stood with the rest of the family on the front row to the right of the center aisle. The left side of the church was empty. Reverend Rucker Wilkes waited near the altar. Everyone seemed angry with him because he was alone. Eager to leave, he tugged at the door but it would not open.*

When Sneed awoke, he was wet with perspiration and his heart was pounding rapidly. Satan was on the march and God would be punishing the earth for its sins! He must act quickly because they would be trying to get him. During the Judgment, Millie and he might spend the rest of their lives peaceably in the garden, and if it were the will of God, they might stay there through all eternity.

He had to be careful. He took the rubber surgical gloves from the satchel and using a moist washrag, carefully rubbed any fingerprints off both sides of each bill. The brown wrapping paper was also thoroughly wiped. The money was stacked compactly and was placed back in the box together with two pennies. The box was then wrapped with heavy brown paper and tied with a strong cord.

He next took a pen from the desk drawer and using the edge of a small calendar to guide it, he printed on the wrapping: MAYOR JOHN FERN FOR THE CITY OF PLAIN OAK. By three-thirty that afternoon, he was again driving north.

When he arrived at Plain Oak early that evening, things seemed different. A number of streets had been freshly paved. There was a parade. Stake-bodied trucks were carrying young cheerleaders to a high-school football game. Sneed drove around the city to look over the drainage works. He also visited the park where several families were picnicking and children were playing happily on the new playground. Everything seemed beautiful. Later in town, Sneed looked for his boyhood home. Soon he remembered it had been demolished years earlier when the new hospital was built.

As the sun was setting he continued aimlessly driving about town until he saw the bright lights of the stadium and heard the marching bands and roar of the crowd at the game. Sneed remembered the package must be delivered and hidden, but he was momentarily confused where the city hall was located. Finally he reached downtown and saw the building on the corner. After parking in front of the new library still being constructed, he carried his package by the cords to the city hall entrance nearest the alley. It was locked so he had to use the side door near the police offices.

Sneed next heard the blaring sounds of a sports announcer giving the details of the game over a radio in the police headquarters. Quite boldly, he walked down the empty hallway and softly mounted the darkened stairs to the mayor's office. Using a handkerchief to conceal fingerprints, he found the entrance locked. Sneed opened his pocketknife and used the blade to ease back the latch. The door opened quietly.

Once inside, he took the handkerchief and gently closed the door behind him. Everything was dark. Sneed struck a wooden match and used it to find his way into the private office and locate Fern's desk. When this had burned out, he blew it cool and placed the ashes in his pocket. He next took the handkerchief and pulled open the large lower left desk drawer. After striking another match, he could tell the drawer was empty. He immediately deposited the package then closed the drawer. His fingers had touched nothing.

Sneed's heart pounded when he heard footsteps in the hallway outside. After praying silently for God's mercy and protection, the sounds ceased.

A few minutes later, he took the handkerchief and eased open the door. There were sounds of somebody mopping the hall floor downstairs. Sneed stood quietly in the darkness for what seemed like a very long time. Finally a voice from below shouted aloud, "Touchdown, Plain Oak!" followed by cheers and other mumbling from the police headquarters. The person swabbing the floor could be heard dropping the mop and running off toward the police desk. Sneed carefully closed the office door and stole quietly down the stairs through the darkened hallway and out the side entrance. No one had seen him enter or leave the building.

Sneed next went into the post office. The counter section was closed off but purchases could be made through vending machines. He bought a postcard and a stamped business envelope.

Ever so careful not to touch this stationery, Sneed used his driver's license as a straightedge and printed on the envelope:

John Fern
Oak View Drive
Plain Oak, WVA

On the card itself, he lettered:

In your office desk
Destroy everything including this.

The card was placed in the envelope which was then sealed and dropped into the slot for local mail. No one else had been in the lobby, and the working area of the post office appeared dark and empty.

The streets outside were vacant. Once inside his automobile, Sneed could not decide exactly where to go. After driving around aimlessly, he became ensnarled in the heavy traffic departing from the football game. Young teenage boys and girls were ringing bells and yelling as they walked briskly alongside the slow-moving, horn-blowing vehicles. Sneed felt like everyone was chasing him and he needed to find Millie.

When he reached Westview Drive, he turned to the right escaping from the creeping traffic. Sneed remembered that Millie lived alone in a large home near the street's dead end. Soon he saw her stately residence with lights shining at the front door and in two of the downstairs rooms. The rest of the house was dark. *She's waiting for me*, he fancied—*waiting to be rescued.*

After parking in a dark spot, he turned off the ignition and his headlights. Sneed's heart pounded with dread over whether to knock on her door. Sixty years ago shyness often engulfed him before calling on her but once in Millie's company everything always turned out well. She had always been kind and gracious to him and made him feel at ease.

After praying for guidance, Sneed suddenly and impulsively opened the car door and marched in nervous haste up the sidewalk past the boxwood to the colonnaded entrance porch.

The instant Sneed pressed the doorbell, a dog inside began barking aggressively. Next he heard a woman's voice trying to quiet the animal. A few seconds later there was a mechanical unlocking sound and then the undoing of a chain latch. The door was opened and Millie Fox Frei, strikingly beautiful and dignified, appeared. "Why Harry Sneed…I don't believe it!" she exclaimed graciously. "What brings you here after all these years?"

At a loss for words, Sneed managed. "I…I just w-wanted to make sure you were a-all right, M-Millie."

"Thank you, Harry. I'm quite fine. Please come in."

"N-N-No," he hesitated. "That wouldn't be right."

"Now really, Harry, you're not so dissipated as to shatter the reputation of a seventy-nine year old widow. Come on in here before I get my lasso and rope you up and pull you through this door. Besides, I'm a tiny bit angry at you…no, not angry—miffed is the word I want but, of course, not much."

"Fuh w-what, Millie?"

"You come on inside," she commanded with eloquence, "and I'll tell you all about it."

With this, Harry Sneed entered her home. As they passed through a large well-decorated living room, he noticed a portrait of Richard Frei staring soberly from above the mantle. Millie instantly caught the soft sneer Sneed had returned to the picture. "Don't pay any attention to Richard, Harry," she declared as they entered the cozy den where she had been reading. "Let bygones be bygones. Do sit down," she entreated as she sat on the sofa. "He didn't get any of your place. Don't hold any of that against me."

"Oh I don't, Millie," he answered soberly as he sat in an armchair.

"What bothered me—but only a little, Harry, was that you didn't come around at all, or write me a note, or sign a condolence book, or send a flower, or come to the funeral, or anything when Richard died," Millie began as she relaxed on the sofa. Obviously uncomfortable and speechless, Sneed merely stared at the floor. "Of course, it's rude of me to call attention to this but because of your and Richard's feuding all the time and when you did absolutely nothing, I felt perhaps some of your animosity to Richard had rubbed off on me. Deep down inside, I knew this could not be."

"Oh, n-no, Millie," Sneed replied in a tone nearing grief, "I-I would never want to hurt you in any way at all." He then took the same handkerchief that had been used to conceal his fingerprints and wiped his eyes gently.

"And the first time I'd so much as laid eyes on you in, I guess, fifteen years was at a city council meeting three years ago. I know you saw me but you didn't say one word to me, Harry," she continued. "This made me think you were angry at me for something."

Straining to keep from bursting into tears, Sneed managed to mutter, "N-No, M-Millie, I'm very sorry."

"Now as rude as it may have been for me to mention all this, I'm glad I did because now I know my worries were not so. All is forgiven and I'm ever so happy to see you. I really am," she announced positively and with a cheerful smile. "Now why were you so sweet as to worry about my being all right? I'm fine."

"I…I don't know, M-Millie," he stammered.

"Harry, your giving all that land out there to the state was a magnificent thing for you to have done. I know Richard wanted part of it for development but, lucky for him, this never happened. I say lucky because he would have gotten overextended and the thing would have gone under. Now it will remain in a natural state. I understand the place is beautiful, Harry."

"Yes," he replied feeling much more relaxed. "It's the most beautiful place I know."

Usually quite talkative, for what was actually only a very few seconds but which seemed much longer, Millie could think of nothing to say. In this brief twinkling she felt a tiny trace of guilt as her mind flashed back to her own coquetry and her hasty decision to marry Richard Frei. She was also strangely happy to be in Sneed's company once again.

"May I get you something, Harry?" she offered politely, also ending what for her was a painful silence. "Coffee, tea, a coke…a drink?"

"No thank you, Millie. Nothing at all."

"Do you know what I think, Harry?" Millie began quietly and quite seriously, "and it will absolutely stay sealed up inside me forever. I'll never tell anyone and even if I should become a convert to Catholicism and somehow…I don't know how…my vows required me to confess it to my priest, I still will remain silent. Harry, you gave our city all that money, didn't you? As soon as I read about it, somehow I knew it had been you. I've never breathed a word of this to a single soul and never will as long as I live. I swear and I promise. You don't have to admit it, and if it isn't true, please don't deny it because I want to believe you were the person even if you weren't. But I know. There's no doubt in my mind, Harry."

"Now M-M-muh-Millie," Sneed began as he reached for words to express the confusion in his own mind. "You've gotta get out of here, Millie!" he urged impulsively. "Come with me. You'll be safe. They won't get us!"

"Who, Harry? Who won't get us?"

"God's gonna punish the earth, Millie. He'll unleash Satan's forces as an instrument of his will!"

"Oh Harry, you're so tired. You may need help," she replied tearfully.

"Millie," he continued in a near frenzy, "it ain't too late! They don't know my car and God's with me! He'll want you to be spared!"

"Harry, believe me. I swear no one—absolutely no one—will ever learn from me what I just said about your helping our city. Please don't fear that."

"Muh-Millie, I…I want to help you. I really do," Sneed offered as his eyes flowed with the tears of conviction.

"Don't you want to rest, Harry? You seem so weary. You can stay here or I'll call Margaret."

"N-No, don't do that, M-Millie," he countered. "I'll be all right. God's with me, you see. He's guiding me. I'll pray fuh you, Millie. I'm hoping he'll spare Plain Oak. I'm certain he will but if he doesn't, he won't destroy my place. You can come there anytime. I'll be waiting for you and you'll be safe, Millie."

"Thank you, Harry," she declared with her eyes also full of tears. "Remember, I won't tell one soul. I swear before God."

"I've got to go, Millie."

"Please be careful, Harry. I'll be glad to help you get help."

"God's with me, Millie."

They both stood and then walked softly through the living room into the front hall. Sneed ignored Frei's portrait as if it were a forbidden abomination. At the front door Millie

Frei extended her soft hand. Sneed clasped it in his own the same way he had some sixty years earlier. With a flicker of encouragement in her eyes, he hugged her tenderly, bringing forth for a few seconds a trace of the passion and happiness they had once known together. Millie's eyes remained moist as she watched him ambling forth into the soft autumn air.

CHAPTER 29
LOST IN THE WOODS

Abe Dillon was standing in the doorway of the Crossroads Store when Sneed drove up.

"Workin' late, Abe?" he asked through the car window.

"I'm here 'til eleven most Fridays."

"It's quarter past already," Sneed noted.

"I'm waitin' on muh boy to fetch me." Abe Dillon replied.

"Can a man still buy a thing or two?"

"Sure, Harry."

Sneed parked and entered the store. After turning on the lights, Dillon remarked, "Say, it ain't none of muh business, Harry, but the law's been nosin' around here again about ya. I ain't never said nothin'. They was talkin' to that nephew of mine...Pat."

"When did they come this time, Abe?"

"Been about two weeks."

Sneed thought for a moment and asked, "I wonder if that boy of yourn—Tommy it is, ain't it—would like to earn some foldin' money by doing a little job. He won't be doin' nothin' wrong or again the law or nothin'."

"Go on," Dillon replied in a show of interest.

"I want him to drive that there car back to the Chattanooga Airport and turn it in to Avis. By then it'll have around nine-hundred trip miles of use. I've had it four days but at Chattanooga there won't be no be no drop-off charge. I'll give him a lot more cash than he'll need. The papers are in the glove box. He'll have to pay something to get back home. Whatever's left over is hissun to keep."

"He can do all that, Harry, and he don't talk."

"Specially to Pat."

"He won't. They don't get on nohow."

"Here's seventeen hundred dollars. It's a lot more than a plenty. When he gets back and looks you in the eye and says, 'Daddy, I done it all,' go ahead and give him the last five hundred from it. Don't let him spend it on no spree. That'd draw attention. It ain't no hot car or stolen or nothin', but he'd best drive real careful and legal-like. The papers ain't in muh name, so I don't want nobody but me and you and the boy to know about it."

"Okay Harry."

A few minutes later a young bearded man drove up, parked and entered the store. "Can you drive down to the Chattanooga Airport early tomorrow morning, Tommy?" Abe Dillon asked. "There's a real good fee in it."

"Yeah man!"

Sneed added to his purchases while listening to Abe Dillon repeat the instructions. "You say this car ain't hot, Mister Harry?" Tommy Dillon sought for reassurance.

"Word of honor, Tommy. It ain't wanted. I'd take it down there muhself but I just can't do it right now. The papers say a man named Owen J. Bartow rented it so you're turning it in fuh him. It all ought to go okay but if the law should really get ta askin' what you're a doin' with it, don't tell no lie and get in trouble. If'n you have to, tell 'em Harry Sneed's a payin' ya to run it down there and turn it back in. It'd be best if you don't have to say nothin' so drive careful and legal. She runs good and yuh daddy's got the money, plenty of it."

"I'll get it done, Mister Harry," the youth assured him, "and I won't say nothin' to nobody lessun I really have to."

"Now would you please run me back home, Abe," Sneed sought.

"Get in the truck, Harry."

Sneed put his purchases together with a satchel and his suitcase from the car onto Dillon's pickup truck. Abe Dillon turned off the lights to the store, locked the door and got into the truck to drive.

The two said nothing for five minutes. When they reached the draw gate, the truck was stopped and Sneed got out and unlocked the mechanism causing the gate to rise without the bell ringing. Back in the cab, he advised, "When you leave, Abe, it should shut behind you. It's automatic."

A short time later, they reached Sneed's cabin. "What do you want me to say if the law asks me if I seen you, Harry?"

"If you gotta, tell 'em you seen me when I come in and bought some stuff. Try not to say no more than that. There ain't no lie in it."

"Okay Harry."

"Thanks, Abe."

"Harry, you're a gonna be out heah all by yuhself with that gate shut up sos it won't spring open. I don't see where you got no car."

"Don't you get ta worryin', Abe. I reckon I know how to keep muhself on this place. I'll be all right."

"Anything else?"

"No, jist drive on out through the gate and if'n it don't shut behind you, come on back and tell me. I don't want no bear a gettin' out on the road."

"Okay Harry."

"After Sneed removed the groceries and luggage, he went to the driver's window to ask Dillon if he owed him anything.

Dillon responded, "You don't owe me a thing." He then shifted gears and drove away.

Once inside, Sneed looked over the cabin, his home for almost fifty years. The sharp contrast with Millie's elegance was unavoidable. He sat in the wooden rocker on the porch and smelled the midnight coolness. His thoughts then returned to Millie. God had informed her about the New Jerusalem. She would tell no one because she had sworn it. *The young children were playing happily in the playground. He ran with them but soon it would rain. There was nothing to worry about anymore* and he awakened feeling good about it.

Sneed thought of the Hoags and begged God to protect the secret by remaining with them during their hours of need. The FBI must never talk with him again because he might boast how clever everything had been.

When he showed her the industrial park and pointed out the men and women working, Millie smiled in admiration, but there was a shrill cry in the night. *The big cat,* Sneed reminded himself while regaining consciousness.

Once again the mountain lion had challenged him to their private game. To see this creature would be the sign sealing God's approval of everything. The animal would remain nearby but always hidden from view.

Sneed put on his tall boots and strapped a knife sheath to his belt. The knapsack was packed with a light sleeping bag, food, a Bible and a picture of his parents. He filled his large canteen, took his hand lantern and went into the heavy darkness. It was almost 4 a.m.

Sneed paused in silence until he heard another scream. He tried to encircle the animal now judged to be two to three hundred yards away. Determined to witness God's sign, Sneed stole through the brush and worked his way around obstacles and over fallen logs. For an hour and half there were no more cries. Quite suddenly, he was stunned by a loud shriek that seemed to be right at him but it was too dark and misty for the cat to be seen.

A soft radiance began tinting the foliage and Sneed could just barely make out a small meadow ahead. An animal jumped up from behind the tall grass and disappeared into the woods. Everything had happened so suddenly and in such haze and shadow, he was not certain whether this was the mountain lion or another creature perhaps frightened by it. Had God sent the sign? Sneed could not be sure.

He must not go back to the cabin because Millie would not be there, and sooner or later Alex Parker and the others would want to ask more questions. For a few moments Sneed pondered what to do. The cat had led him to a place where he had lost his way. Part of the confusion came from knowing he must not return and partly it reflected an old wish that the garden should become so large he could easily get lost inside.

While bewildered, Sneed was strangely happy. The morning birds were beginning their orchestral tuning, and the early sunlight was casting a dim gold over the tiny meadow and onto the trees. He remembered the Indian who had lived on the place many years back. When this man disappeared, no one ever knew what had happened to him. Although the Indian would be just over one hundred years old, he was perhaps still alive and they might share the wilderness together.

When the daylight became stronger, Sneed arose, remounted his knapsack and drank from the canteen. He then walked toward the thicket where the animal had disappeared.

The End

Made in the USA
Lexington, KY
17 May 2013